SAVE ME

FORGIVE ME
BOOK 3

A. NASH

Save Me, Forgive Me #3

Ariana Nash

Subscribe to Ariana's mailing list & get the exclusive story 'Sealed with a Kiss' free.

Join the Ariana Nash Facebook group for all the news, as it happens.

Authors note on languages and content:

In this series, "Mafia" is used as a catch-all term for Italian organized crime. For legal reasons, the author has chosen to use the fictional name "Battaglia" in place of real crime syndicate names.

The opinions and beliefs of any characters within this series are those of fictional characters and are not indicative of the author's personal views.

www.ariananashbooks.com

CHAPTER ONE

Francis

Francis opened the door into the casa and stopped, alarmed at the sight in the living room. Vitari glanced up from the stacks of cash on the coffee table, raised his eyebrows, and resumed counting.

The fact Vitari was home might have been surprise enough. But the counting out of money... Pile after pile of it. There had to be tens of thousands there. Where had it come from?

Francis veered toward the open-plan kitchen area and flicked on the coffee machine. The air conditioning hummed, holding off Panama's sticky heat. He eyed Vitari again. He didn't want to start throwing accusations around but normal people didn't count cash on their coffee tables, and while he knew their circumstances weren't normal, he'd perhaps been foolish to believe all illegal activities had ceased since they'd fled Europe.

They'd been living in Gamboa, Panama, for over a

month, and in the last few weeks, a familiar pattern had emerged. Just like Venezuela. Vitari was gone for most days and nights, and when he returned, he was either too lost in his own head to talk or he crashed, too exhausted to give Francis more than a polite peck on the cheek.

"You're doin' the thing." Vitari finally spoke, having finished his counting, and when Francis glanced over, Vitari swept all the stacks together.

"'Thing'?"

"The quiet brooding thing because you don't want to say what's on your mind. Just say it."

Fine then, he would. "Where did you get the money?"

"Did some deals." Vitari reclined, resting his arms over the back of the couch cushions, and he smirked—his satisfied smirk. His unbuttoned collar revealed a V of golden skin, and the rolled-up sleeves exposed fine forearms. His watch gleamed, shining like his shoes, although those had some crusted mud on them. "And there's that judgmental expression." He sighed. "I knew it wouldn't be far away. Before you get all high and mighty, this cash is going to save our asses, Padre."

"Is it illegal?" Francis almost winced at his own idiocy. *Of course* it was illegal.

Vitari's grin grew.

Francis wasn't sure what he expected. They were in hiding, tucked away in a jungle town an hour from Panama City, so their options for attempting to start a new life were limited. He knew it was going to be tough. But it hadn't occurred to him that Vitari would be *dealing*. It had to be drugs, didn't it? What else could it be? Where did he get the drugs to deal them?

Francis's heart sank a little. They needed the money, but not at the expense of vulnerable people.

Vitari pushed from the couch and sauntered over. "We can't all be saints like you."

Francis snorted and busied himself using the plunger on the French press, squeezing out fresh coffee. "You *could*, you just don't want to try."

Vitari's arms looped around his waist, drawing Francis backward against his firm, warm body. "Hm," he purred in his ear. "This is what I do," he said, and the words skimmed Francis's neck, just below his ear, delivering a shot of lust to his veins. "I'm good at it."

Francis caught a glimpse of the money in the corner of his eye. Was it risky, whatever Vitari did to get that money? Would someone recognize him? Would it bring the police to their door, or the Battaglia? The DeSica?

He didn't want to move house again. He liked it here, despite being alone most days. The town only housed a few hundred people, and most of them worked at the luxury hotel a few miles up the hill. There was a church, a store, and little else. But he'd begun to feel settled, like he had in El Cristo. But that had ended badly. Would this one too?

"You could do something *less* illegal?" he suggested.

Vitari stiffened. It had been the wrong thing to say.

Francis turned in his arms and tried to smile away the tension, but Vitari was already easing off. He took his coffee and leaned against the opposite counter. "What am I going to do?" he asked, taking a sip of coffee and raising his dark eyes. "Work a shop counter?"

He wasn't smiling now, and it seemed as though Francis was walking toward a trap. He swallowed. "I don't know, you could do anything. The hotel has jobs."

Vitari gave him the dead stare, while the rest of him remained very still. "I'm going to assume you're joking."

"No, this..." Francis waved at the house around them.

"This could be a new start for us. A new place, new names, we could make a life..." He swallowed the rest of the words, not sure if this was the right moment to explain how he'd been thinking about the future... with Vitari. Together. But they couldn't have a future if Vitari continued to do *illegal* things.

"Jesus." Vitari laughed but it was one of those short, sharp laughs that had nothing to do with humor. "I can't wait tables, Francis. That's not me."

"Why not? It's not going to earn money like... well, like selling whatever you're selling, but it's good, honest work."

Vitari's smile was long gone now. "You want me to play house? Get a mind-numbing nine-to-five job? I'll fuckin' shoot myself now." He carried his coffee across the room toward the piles of cash.

Francis sipped his drink, needing the hot, bitter taste to buy a few seconds so the hurt didn't show on his face. He hadn't really thought far ahead. The last few weeks had been good, but he'd assumed they'd left all the criminality behind. Or so he'd thought, until he'd come home to find Vitari counting drug money.

He *had* thought they could make something of their lives here. Clearly, Vitari hadn't been thinking of their future at all.

"You trying to change me, Padre?" Vitari said, scooping up his stacks of hundred dollar bills. "Don't. This is who I am."

Francis had known, hadn't he? Of course he had. He'd seen Vitari's life; he knew what he did and could guess the things he'd done in the past. But he'd been sure Vitari didn't *want* that life. Nobody wanted to be a criminal, did they? He'd said, long ago, in an Italian restaurant in a Spanish port, being a criminal wasn't a choice.

This was their chance to start over, but perhaps Vitari didn't want to.

Francis had been wrong, and naïve, to hope for a happy ending. They could leave their lives behind, but they were still products of the Mafia, and the Church. Changing was never going to be easy, or even possible.

"Go get a job at the local store if you want," Vitari continued, his tone dismissive. "We don't need the cash, but if it'll help you sleep at night, Father Scott, then do it. Just don't use your real name."

"If we're staying then I will," Francis said, adding his own defiant note. "But there's no point in trying to make a life if we're on the run again tomorrow."

"We'll be here a while yet." Vitari opened one of the kitchen cupboards, took out the back panel, and stuffed the cash behind it, among a whole lot more stacks. How long had he been dealing? Since they'd arrived? There had to be fifty thousand dollars stashed back there—maybe more—and Francis hadn't a clue this whole time.

With the cash safely stowed, Vitari passed him, then paused at the top of the stairs leading down to the bedrooms on the ground floor. "I'm going to take a shower." He glanced up. "You wanna join me, Padre?"

Francis did want to. He always wanted to be with Vitari, which was why his absence had been so painful.

"I'll bring a gun..." Vitari added.

"I don't think so." Francis stared out of the windows, resisting temptation, and when he looked over, Vitari had gone. He *did* want to join him, wanted to join him more than anything else. He missed their intimacies, missed having Vitari's arms around him, having his hands all over his body, his mouth scorching his skin, and other parts, having him buried deep, bringing him alive. He wanted that again, like they'd had when they'd first arrived, ached for it, but his own naïve foolishness had ruined his mood, and the moment.

Francis looked out at the jungle and the gaping mouth of the Chagres River where it joined the infamous canal far beyond, and for the first time since leaving Westminster, an old, familiar feeling began to creep back in—being trapped.

It was just cabin fever. He'd been alone for too long. He needed to get out, to find a place, a purpose, or he'd lose his damn mind.

Tomorrow, he'd walk into town and find a job.

CHAPTER TWO

Vitari

Vitari popped the lid on the crate of guns and stepped back, allowing the buyers to examine the product. *Stolen* product. It would be months before the Battaglia realized their local cache of guns was missing. By then, Vitari planned to be long gone.

He planted a hand on his hip and squinted at the guards the buyer—a stoic, tall man named Aiken—had brought along. Big men. Five of them. Each armed with semiautomatic rifles. If they had it in mind to point those guns at Vitari, there wasn't much he could do to stop them. He'd narrowly missed a firefight during the last sale. Francis would lose his mind if he knew how close he'd come to trouble. Which was why Vitari kept all this to himself. They needed the money. Once they had enough to set them up far away, he'd ditch this life and start a new one in Belize, where the authorities would look the other way for enough American dollars.

He just needed to survive a few more deals and they'd be free.

"Good," Aiken said in Spanish. "But I want more." He removed his wide-brimmed hat and patted it free of dust, then swept his slick dark hair back and tucked the hat back on.

"How much more?" Vitari replied.

"Five crates."

Jesus, what was he arming, a militia? Five crates worth of cash would be enough to get out of this jungle backwater. "I need a week. But I'll get it."

Aiken nodded. "You want a drink? My men will sort out payment for this crate as we discuss what happens next."

Never say no to an invite of food or drink during business. Giancarlo had taught him that. More lucrative deals were sealed over dinner than over a desk.

Vitari sauntered along the poorly lit street beside Aiken, although calling it a street was a stretch. This part of Gamboa had long been forgotten and left to crumble. Concrete breeze-block houses remained unfinished, and the roads leading to them had buckled under the weight of minimal repairs and scorching sun.

He sat with Aiken at an outdoor bar and talked guns into the late hours. Aiken was absolutely trying to feel him out—his past, his associations, who he worked for. Vitari remained tight-lipped. His product talked for him. At two a.m., he climbed behind the Jeep's wheel, placed the stacks of cash behind the passenger seat, and began the drive back to the casa, taking the long way around and doubling back to lose any tails.

A mile from the house, he pulled over, flicked the Jeep's lights off, and waited for any movement in the mirrors. He wasn't expecting trouble, but he also didn't want to take any of this shit back to Francis. He'd been through enough.

Closing his eyes, he dropped his head back and sighed.

Francis wasn't supposed to see the cash. Vitari had known he'd hate the whole idea of it.

He was losing him. He knew it. Expected it, even. He wasn't worthy, didn't know how to make himself worthy. He couldn't change who he was, and it was clear, Francis *wanted* him to change. Wanted things he couldn't give, like a future. A mile up the road, Francis would be waiting for him, and he'd look at him, judge him with those disappointed eyes, and it would wreck Vitari's heart.

With any luck, Francis would be asleep when Vitari returned.

He'd always known he couldn't keep Francis. This wasn't some fuckin' fairy tale. Francis was realizing he needed more than sex—he hadn't even been getting that lately. Maybe Vitari should split the money and tell him to go set up a life somewhere without him. *So long, and thanks for the memories, Padre.*

"Jesus." Vitari dragged a hand down his face, clearing away his grim mood, and started the Jeep's engine. It was just the alcohol, the sleepless nights, the wretched jungle, and the fact he was trapped in the ass-end of Central America, with few options and fewer prospects. Shit would get better soon. It had to.

He pulled the Jeep up outside the casa, climbed the stairs, and unlocked the door. The house was quiet, which meant Francis was asleep downstairs. He stashed the money with the rest, poured himself a drink, and braced against the wall of windows. With the lights off, the view stretched far across the jungle canopy and down to the river, where ship lights blinked like slow-moving stars.

Vitari was doing all this *for* Francis. The thought of cutting him loose crushed his heart, but holding on to him was selfish.

He kicked off his shoes and padded down the stairs, then propped a shoulder against the bedroom doorframe, sipped his drink, and watched Francis sleep. He lay on his side, sheet kicked halfway down his body and tangled in one leg. He always looked so fucking innocent asleep, but serious too, as though even the business of sleeping should be done with conviction.

Vitari's heart stuttered. He tried to snuff out the fear with a few gulps of potent whisky but failed.

If Vitari had never met him, if the DeSica hadn't wanted to get their hands on him, Francis would still be in his little England parish church tending his flock. Although, Francis had hated that life, but he'd have made it work, like he'd made Venezuela work, like he'd probably make Panama work if they stayed long enough. He had a knack for getting on with shit, wherever he ended up. Francis could land at the North Pole and he'd find a little village to adopt as his flock. It was remarkable, really, how everyone warmed to him. Everyone liked Father Francis Scott. But nobody liked him the same way Vitari did. Liked him so much, Vitari would rip out his own heart and hand it to him, if he asked. Loved him.

Francis was his.

He should crawl into bed beside him, pull him close, whisper in his ear all the things he wanted to say, all the fears gathering like storm clouds, and he'd kiss him awake. But it wouldn't go like that because Francis didn't want him anymore, and Vitari couldn't stand it if he reached for him only to have Francis pull away again.

Vitari left him sleeping, returned to the living room, and

stretched out on the couch. The ceiling fan spun overhead, churning stuffy air.

He just had to get through this one last deal, get enough cash to leave Panama, travel up the coast, and then they'd talk. And maybe, they'd have a future together.

If Vitari didn't fuck it up before then.

CHAPTER THREE

Francis

He secured a job at the hotel bar and restaurant clearing tables, refilling the beer taps, and helping the hotel guests, since he spoke English and could throw together some Spanish. It wasn't the most glamourous of jobs, but it got him out of the house, meeting people, and none of the staff asked why a young English man was waiting tables.

During his first few days, the staff helped him settle in, mostly laughing at his attempts to speak the language. But they were kind and welcoming. And it felt good, doing something productive. Keeping busy.

On the fourth day, as he helped tidy the restaurant tables after breakfast, he spotted a man sitting by the window. He'd been there throughout the entire breakfast service. Most people ate breakfast in half an hour and then left for their day's hiking. This man had been speaking with the staff and showing them something on his phone. Francis had been too busy to find out what he wanted, but with the restaurant almost empty, and the man still sitting there, he ambled over and set about stacking the plates from a nearby table on his arms.

The man looked up from his phone and asked him something in rapid Spanish.

Francis smiled. "No hablo español." He could speak a little, but it was a colloquial mess of Spanish he'd learned in Venezuela.

"Inglés?"

"Yes."

"You see this man?" the stranger asked, turning his phone toward Francis.

Francis blinked and froze his smile. "Uh, no. I don't think so." The photo showed Vitari crossing a road, glancing over his shoulder. His surroundings appeared to be somewhere in Rome, and he wore his flashy expensive clothes.

"Your name?" the man asked.

Francis swallowed again. "John." It had been the most uninteresting name he could think of when he and Vitari had come up with pseudonyms to use locally.

"John. You sure? Look again."

"No. Haven't seen him. Can I get you some more coffee?"

"No, no." He waved his hand and closed his phone, setting it down on the table top.

"Buenos dias." He hurried away, dumped the plates in the kitchen, and walked from the hotel, through the grounds, and out onto the road. With every uneven step he took, he ran through the conversation again in his head. Someone was here, asking after Vitari. That had to mean this life was already over.

He checked over his shoulder. Nobody followed. His heart thumped in his throat. He didn't want it to be over, not yet. But Vitari was supposed to be dead, so why then would a Spanish man be asking after him?

Unless he worked for Giancarlo.

Giancarlo knew his son wasn't dead. Because Francis had told him.

He still believed calling Giancarlo had been the right thing to do. A father had a right to know their son was alive, even if that father happened to be as horrible as Vitari's. Giancarlo was many things, but not stupid. Francis's call had hopefully earned them some breathing room and some grace with the Battaglia.

Vitari didn't know he'd made the call. With any luck, he'd never find out.

Would Giancarlo send someone?

As he turned onto their track, he spotted the empty driveway, the Jeep absent. He jogged up the outside steps, mud on his shoes and his damp shirt clinging to him, and entered the house.

"Vitari?"

Nobody replied.

Francis grabbed the emergency mobile from the kitchen drawer but as he tried to turn it on, it remained dead. He muttered a curse. He had another phone—his phone, left in the drawer beside the bed. He'd charged it not long after arriving in Panama, then switched it off and set it aside, as though setting aside that life.

After dashing downstairs, he dug the phone out of the drawer, turned it on, and dialed Vitari's number.

"Come on, pick up." Where was he? An answer service rattled off Spanish and then beeped. "Call me back, it's urgent."

He tried to call again, but it rang out again, so he hung up, dropped the phone in his pocket, and paced.

The man in the restaurant had been casually dressed—not like a tourist, prepared for hiking. But he hadn't known *where* in Gamboa Vitari was. They had time. Just so long as none of the hotel staff recognized Vitari from the photo shown. It wasn't likely. The immaculately dressed Rome-Vitari in the picture had been unrecognizable from the loose shirt and linen pants of Panama-Vitari, although he still had the Italian beauty that didn't vanish from shedding expensive clothes.

Still, the man hadn't recognized Francis, so it was only Vitari he was looking for. Did that mean something?

They'd left a mess behind in England and Italy: fake deaths, a murdered archbishop... Panama should have been far enough from Europe to hide from it all, but sins like theirs would always find them.

He closed his eyes and heard the shot again. A single round that had pierced Charles Montague's skull. The gunfire had echoed around the vast cathedral, like it reverberated through Francis's soul now.

Francis opened the balcony door and stepped out into the jungle heat.

Vitari would be back soon.

All Francis had to do was wait.

CHAPTER FOUR

Vitari

Three of Aiken's guards loaded the crates into the back of a panel truck, while two stood back, eyeing Vitari hard.

Trust was fragile deep in the jungle where the law didn't reach. Vitari had picked the location for the trade, making sure they were a long way from witnesses, but the isolated location also left him vulnerable. And the tingling down the back of his neck reminded him he had several hundred thousand dollars wrapped up in duffel bags and a single gun to defend it.

The men slammed the truck's back doors closed. Aiken had his product. It was time to leave.

He caught Aiken's eye and joined him near the back of the truck. "Are we done here?"

Aiken extended his hand, and they shook. He smirked in the shadow cast by his hat. "It is good doing business with you, *Angelo della Morte*."

He dropped Aiken's hand and swallowed his thumping heart. "Who told you?"

A glint of knowing shone in his eye. "It is not that difficult to figure out. Italian accent, Battaglia guns. You are a long way from home."

Vitari backed up. It was *definitely* time to leave. If they knew who he was, then they likely knew he was supposed to be dead, and the guns weren't his to sell.

Aiken nodded at his guards. They shouldered their weapons and aimed at Vitari.

Fuck.

Vitari reached for his own gun.

"I wouldn't do that," Aiken warned.

He froze, then raised his hands. His heart sank. He'd been so fucking close to making it. "You goin' back on your word, Aiken? I thought we had an understanding."

Aiken nodded again at the rest of his people—the ones who had been loading the truck—and they started forward, toward the Jeep, where he'd stowed the bags of cash. Vitari could only watch as they grabbed the bags and hauled them to their truck.

He'd lost the guns *and* the money.

"You should be happy," Aiken said. "I'm letting you live. You have enemies who will not be as generous."

"I'm thrilled," he drawled, watching the rest of his escape money vanish behind slamming truck doors. If Aiken hadn't told anyone he was here, he would soon. People would pay handsomely to know the location of L' Angelo della Morte. People like Giancarlo. Like Sasha.

Their trip to Panama was over.

Francis would leave him after this.

Aiken climbed into one of the cars, and his armed men closed in on Vitari.

"Hey, come on, I'm not resisting. Just take the product and go—"

One at the front lunged. Vitari swung a punch, danced back, and tried to grab for his gun, but they were on him. A rifle butt slammed into his cheek, the skin splitting. Someone kicked his leg out, and he dropped, knees in the mud. A kick to the gut made sure he stayed down. He coughed and wheezed around crackling rib pain.

He blinked through watery tears as the truck, and his future with Francis, disappeared into the jungle.

He stumbled to his feet, winced around a riot of new bruises, and hitched himself behind the Jeep's wheel. A glimpse at his reflection in the rearview mirror revealed blood and mud smeared along his cheekbone.

Fuck, he was a mess. Francis was going to kill him.

Wincing and groaning, he drove his sorry ass back to the house. By the time he pulled up outside the steps, it was dark, and as he cut the lights, Francis appeared on the top step, all haggard and furious.

Jesus, this might be the final straw, the thing that pushed them too far apart...

Vitari opened the Jeep door.

"Thank the Lord, you're back." Francis hammered down the steps. "I've been calling you! Why didn't you answer your phone?!"

"You called me?" Vitari climbed from the Jeep and gasped as bruises in his gut sparked alive. Francis had been trying to reach him? The phone... He'd left it in the glove box. Francis was only supposed to use it in an emergency. "Why were you calling? What's wrong?"

"Your face!" Francis was in front of him, his soft hands on Vitari's face, thumb scraping the swollen split. Vitari's cheek burned, and he hissed. "You look terrible. Were you attacked?"

"No. It's nothing." Vitari brushed him off and started up the stairs.

"'Nothing'?"

He didn't need to look behind him to see Francis's judgmental frown, it was right there, in his voice. "It doesn't matter." Vitari made it inside and went straight for the whiskey cupboard. "We need to leave." He sensed Francis simmering behind him, and since he hadn't replied, Vitari filled a glass and stared at it, waiting for the accusations to fly.

A drawer slammed. Utensils rattled. He glanced over his shoulder. Francis wet some cloths and opened a first aid kit. "Come over here."

His voice was all cold, flat efficiency.

Vitari shifted to the opposite counter and watched as Francis's quick fingers opened the antiseptic wipes. He straightened and peered into Vitari's eyes. "Hold still. This might sting."

The cloth touched Vitari's face, shocking him. He hissed.

Francis winced. "Does it hurt?"

"It's cold."

He wiped at the blood and mud, focused on that, while Vitari studied his face up close. His freckles had bloomed in the Panama heat, and his chestnut hair had lightened, turning more sandy blond than brown. Vitari hadn't been this close to him in weeks and missed the view. He shouldn't have shut him out, but then Francis had gotten all withdrawn and icy, and Vitari had been afraid to try to fix whatever was wrong with them, knowing *he* was the problem.

He couldn't fix himself.

"I'm going to ask again," Francis said. "Please don't lie, Vitari. What happened?"

He huffed. "I fucked up."

Francis's gaze lifted, lashes fluttering as his eyes widened. "Your drug deal went wrong?"

"Yeah." In a break between Francis fussing over wipes and cloths and poking at Vitari's face, Vitari sipped his drink. "I got made and lost the product. It's not drugs, if that matters..."

"So, what was it?"

"Guns. Battaglia guns. I remembered we had a stash here and took advantage of it. We need the money if we're going to survive this."

Francis sighed. "Someone at the hotel was asking around for you today. That's why I called." He straightened again and dabbed at the cut.

Vitari winced, gritting his teeth against the burn. "Did they know my name?"

"He had your picture." Francis chewed on his lip as he concentrated on the cut. "But he didn't say your name, no."

Vitari closed his eyes and tilted his head, letting him work. The fact Francis wasn't raging or throwing things proved he was better than Vitari deserved. He should have talked with Francis, should have discussed it all, but this, them, being a pair—he'd never fucking done this before. He'd always been alone. He didn't trust people. Alone meant safe. Francis wasn't like that. "I'm sorry," Vitari said.

"For what?"

"For being an asshole."

Francis stopped poking at Vitari's cheek and stood back. "Is that all you're sorry for?"

Yeah, he was mad. "I'm sorry... for not being good enough."

His frown hardened into a glare, and now he resembled the infamous Padre Blanco who killed men who wronged him. He tossed the wipes, grabbed a butterfly strip, and jabbed it at Vitari's face.

"Ow! Jesus." Vitari flinched.

"Why do you have to be so... *you*." He scooped up the used wipes and dumped them into the trash, his every motion jagged with anger.

His rage made Vitari's insides tighten, made him feel small and vulnerable, and he hated it, hated feeling weak, hated how one glance from Francis could make him feel so ashamed that he wanted to drop to his knees. "Maybe you should throw something? Huh? Will that make you feel better?" Vitari had no right to be angry back, he should be on his knees, but old habits filled his blood with fire.

Francis grabbed the first aid kit and slammed it onto the countertop. "Maybe I will."

"I don't know what the fuck you want me to say. You know what? It doesn't matter. Pack up your shit. We need to be out of the house *now*."

"*Thank you, Francis, for fixing my face.*" Francis folded his arms and glared, red faced and fuming.

Vitari glared back, at a loss. He'd said sorry. What more did Francis want? "I have enough cash to set us up for a few months somewhere else—south, Cartagena maybe? Once there, I'll get you on a boat to Belize. You'll be safer there, without me."

Francis's face fell. And Vitari's heart broke open. He turned away so Francis didn't see how this wounded him more than any stupid split on his cheek. God, why did Vitari have to love him? Why couldn't he make his heart *stop* loving him, when they both knew it was pointless anyway.

"Is that what you want?" Francis asked quietly.

"Yeah, sure." He reached up and removed the cash cupboard back panel, then began emptying the stacks onto the counter. "It's not as though we have to stay together."

"Vitari?"

Vitari continued emptying the cupboard. He couldn't turn, he didn't dare look. If he saw the goodbye on Francis's face, it would break him wide open.

After he'd removed the last of the stacks, he checked over his shoulder, but Francis had gone—probably downstairs to gather his belongings. Vitari muttered a curse and sighed. Everything he touched turned to dust, so why should this be any different?

The front door flew open. Armed men poured in, yelling in Spanish for him to raise his hands. There was no time to go for his gun, they were almost on him.

"Francis, run!"

The men grabbed him—dragged him to his knees.

Aiken strode in, as though he had every right to wave guns around their home.

"Vaffanculo, stronzo!" Vitari snarled. In his rush to return home, he'd led him straight to their front door.

The men yanked Vitari's arms behind his back and tossed his gun onto the countertop, while two more ran down the stairs. If Francis had gotten out, he'd be all right. He just had to run and get the hell away from Vitari. He'd be safer on his own anyway.

Aiken loomed, straight faced and businesslike. "You're not going to give me any trouble, are you, Angel?"

"Depends. Who's paying you?"

Aiken eyed the fresh piles of cash, told his men to bag it

up, and settled his glare on Vitari once more. "That has yet to be decided."

He was going to ransom them off to the highest bidder. Vitari would have done the same in his position. If the DeSica or Battaglia got hold of them, they were dead men.

That couldn't happen.

A gunshot boomed from the bedrooms.

"*Francis?!*" Vitari bucked and flung his head back, smashing his skull into the nose of the bastard holding him. No, fuck, it wasn't ending like this, it couldn't. He twisted, and the grip on his wrist vanished. Vitari lunged, snatched the gun off the counter, and spun. Aiming up, he pulled the trigger, spinning the nearest armed guard around.

But there were two others, lifting their rifles.

Vitari grabbed Aiken, thrust the gun under his chin, and held him close, as a shield. "Point those fucking guns at me and your boss eats a bullet!"

Aiken raised his hands. "Relax, Angel, relax. Nobody needs to die for this."

"Don't fuckin' tell me to relax. *Francis?!*" Vitari backed toward the stairwell, dragging Aiken with him while keeping an eye on the two twitchy guards. "Francis, answer me!"

"I'm okay!"

A gasp that sounded a lot like a sob fell out of Vitari. "You need to go," he called down to him. "Get out of here." He wouldn't listen. He never did. Vitari loved that about him. And hated it.

"I don't think I can..." Francis called.

"Are you hurt?"

"Yes."

Blinding rage surged through him. His finger twitched on the trigger. They'd hurt Francis—*nobody* hurt Francis.

"Tell your men to put their guns down or I will blow your fuckin' brains out."

The guards didn't move.

"Fuckin' do it!"

Aiken nodded, and the men dropped their rifles.

"Kick them over here."

Reluctantly, the guards obeyed. Vitari—still clutching Aiken—maneuvered closer and kicked the rifles under the couch. "Over by the window, all of you, go. Turn your backs. Hands up."

They obeyed, albeit too fucking slowly.

"This won't save you, Angel," Aiken said through clenched teeth. "They know where you are."

"You think I give a shit about me?" Vitari snarled in Aiken's ear. "If he's been shot, you have no idea the hurt I'm going to rain down on you. You hurt my priest, all bets are off. You fuck with L' Angelo della Morte, you die." He could feel it, the surge of power, the taste for violence, feel it bringing him to life.

Aiken knew who he was. The second Vitari let him go, he'd tell Giancarlo where they were and that Vitari was alive, if he didn't already know.

Neo, back in London, had been right about one thing— his chances of fighting the Battaglia *and* DeSica were slim. But he'd kill anyone and everyone before dying on that hill.

"Francis?" Vitari called.

"Yeah."

"Can you make it up here?"

He paused for too long. "Is it safe?"

"Mostly."

"I'm coming up."

Good. That was good. If he was coming up, then he could still walk. He was going to be okay.

Aiken writhed and Vitari dug the gun deeper. "Your life depends on how bad he's hurt, so you had better fuckin' hope he's fine."

"They will come for you eventually. You're a dead man."

"You should have taken the guns and left the money, Aiken. We had a deal. You screwed me over."

He caught movement in the corner of his eye and spotted one of the guards making his way up the stairs, hands raised. Then Francis limped up after him, pistol aimed at the guard's back, his expression determined. Blood soaked his left leg and Vitari fought the violent urge to pull the trigger and end Aiken.

"Where's the other guard?" Vitari asked.

Francis blinked. His face was pale, freckles dark. Or were those specks of blood?

"He's uh... He's not coming." Francis said. He jerked the gun, indicating his prisoner should join the others at the window.

There had been one more man at the sale—that prick was probably outside, guarding the truck loaded with guns and a whole lot of money they'd stolen from Vitari.

He glanced again at Francis. Shit, he was pale. "Where were you hit?"

"My leg."

"I see that, Francis. Where?" He kept his voice level, calm, and controlled, despite the feral urge to murder the whole fucking lot of them. "Is it still bleeding?"

"I'm not looking," he said, swallowing hard. He kept his gun trained on the third guard, like a fucking pro.

Vitari's heart swelled. Father Francis Scott, the most bad-ass priest in the whole Catholic Church. All the dead popes would be turning in their graves if they knew. "It *really* hurts," Francis added, turning whiter by the second.

"Yeah, okay. It's going to be okay." Vitari wanted to kill them all for this. He would have done, once. Before Francis. "What do you want to do?"

"What?" Francis glanced over, so wide-eyed and innocent that Vitari loved him even more, if that were even possible.

"You want to kill them?" Vitari asked.

"What?! No. I... No. God, no."

"You hear that?" Vitari asked Aiken. "You're lucky you got yourself an angel today, Aiken, and it ain't me." He shoved him from his hold, toward the windows, and sneered at Aiken's fearful glance over his shoulder. "Get over there with the rest. Stay there. Francis, keep the gun on them."

Vitari grabbed a bag from inside a kitchen cupboard and loaded up the cash, then hurried to Francis's side.

Kneeling, he checked his leg and found the hole in his trousers, high up on his thigh, but on the outside, not inner. It looked as though the round had passed through, not lodged in the muscle, but it would probably need medical attention. He grabbed the first aid kit and shoved that into the money bag. "We're going to go outside," he told Francis. "Go straight to the Jeep. I'll do the rest."

Francis turned his head and peered into Vitari's eyes. He was afraid, more afraid then he was letting on. He was too damn precious for this shit. "We need to be fast, can you do this?" Vitari asked.

He nodded.

"Go."

Francis limped for the door.

Vitari raised his gun and fixed Aiken down the sight. The warning was clear. *Come after me, and you're a dead man.* Then he dropped his aim and shot him in the leg, the same place as Francis. Aiken barked and dropped.

Vitari dashed outside after Francis. He aimed the gun at the truck and sprayed the windshield with bullets. "Go! The Jeep!"

Francis skidded around the front of the Jeep and threw himself into the passenger seat.

Vitari shot out the truck tires, opened the cab door, snarled at the terrified driver, and grabbed his stolen duffel bags of cash. "Grazie." He tossed the bags into the Jeep, slid in behind the wheel, and gunned the engine, then lurched the little Jeep out of the driveway.

With the Jeep's wheels spinning, they sped down the track, passing the crippled truck.

Francis twisted in the seat. "Nobody is following."

"Good. Aiken knows when to back off. The glove box, my phone, grab it for me?"

Francis handed it over and Vitari one-handed dialed the police, then told them in Spanish where to find a broken down truck full of illegal weapons. That should keep Aiken off his tail for the next few days, should he get any ideas about tracking them down.

The Jeep bounced through a pothole, and Francis tensed, wincing. He clutched the door with blood-smeared hands.

"Hey, you did good back there." Had he killed the other guard? "We'll get some distance under us, then check out that leg, all right?"

He nodded, determinedly *not* looking at his leg.

Vitari smiled. "You'll be all right, Padre."

All things considered, it hadn't turned out too bad. They had money, and a long road ahead, but they were alive. And Vitari hadn't killed anyone. Yet. "There's still time to make an angel out of me, Padre Blanco."

Francis's mouth finally found a little smile as he glanced over. "I uh... I feel uhm..." His eyes rolled, his head lolled, and then he slumped unconscious in the seat.

"Fuck." Vitari skidded the Jeep onto a side track and jammed on the brakes, rocking it to a halt. "Francis?"

He clambered over the gear stick, unbelted Francis's trousers, and tried to tug the pants out of the way to examine the gunshot wound. Passing out was bad, passing out was near-death bad. Not Francis, death couldn't have him. *Never* him. "Fuck, no."

Among the blood, he found the wound. The round had taken a chunk of flesh out of his thigh, but the bleeding had slowed. The round hadn't hit an artery. He was lucky. It would scar but wouldn't kill him, as long as he kept it clean. Vitari breathed, relieved. He'd passed out from shock, not blood loss.

Straddling his legs, Vitari patted his face. "Hey, Francis... Hey, wake up, you're all right."

His lashes fluttered and his lips mumbled something that sounded a lot like a prayer. Vitari bowed his head, pressed his forehead to Francis's, and thanked his god for looking out for him.

Vitari needed him, and even if that meant letting him go, he'd do it. Whatever he wanted, Vitari would make it happen.

Just so long as he was safe.

And safe meant he could not be with Vitari.

CHAPTER FIVE

He blinked awake into glaring sunlight, already sticky with sweat, and swept his tongue around his mouth, clearing the foul dust. "God."

"No, just the devil," Vitari said. "Here." He handed over a pink bottle with italic Spanish writing on the side. Francis shuffled upright in the Jeep's reclined passenger seat and took a few glugs.

Fire surged up his leg. He glanced down and wished he hadn't. Blood stained his pants and his leg, which was exposed where Vitari had cut the fabric to get to his thigh. His head spun. He blinked away, taking more sips of water, and tried to remember how to breathe.

At least Vitari had bandaged it up. Francis recalled that happening like a horrible dream he was still trying to wake from.

He glugged more water.

"It looks worse than it is," Vitari said. "You'll scar, but

keep it clean, go easy on that leg, and it'll heal in a few weeks."

He squeezed his eyes closed and tried not to think about the chaos of last night—the armed men who had stormed the house, and how he'd shot one of them. "Where are we?" he croaked, glancing at the quiet street. A chained dog lay asleep under a palm tree in someone's yard, but the timber-clad houses were all quiet.

"A few miles from La Mesa. While you were out cold, I stopped at a local store and bought you some slacks to replace those. And the water."

Francis followed Vitari's glance to the folded slacks on the back seat, next to the huge bags of cash. His head and leg throbbed with the same heavy beat. Was this his life now? Was it always going to be like this? Forever running from the past? He couldn't think on it, or he might break down, or explode, or yell at Vitari. He didn't blame him. The choices that brought him here were his own.

"Thank you." He took another sip of water, then eyed the slanted wording on the side of the bottle. "What does it say?" He recognized some of the words. Agua, chicas...

Vitari smiled softly and shifted in the driver's seat, draping his arm over the wheel. "*Good Girls Drink Water. It's the only bottle the store had."

"Oh." He side-eyed Vitari and held out the bottle. "Well then, you should drink some. Like a good girl."

Vitari snorted. "I'm none of those things."

"If that's the dehydration hill you want to die on." He waggled the bottle, enjoying Vitari's evasiveness. Was a pink bottle not masculine enough for the Mafia don's son? Now Francis *needed* to see him drink from it and grinned as he teased, "If you were confident in your masculinity, you'd drink from a pink bottle."

"Feeling better, are you?"

"Watching you get evasive is a good distraction from my bloody leg and everything else."

"Fine." He snatched it, gulped heartily, throat moving, then lowered the bottle and licked his lips dry. "Do I look gay?"

"So gay." Francis grinned. "Good girl."

"Fuck you, Padre." Vitari laughed and handed the bottle back. It was good, hearing his laugh, as though maybe everything wasn't as dire as it seemed. They had each other. And several bags of cash. And a pink water bottle. Or maybe Francis was delirious from the heat, or a fever.

"Listen, I'm sorry," Vitari said, still smiling. "It wasn't supposed to go down this way. I fucked up." He circled his hand in the air, watch glinting. "Like I always do. On the plus side, we're where we need to be."

"You have a plan? We aren't just in the wind?"

"I can make this work. We'll head northeast, hire a local boat to Cartagena. It's easier to get into Colombia than get out. Once there, I know a guy with a small plane. He'll take you up the coast to Belize. It's going to be fine."

"Can't we fly from Panama?"

"Now I've been made? No. Colombia is... easier."

He said easier as though what he really meant was Colombia had more officials who could be bought. At least they *had* the cash.

"It's nice in Belize," Vitari explained. "You'll like it. It's like Venezuela but more refined. Once set up there, you'll be fine."

"Me? Aren't you coming?"

Vitari turned his face away. Francis had his answer. He wasn't sure what he'd done wrong, but Vitari had made it clear last night and right now that they had no future together.

What was the point in all of this if he couldn't be with the man he loved? He'd given up everything—his life, his Church—and he'd sacrifice it all again, without question. Well, a few questions. But the outcome would be the same. Had he given up his old life for nothing?

He shuffled down in the hot seat, trying to find a position that didn't make his leg feel as though it was on fire, and stared out of the window. "Cartagena." Which was in Colombia, the drug capital of the world. Francis knew that much from old movies. He snorted. "You take me to all the best places."

"I know, right." Vitari's grin returned, as bright as ever. "We'll make a cartel boss out of you yet, Padre Blanco." He shifted in the seat and jabbed the Jeep's start button. The engine grumbled to life, and they were on the move again, bumping down a cracked road.

Francis clutched the pink bottle and watched the palm trees blur past the windows. His leg throbbed, but all things considered, he didn't feel so bad. He'd have felt better if he'd known Vitari was staying with him. Panama, Belize, Colombia—Vitari made it sound so simple. Hop on a plane, run from their enemies. But he was tired of running from yesterday. He wanted a tomorrow. And now, maybe that wasn't ever happening. Not with Vitari.

"They used to put on a film about a cowboy and a writer who went to Cartagena. They crashed a bus in the Colombian jungle—or they were on the bus and it crashed—and there were these drug dealers after them..." Francis trailed off as Vitari glanced over, frowning. "At Stanmore, I mean. One of the managers had a thing for Michael Douglas. She'd put the DVD on every Saturday."

Vitari flexed his grip on the wheel. "I didn't get the all-inclusive, Saturday morning TV Stanmore experience."

Francis winced, recalling the horrible windowless room and Vitari's initials on the wall. Maybe, when all this was over, he'd take Vitari back there, and together they'd burn what was left of Stanmore down to ash. Someone needed to destroy that place, and he didn't see how they could.

"What happened?" Vitari asked. "In the movie?"

"I don't remember much. Except they had to get to Cartagena, and there was a yacht in New York at the end, and they got married, or something. Michael Douglas wore crocodile boots. I remember they were awesome, when I was ten."

"Sounds like a weird-ass film."

"They skipped the romantic parts. I didn't care because Michael Douglas was... you know... all rugged and interesting."

"'Rugged and interesting'?" Vitari snickered. "So you watched it because he got you hard?"

"I was ten." Francis tried to hide his grin behind a hand and failed.

"You know Michael Douglas is probably a hundred years old now?" Vitari said.

"He wasn't a hundred then. And he had crocodile boots. It's an old film, okay?"

"All right, no need to get defensive. I know you like 'em old."

Francis raised his eyebrows. This was payback, for making him drink from the Good Girl bottle.

"Too soon, amore?" Vitari smirked.

"You're outrageous." Francis laughed, even though he knew he shouldn't, not about any of the past, but Vitari's grin made it all right to laugh. He'd missed this with him, missed a lot of things, but mostly just missed being inside Vitari's orbit instead of cast out on its fringes.

"I missed that laugh," Vitari said. Smiling, he added, "Missed you, you know?"

Francis smiled sadly and nodded, not trusting his voice. He knew, because he felt it too, but he had no idea how to make the distance between them go away.

"The guard...?" Vitari asked, changing the subject. "Back at the house?"

Francis looked up and winced at the raw concern on Vitari's face. "Oh, he's not dead. I shot him in the leg. I think. It happened fast. He was alive though, when I left him."

"Good, that's good." He sighed, relieved.

Why did it feel as though there was still a chasm between them, growing larger by the minute? "You can tell me things, you know," Francis said. "I won't fall apart."

Vitari breathed in and glanced over. "Things like...?"

"All of it. Whatever you've been doing, who those people were, what you were selling. You could have talked to me. Still can."

"You made it clear you want nothing to do with shit like that."

"That's true, but only because I stupidly thought *all that shit* was over. You let me believe it was over."

"What did you think I've been doing at night? You're not stupid, Francis."

"I know." He felt pretty stupid. "I just, I hoped—"

Vitari checked the mirror, then yanked on the wheel and pulled the Jeep to a skidding stop. He leaned over. His fingers skimmed Francis's jaw and tilted his head up. The touch stole Francis's next breath. "All of this, everything I did these past few weeks, I've been trying to save you, save us. I don't know any other way, and I'm sorry it's not good enough, but the criminal shit is all I've got to give."

Francis caught his hand, holding it still. "You shut me out, Vitari. I thought we... I wanted—" *A future, with you.* He couldn't say it. Vitari would laugh, and Francis's heart might shatter.

"Kiss me," Vitari said.

"What?"

"Kiss me now. So I know it's real, and what we have isn't just in my head."

Francis swallowed and glanced around them at the empty track. What if somebody saw?

"Nobody is out there." Vitari shifted closer, kneeling over the gear shift, and whispered, "Kiss me, Francis, so I know I'm not losing you."

Francis fell into his dark eyes, into the breathless way he begged. They were sweaty and bloody, both a mess, but as he reached up and brushed his fingers over Vitari's beautiful face, traced the proud line of his jaw and down his bruised cheekbone, all his fears faded. It had been so long since they'd touched. Weeks that felt like months. He so desperately missed the feel of Vitari, the *taste* of him. Francis shifted forward. The wound in his leg flared up. His vision blurred, and a whistling started up in his ears. "Ugh..."

Vitari smiled and dropped back into the driver's seat. "We'll come back to that, when you're healed up."

He'd almost had him, almost kissed him, and wanted it, wanted it enough to try to climb over there and take it, take him. But if he tried it, he might pass out again. "Sorry."

"I'll find us something to eat," Vitari said, pulling the Jeep back onto the road. "And you some Advil. We've got a long drive ahead."

He caught Vitari's smirk and that knowing flicker of

delight in his eyes, the anticipation of what was to come the next time they were alone together.

Would it be wrong to blurt out how he loved him now, and beg him to come to Belize, to stay with him? What if Vitari laughed him off? What if he told him the truth, that this couldn't ever be love.

Vitari would do anything to keep him safe. Except *be* with him.

And maybe, if Vitari didn't love him, then he was right.

In the next town, Vitari stocked up on supplies for the road and Francis cleaned up in a restroom, ditching his bloody pants in the trash. The grocery store didn't have cameras and nobody was around to see him stuff blood-stained clothes in a trash can. He limped back to the Jeep, and they got underway. The paved roads became rough dirt tracks, then overgrown trails, and Vitari had to switch to four-wheel drive for some sections, just to get through.

Francis drifted somewhere between asleep and awake, nodding off, then jolting his eyes open when the Jeep hit a pothole. He dreamed of crocodile boots and a yacht floating in brilliant azure waters, but then the motion made him sick, and he woke feeling grim all over again.

"Hey." Vitari woke Francis. "Come, see this." He opened the Jeep door and climbed out.

Francis rubbed sleep from his eyes and blinked to clear his blurred vision. Stars winked in the maroon sky. He climbed down, hissing as his leg complained with a whole array of new throbs, then limped over to where the trees had been cleared and the edge of the road dropped away. He stopped beside Vitari and took in the breathtaking view of the jungle spilling down a hillside into a valley, and a splash of an oceanside town in the distance. Town lights glistened along the shoreline, as though someone had sprinkled glitter on black paper.

Vitari glanced over, his smile brightening his whole face.

The view was stunning, but Vitari standing with his hand on a hip, shirt untucked and unbuttoned halfway down his chest, hair a mess, his priceless smile—that view was worth a thousand sparkling towns in a faraway land.

"San Blas," Vitari said. "We'll get a local ferry from there to Cartagena."

Francis heard him but lost any reply somewhere in admiring Vitari.

"The roads are going to be rough, Padre. We need to stick to the tracks, stay off the main routes. You up for this?"

"What? Yes." He swallowed and turned his face toward the glistening lights in the distance. "How are we going to get into Colombia without passports?"

Vitari's grin was the only answer he gave. Did he have a plan, or was all of this improvised? How did he even know where to go and who to speak with to get there?

"Francis?"

Francis smiled over at him and saw how Vitari's smile had faded.

Vitari stepped closer and gathered up Francis's hand. "You're going to be okay." He swept Francis's bangs back. "Whatever happens, I'll always make sure you're safe. Nobody is going to hurt you."

What about *Vitari*? Who was keeping him safe? After putting Francis on a flight to Belize, would he disappear, never to be seen again? The thought of losing him jabbed him in the chest. The way he talked, almost as though he were saying goodbye. But if Francis asked him to go with him to Belize, he'd get the same response as when he'd asked him to look for a job. Vitari didn't do happy ever afters. He didn't settle down. He didn't want that life. *Criminal shit* was all he had to give.

What sin brought you to me?

You did.

"Smile, Padre." He moved in, closer still, pressed so close his every breath brushed Francis's lips and his long-lashed dark eyes pulled Francis deeper. Francis's heart fluttered in his throat. If he leaned in, he'd kiss Vitari, and it wouldn't stop there, even with a wounded leg. He craved Vitari. More so because he'd been starved of him. He needed him to make his heart beat. But if he fell into the kiss, he'd never want it to end, and soon, it would be over. So why torture himself? If they drew closer again now, it would only hurt more later, when Vitari let him go.

Swallowing, Francis bowed his head, bumping against Vitari's forehead. "Let's go, then," he croaked, leaving him to climb back into the Jeep. Vitari waited a while, his back to Francis, then returned and got the Jeep underway again. He didn't speak, only stared ahead, concentrating on the broken road.

Francis clutched at the handle above the door. The little Jeep clambered over washed-out gullies, engine humming, and it seemed as though they were making good time, all things considered.

Sometimes, headlights would gain on them, out of the gloom, and a few locals went by on trail bikes.

Francis clung on, trying not to whimper every time they hit a rough bump or one of the Jeep's wheels slid down a rock and struck the ground hard. It might have been easier to get out and walk.

"Do you have any more of the painkillers?" Francis asked. The throbbing heat turned his stomach over.

"Sure, in the bag in the back."

Vitari stopped the Jeep, and Francis rummaged through the bags of cash to find their supplies. He took a few tablets and washed them down with the water from the Good Girl bottle.

"You okay?" Vitari asked, his face troubled.

"I will be after these kick in," he said, slumping back in the seat. Slick with sweat, he really needed the journey to end.

"We'll change that dressing soon." Vitari stared ahead and flicked out his hands, flexing his fingers. The terrain was brutal on him too.

"Maybe we should wait until daylight?"

"It'll be worse then, busier and hotter." He put the Jeep in gear and started forward again. "We do not want to meet a bus coming the other way."

"A bus? Surely not on this road."

Vitari laughed. "Only the strong survive this journey, Padre."

His words were proven as they approached an abandoned SUV by the side of the road. It looked to have been shoved to the side and left there to sweat and rot in the heat while the jungle tried to swallow it.

Exhaustion alone tried to pull Francis under, but there was no chance of sleep in the jolting, rocking Jeep. He gritted his teeth. It would end, eventually. The Lord taught how endurance produced character, producing hope. Pain never lasted.

Vitari pulled the Jeep to the side and let a pickup truck clamber by. Francis watched its taillights disappear ahead.

"Hey, Francis?"

"Huh?" He blinked at Vitari's ghostlike face in the glow of the Jeep's instrument panel.

Vitari leaned over. His cold hand touched Francis's forehead, burning like a brand. "Fuck, you have a fever."

"It's fine."

"It's not fine, Padre. You need a doctor." He pulled the emergency phone from the glove box. The glow from the screen lit up his stern face. He growled. "We have a few more hours of this, then we'll be back in civilization."

"I really am fine." He just needed a bed and some sleep, and he'd be all right. He dropped his head back and closed his eyes.

"Hold on." Vitari revved the engine and lurched the Jeep back onto the track, plowing ahead and rattling Francis like a pea in can. But everything really would be fine, if he could close his eyes and sleep and dream of an avenging angel—who would leave him, once his mission was complete.

CHAPTER SIX

They rolled into San Blas as the sun rose over the endless ocean bay.

There would be a doctor, but finding one at four a.m. wasn't going to be easy. A quick search on his phone revealed a resort at the south end of the town. A hotel would have a doctor and medical supplies, but on the way there, he spotted the church and pulled the Jeep to a stop outside.

Leaving Francis, he hurried up the steps. The man inside wore casual clothes but also a priest's collar, the universal language of Catholicism, and introduced himself as Padre Federico. Vitari asked after a doctor in Spanish, and Federico took him across the street.

A sleepy-eyed woman answered her door, and the rest happened in a blur. Vitari maneuvered the Jeep up alongside her house. Together with Federico, they guided a mumbling Francis inside, where Mia, the doctor, administered a shot of antibiotics, laid Francis down on her examination bed, and removed the sweat-slick bandage.

Vitari winced at the state of Francis's thigh. A few painkillers weren't going to fix the angry wound. Mia said a whole lot about tidying his leg up and getting his temperature down, then went to work. Francis was in safe hands, and with nothing to do but rattle around the tiny room, Vitari headed back outside, tossed a blanket over the bags of cash in the Jeep, and sat on Mia's porch steps, watching the people of San Blas go about their morning routines while he fretted over Francis.

Maybe he should pray? The church was opposite.

Francis's God would have to listen there.

And he deserved a break. All of this—the chaos, the murder, the blood—Francis hadn't wanted any of it.

Fuck, Vitari had ruined his life.

"He's going to be fine," Mia said in Spanish as she joined Vitari on the porch. She tucked her long dark hair behind her ear and nodded at the Jeep. "But he needs to rest for a few days. I'll give him another shot of antibiotics tomorrow, then watch him to make sure he's healing up and the fever is gone."

Vitari nodded. "Gracias."

"You know—" She sighed and tucked her hands into her pant pockets. "—I'm obliged to report gunshot wounds."

He tried to read her face and get an idea whether she'd take a bribe or if she was going to be a righteous pain in his ass. "Are you, though?"

"Depends." She sat on the step beside him. "He doesn't look the sort to attract trouble, but you?"

"What do I look like?"

"Like you thrive on it."

He arched an eyebrow. "Two hundred American

dollars might do a lot for your clinic, doctor? Buy some much needed medicine?"

She smiled and nodded at the church across the road. "Give it to the church."

Her and Francis would get along like a house on fire. "Rough night?" she asked, reading too much on his face—everything he was too tired to hide.

He laughed dryly. He reeked, he was certain the crusted dark stuff under his nails was blood, and he had a few days' worth of stubble on his chin. But it was his heart that hurt the most. If he could stop that part of him from aching, he might be able to think straight.

"He's going to be okay. Really," Mia said, sensing the route of his pain. "I'm making coffee, do you want some?"

"Thank you," Vitari said again, revealing too much emotion in his voice. Shit, he was a mess.

"Come inside, Vitari."

In his panic to find someone to help, he'd told her their real names. Hopefully it hadn't been a mistake.

He nodded. He would join her inside, he just needed a minute on the steps, alone, so he didn't fall apart in there as soon as she said more nice things.

The church doors beckoned. He stood and ambled across the street but didn't climb the steps. He rubbed at his face, wiping away the grit and sweat. It wasn't meant to be like this. If anyone should get sick, get hurt, it was Vitari. Maybe God would agree?

Inside, prayer candles flickered to the left of the altar. Father Federico had made himself scarce, which suited Vitari. He knelt in the first pew and clasped his hands together. The last time he'd prayed it had been for Francis too, in his English church. He'd prayed that Father Francis Scott should be given a chance to be free, because in the week before they'd met, the week Vitari had spent watching him, he'd obviously been trapped. Now, Vitari was praying that Francis would find somewhere safe, and maybe someone to keep him safe. Because Vitari couldn't. These last few days were proof of that.

If things continued as they were, he'd get Francis killed.

Vitari opened his eyes and caught Father Federico in his peripheral vision. "Your kind have a knack for lurking."

"My kind?" The older man chuckled in Spanish.

"Priests."

"Ah. Yes, we do like to lurk. How is your friend?" He made his way over and stood facing Vitari with his back to the prayer candles. He was in his late fifties, with a kindly, wrinkled face, tanned by a life in the sun, aging him further.

"He'll be fine, just so long as he's far away from me." Vitari slumped back in the pew and lifted his gaze to Christ pinned to a cross.

"Does he think the same?" Father Federico asked.

"We're too different, you know?" Vitari recalled how Francis had shut him down at the view over San Blas, exactly as he'd feared he would. It was stupid to want something good in his life, to want to keep Francis for himself.

"Perhaps you should ask him?" the priest said, sticking his religious oar into things he didn't understand.

Vitari swallowed the urge to tell the priest to keep his opinions to himself. "Thank you, for helping me earlier."

The priest spread his hands. "Help is what God is here for."

"I don't think God has any interest in helping me."

"His help often manifests in subtle ways."

"And what of sinners?" Vitari asked. "And I'm not talking about little sins, what are they called?" Francis had told him once. "The trivial shit?"

"Venial sins." The priest smiled and gave a soft puff of a sigh. "Those who have lost their way are in the most need of a guiding light."

"My friend would agree with you."

"Your friend is wise."

Vitari smiled. "Yeah, he is."

"You care for him?"

Vitari lifted his gaze. Could this stranger know how much he cared for Francis just from meeting for a few minutes? Was Vitari's heart that obvious?

"You should tell him," Father Federico said.

He almost laughed. As though telling Francis he loved him was such an easy thing to say. What did this priest know of love? Still, he had the kind, aged eyes of a man who knew regret, or even remorse. Before meeting Francis, Vitari had always assumed priests had it easy. Follow God, get paid, go to Heaven. But Francis had taught him there was nothing easy in devoting your life to faith, and there was nothing easy about love either.

"Will you light a candle for my friend, Father?" Vitari asked, leaving the pew.

"I'll light two," Federico said as Vitari let the church doors swing shut behind him.

Vitari booked three days at a local resort hotel, then returned to the doctor's house to find Francis sitting at Mia's kitchen table and chatting with a young girl and her mother as though he belonged.

He watched him through the screen door, marveling at his resilience, until Francis noticed and waved him inside.

Vitari said his hellos and managed to pry Francis away

from the doctor's, then walked him down the small main street and toward the resort. They made slow progress, but after he'd shown him to their little cabana on stilts, set above the water's edge, he left him to get cleaned up.

"I'll meet you at the bar," Vitari called over the sounds of the shower, then left and went in search of a cold beer and a quiet sun lounger.

Francis joined him a little while later, fresh faced and clear eyed. He still limped but had recovered well since that morning.

"Here." Vitari handed him a beer as he sat on the lounger beside him.

Francis cringed at the bottle. "I shouldn't, not with the painkillers."

"One won't hurt. We've earned it." He took it, and Vitari chinked their bottles together. "To surviving, Padre."

As Vitari took a swig, Francis stared at his bottle, thoughts far away.

"What did I say to ruin everything now?"

"I uh..." He gazed out over the ocean and the tiny waves tickling the shoreline. His cheek flickered. "When I thought you were gone, back in England, I lost myself for a while," he admitted.

"Yeah, bought a gun, huh?" Vitari grinned. "I'm intrigued how a priest gets hold of a gun in a country with some of the strictest gun laws in the world."

"Oh, yes." He beamed. That smile lit up his face, making Vitari's heart flip-flop. "It was quite something. I got mugged early on. But I was undeterred. I thought I was being clever, but in all honesty, I suspect that Neo character had been watching me for a while."

Mention of Neo soured Vitari's mood. "That slippery fuckin' bastard. I never should have trusted him. I'm good at spotting liars, but he had me fooled. If I ever get my hands on him again, I'm going to remind him what it means to be a rat in the Battaglia."

"Uh... Yes, well... I erm... I started to drink a lot, after you were gone, and on one of those nights when I couldn't see a tomorrow, I raised a glass to you, my uh... my friend... and I toasted *to surviving*. Like we did, remember?" His voice cracked, and the next words fell out as a whisper, "I was so alone."

Vitari rolled his lips together and swallowed the sudden lump in his throat. He tried to hold on to his smile so Francis didn't see how his words hurt him too, but he could no more hold his smile than he could hold on to Francis's laugh.

The fact he'd hurt Francis proved how much of a piece of shit Vitari was.

"You just reminded me." Francis laughed softly, trying to make light of it, and picked at the beer label. "That's all."

"I'm so fuckin' sorry." Vitari briefly closed his eyes as his insides twisted. He didn't deserve to be forgiven, even if he wanted to drop to his knees and beg Francis for it.

"I know, it's okay, it's fine." Francis shrugged and took his first swig of beer.

Vitari hadn't believed Francis would care that he'd gone, but he should have, should have gotten out of his own head and started thinking about others. The fake death hadn't done any good anyway. Everyone knew he was alive, probably because he hadn't killed Neo, and that prick had talked.

He should have executed that asshole outside the cathedral.

"Have you checked the news?" Francis asked. "To see if anything has happened at home, anything about the

Battaglia?" he whispered, glancing around, checking they weren't within earshot of the handful of other beachgoers.

"No." He hadn't dared Google their names, just in case he saw his own face plastered over every news report.

However, it made sense to look now, since they were back among people, and someone clearly knew they were in Central America.

He pulled the phone from his pocket, connected to the hotel's weak Wi-Fi, and hovered his thumbs over the screen. What if it was bad? It had to be, didn't it? Not knowing meant he still had a shred of hope that everything was fine back home, even though it couldn't be.

"Do you want me to do it?" Francis asked.

Vitari handed over the phone and stared at the ocean as Francis tapped away. He didn't want to know what chaos he'd left behind, didn't want to face the repercussions of his actions, knowing it had to be dire. He'd faked his own death and figuratively thrown his father under a bus, using Sasha Zhokov to do it. Whatever Francis said next, it would be bad.

"Oh."

"You going to keep me in suspense?"

"Your father was arrested. He's been released on bail."

"They released him?" Vitari laughed. "Of course they did." His father would have paid the judge, and he'd be in the process of finding every single person connected to his case—to coerce, bribe, or worse. A fucking tale as old as time. Justice could be bought. "Anything on Sasha?"

Francis searched. "Nothing new."

"Then he's pulling strings behind the scenes. Keeping his name out of the fire. Clever." Vitari gulped the rest of his beer and shoved the empty bottle upright into the sand. "And the archbishop? Montague?" he asked carefully.

Francis's thumbs paused over the screen. He looked up, stricken. Despite the vile things Montague had done, Francis would probably struggle with witnessing his execution for the rest of his life. He blamed himself, even though Vitari had been the one to pull the trigger.

"Want me to look?" Vitari asked.

Francis nodded and handed the phone back. Vitari leaned back in the lounger and typed Montague's name in the search bar. A whole array of news links popped up. He scanned the headlines and clicked on the most reliable link. "He's missing, apparently."

"Missing?" Francis squeaked. "He was very dead though, right?"

"Oh yeah." He skimmed the article, picking out the pertinent details, or lack of them. "There's nothing, which means the Battaglia, or someone, sent in the cleaners. Charles Montague is missing, that's all."

"What does that mean?"

This was good news. At least, for Francis. "It means his body will never be found. No body, no murder charge."

Francis sighed hard. "The authorities aren't looking for us?"

"There's no mention of you." He clicked a few more articles and then searched for Father Scott, but no new articles popped up, just old ones regarding his kidnap at the hands of suspected Mafia.

"How does that happen," Francis whispered. "How does... How does a *thing like murder* get missed?"

"My guess is Neo was there for cleanup. After he sold you that gun, it was pretty fucking obvious to Sasha what was going to happen. The DeSica, the Battaglia... A dead archbishop is heat nobody needs."

"He uh… He said, when he sold the gun, his boss wanted to see how it played out."

Vitari nodded. "His boss being Sasha—the fucking Russian. Makes sense."

"I thought he meant Giancarlo."

"Like I said, Neo was a good liar."

"Then I'm—we're not wanted for murder?"

"Doesn't look like it."

Francis hiccupped a relieved laugh and leaned back on the lounger.

The small waves lapped the shore, and the nearby palms swayed in a soft breeze. Francis had that faraway look about him again; the frantic edge of panic had vanished from his eyes. Vitari let him have the relief for a few moments. The cops weren't after them, but they still had a whole lot of professional killers on their tails—killers with zero morals who didn't give a shit for laws.

"Who do you think was the man asking after you in the hotel back in Panama?" Francis asked, with a little more color in his face.

"Could have been any number of people. DeSica, Battaglia… If there's a hit with my name on it, any number of opportunistic assholes will want a piece of the turncoat Battaglia don's son. And you."

"There's a hit out on me?"

He was so fucking adorable sometimes it hurt Vitari's heart. "Padre, you had a hit out on you before the most recent clusterfuck. That shot in St Peter's Square?" Francis touched his forehead. "We still don't know who pulled the trigger," Vitari added.

Francis grimaced, probably remembering how close he'd come to losing his life that day. "I thought it was DeSica?"

"No, I asked, and it wasn't them."

"You *asked?*"

"Sasha helped with the fake-death act—the Russian bastard *really* wanted that Battaglia trafficking info. But he assured me your hit wasn't them. Wasn't my father either. So... I don't know. Someone wanted you gone."

Francis fell quiet, like he did sometimes when he had something to say that he knew Vitari wouldn't like. He looked down at the burn on his palm, the scar Vitari's father had put there. Vitari would hate Giancarlo for that and that alone, never mind all the other shit he'd done. He'd hurt Francis knowing Vitari cared for him. Perhaps because of it.

"Giancarlo offered me five million euros to walk away."

"Fuck," Vitari gasped. He hadn't known that. Jesus, the depths his father would dredge to ruin Vitari's life were unfathomable.

"I keep asking myself why? Why not just kill me? He could have."

"Was that before or after he burned your hand?" Vitari asked, sounding cold.

"Before." Francis glanced at his palm. "Do you think he maybe... didn't want to kill me?"

"You were *protected*. He couldn't."

"Maybe..."

"There's no maybe about it." Giancarlo was a butcher, but the things Francis had said about Stanmore, about Giancarlo's role in it all... "You believe Montague's last words, don't you?" Vitari asked. "About Sasha being behind Stanmore?"

Francis lifted his gaze. "Montague knew too much for it all to be lies."

Vitari had been wondering about that for weeks too, wondering if he'd made a mistake. But his father had known about Stanmore, known everything he'd gone through, and he'd done nothing. He'd let Vitari believe he was a worthless mongrel and his mother a whore. Giancarlo deserved to be caught. It didn't matter what Vitari thought. It was too late now anyway. He'd fucked over the Family, given Sasha everything he needed to bring them down. It was done. He was done. They'd come for him. Today, tomorrow, next month. He was dead.

But since Montague's body had been *cleaned* and there was no murder, Francis still had a chance to be free. And Vitari was going to make damn sure he took it.

"Do you trust Sasha?" Francis asked.

"Trust him? Fuck no. The DeSica have no honor. They'll kill each other to get ahead. It's not like the Family. We have a hierarchy, a code, we have fucking rules. Family first, then business, then country. We don't kill each other. Actually, that's bullshit—sometimes we do, but only to protect the business. Family is everything. There are no rules in the DeSica, just Sasha. So, no, I don't trust that fucker."

"Then he could have lied about not being behind my shooting." Francis flicked his fingers at his forehead. "Made you think it wasn't him so you got him what he wanted. If you knew he was behind the hit, would you have gotten the trafficking evidence he wanted?"

Vitari narrowed his eyes. "No."

"Could he have been playing you?"

He hated to think he'd been so fucking gullible as to be pulled in by the Russian *and* Neo, but it was possible. "Maybe. He said to look closer to home for the source of your contract. Why would he say that if he was behind it? Why not just demand the trafficking information or you get a shot between the eyes, like he started out with? He didn't need to point a finger elsewhere."

"Good point."

They fell into a thoughtful silence again. A whole lot about Sasha's motives weren't adding up. He could have admitted to hiring a killer to take out Francis, but he also clearly liked to play games. He'd known Vitari's mother but claimed he hadn't. He was a liar, like all the DeSica.

"It doesn't matter anyway, DeSica, Battaglia, we're in a whole lot of crosshairs."

"What if your father knew you didn't mean to hurt him?" Francis asked, staring out to sea.

"But I did."

"Okay, but what if it's not like that? What if he somehow knew you'd made a mistake? Would he send people to kill you then?"

Vitari laughed. "A mistake is accidentally getting caught blowing a priest's cock. Betraying your own father to the man who murdered the love of his life? That is no mistake." Vitari tilted the beer bottle and raised an eyebrow. "That's suicide."

Francis's gaze stayed on him a few beats too long, then he looked away. "You think we're a mistake?"

Vitari grinned. "Sure we are." Francis's face fell. "The best mistake of my life, Padre." As his face brightened, Vitari caught his heart hiccupping over all the hope and possibilities he shouldn't want and couldn't have. God, he was a fool for Francis. He'd do anything just to see that little smile and how it made his handsome face brighten.

He was so fucking adorable, Vitari wanted to crawl over there, straddle his thighs, and kiss him into the lounger, saying all the things with his body he couldn't say with words, but they weren't alone on the beach. Tonight, though. Tonight he was going to unravel Francis with his tongue and reacquaint him with the parts of Vitari that craved him the most, including his heart. "Want another beer?"

"I should probably stick to water."

"Another beer it is." Vitari heard his chuckle as he left for the bar. If Francis could laugh, then things weren't so bad.

Hopefully, with a little luck and God on their side, the worst was far behind them.

CHAPTER SEVEN

Francis

"*Sure we are. The best mistake of my life.*" Those words had flipped Francis's heart into a gallop, making him light-headed. Or perhaps that was the beer.

They stayed on the loungers, talking about nothing, sometimes falling quiet, then the conversation dug deeper. Francis told Vitari how he'd spiraled the last few weeks in Westminster, and how Montague had drugged him, to which Vitari had snarled something vicious sounding in Italian and said again how he wished he'd taken the time to cut Montague's balls off. But then Vitari had gone on to explain how he'd tried to save the trafficked kids in Spain and wasn't sure if he'd succeeded.

Catalina Diaz had told Francis that Vitari *had* succeeded, and when Francis was able to confirm it, all the fake flashiness vanished from Vitari's grin and relief softened his eyes. The same relief he'd seen on his face when they'd saved the Venezuelan kids on the Italian farm. "Grazie, Padre," Vitari said, meaning it. "I needed that."

It felt good, being with Vitari, *talking* with him—really talking, like they should have months ago—spending time with him, without the gunfire, running, murder, or some other dire circumstances trying to pull them apart. It felt like a future together might feel, and was it so bad to want that? They deserved it, didn't they?

"Francis, amore mio?"

Francis blinked awake and smiled at Vitari's warm face. The glow from the sunset caught in his eyes, like fire. "I fell asleep?" The beer and medication had definitely made him sleepy.

"You're so fucking adorable. Come on, let's get inside."

He laughed at himself and limped alongside Vitari to their resort cabana. Theirs appeared to be half suspended above the water, and it was one of the smaller homes, set far back from the others. Vitari must have paid a fortune for it.

"What did you do with the cash?" Francis asked. Vitari wouldn't have left tens, maybe hundreds of thousands of pounds on the Jeep's back seat, would he?

They entered the house, flicking on lights. A lounge at the front had double doors opening onto the balcony over the water, then the kitchen, where they'd entered. The bedrooms and bathrooms were at the back.

"Yeah, the cash." Vitari flopped onto the couch among its dozens of cushions. "We can't take it with us, not like it is. I've stashed most of it under Father Federico's church. What we'll need to get out of Colombia I've hidden in the seams of our bags. You've got enough to get you settled in Belize until I can ship the rest up to you."

Francis hid any revealing frustrations on his face by

heading out onto the balcony. He leaned on the rail and watched the ocean ripple under a rising moon.

He'd lost Vitari once. Thought him dead and gone forever. But he'd come back. A miracle. Only for him to lose him a second time when Francis went to Belize? Perhaps he deserved it, for pushing Vitari away, for breaking his heart?

If Vitari hadn't come back, that night at the cathedral would have ended very differently. Francis would have shot Montague and then turned the gun on himself. Vitari, his angel, had saved him.

Vitari's hand settled on Francis's back and stroked up his spine. Then those warm fingers gently rubbed his neck, and it would have been the easiest thing in the world to let it happen, to lean back and let Vitari do this—he wanted him to, but at the same time didn't, if it meant it would hurt so much more when they said goodbye.

He rolled his shoulders, brushing him off.

Vitari took the hint and moved away.

"Good night, amore," Vitari said.

"Good night." Francis glared at the ocean and forced the words through his teeth. He didn't want this to be how it ended, didn't want to push him away, but what choice had he given him? What was the point in sex if Vitari was going to put him on a plane and send him away? He couldn't stand it, couldn't stand craving him, needing him, knowing it was all for nothing.

Why did he call him his love if he didn't mean it?

Francis bowed his head.

He had to tell him. Before it was too late. *No regrets, Padre.*

What sin brought you here?

You did.

"Vitari, wait." He turned so fast his head spun.

Vitari stopped on the other side of the balcony doors, and when he turned, he wasn't smiling. He just looked tired and alone and hurting. But he didn't have to be alone. Francis was his, if he'd have him. He'd *forever* be his, if he wanted to, in whatever form that forever took. Whether it was white picket fences or stacks of ill-begotten cash. Whatever life Vitari wanted, Francis would stand beside him. That was who they were.

He opened his mouth and stalled. How did he even begin to explain all of that?

"It's late—" Vitari began.

"I don't know why you're doing this, but it doesn't have to be this way."

"Doing what?" he asked.

"Pushing me away."

"I'm not—"

"Don't talk, just listen." Francis moved closer. "Or I won't ever get this out. I know I'm not a part of your world, and I probably never will be. I don't understand much of your life, and maybe I don't agree with most of it either, but that doesn't mean—" The words wedged in his throat. He wasn't sure how to explain everything he felt. It was all so visceral, words failed him.

Vitari's eyebrows lifted. "Doesn't mean what?"

Dear Lord, help me say the right thing. "I'm sorry about what I said, about trying to tame you."

"Tame me?" Vitari laughed. "What am I, an animal?"

"No, that's not what I meant." Oh God, give him strength not to mess this up. "I'm saying it all wrong." He moved closer again. "I lost you once, Vitari. I lost you and it hurt, it hurt like I've never known."

"I'm sorry, I never meant to—"

"Just—hush up. I need to get this out."

A knowing glimmer of mischief sparkled in Vitari's eyes. "Are you mad at me, Padre?"

"Yes, I'm mad at you! I'm always mad at you, and maybe a little mad *about* you." He winced. This was terrible; he sounded like a fool. He wasn't making any sense. The more he talked, the further away he got from the point.

Vitari frowned. "Are you all right? Maybe those beers weren't a good idea—"

Another step brought him almost within grabbing distance, and Francis ached to hold him, to kiss him, to taste him until there was nothing else, but he needed to use words, needed Vitari to understand why all of this was so difficult. "I've never done this before, never really had someone. And I know you don't want a future with me. I get it. I do. But I lost you Vitari and when you came back, it was... I don't know, it was a second chance, a chance to see what I didn't want to see before, what I couldn't see. Everything was so confusing. A lot happened. And there you were, and it was hard, I mean you were hard—"

Vitari's frown tilted, turning confused. "Maybe you should sit down?"

"I'm not sitting down. I have to say this, I have to..." He stepped close enough that Vitari had to lift his chin, that they almost touched; so close it was just him and Vitari and the sound of the ocean. "My whole life, I've been trying to fit in somewhere, trying to make myself into something I'm not. When I'm with you, I'm just me. And it's right. I fit."

The corner of Vitari's mouth twitched, hinting at his smile. "Go on."

"Damn you, Vitari. I think you know what I'm trying and failing to say."

"Do I?"

Here it came, the truth—the only real truth that mattered. "I love you. There it is. I said it. And I mean it."

Vitari's eyes widened, then his smile lifted his lips. "Are you sure? You sound pretty high right now. Painkillers and beers—"

Francis clutched his face, looked him in the eyes, and said, "I. Love. You."

But instead of smiling, Vitari's face crumpled. His smile broke apart and fell away. God, was he about to... cry? Francis flung his arms around him and crushed him close. Vitari clung to his shirt at his back, and he buried his face in his neck. Francis hadn't meant to hurt him, not like this. He'd thought it was a good thing? Love. And he *did* love him; as soon as he'd said it, he'd known it was true. He loved Vitari with every part of himself—mind, body, and soul. He loved him as though a fire burned within, ever brighter and hotter.

"You can't," Vitari whispered. "You can't love me." His cheek brushed Francis's, leaving a touch of wetness behind.

"I can. I do. Please, don't put me on that plane without you. I can't stand losing you again, I can't do it. I *won't* do it."

"Goddammit, Francis. Why are you doing this to me?"

"It's the truth." He spoke the words into Vitari's ear and felt his shudder, felt his fingers dig in, felt him hold on, as though Francis were the only thing in his life worth holding on to. "Your father asked me if the truth was worth my future, and it is. You are." He leaned back, bracketed Vitari's face, and almost sobbed when he saw the tears shining in his eyes. "I love you, Vitari Angelini. I know it because when you were gone, so was my heart."

"Fuck, stop." A tear left a wet trail down his face.

He'd said what he'd said, and maybe, finally, Vitari was

listening and believing he was worthy, because he was everything to Francis—his life, his love, his heart. He slammed a kiss on his mouth, but as Vitari clutched him close and kissed him back, Francis slowed, kissing him softly, carefully, needing him to know, to feel how much this meant and how real it was. Mouth to mouth, soft and hard, so very right that Francis wanted to crawl inside him.

Vitari gasped free and clutched at Francis, bowing their heads together. He drilled his stare into Francis, pinning him still. "If you stay with me, you'll die with me."

He nodded. "I know."

Vitari winced as though Francis wanting to be with him *hurt* him. Why would it hurt? What did he flinch from?

"You deserve so much more."

"There is no more I want than you."

"Francis, I..." He laughed and then kissed him, thrusting his tongue in, rocking Francis back while holding him close. Vitari took his hand and pressed it to his chest, and when the kisses ended, the next words were dragged as though he'd dragged them up from his soul to speak them. "Ti amo con tutto il cuore, ti amo più della mia vita."

Francis didn't know what it meant, but he could guess from how Vitari's voice trembled. He loved him, they loved each other, and wasn't that all that really mattered?

"I love you with all my heart," Vitari said, holding his gaze. "More than life itself. And it scares me like nothing else, you scare me, losing you..."

Oh. Fear, doubt, relief too—it all rushed over Francis, stealing his voice. He swallowed and tried to find the words but none would come. Then Vitari's mouth was on his, his hands on his face, and the dam broke, filling the chasm that had opened between them, bringing them back together.

Vitari laughed free and yanked at Francis's shirt,

sending a button flying. "I need to feel you." He tore at the remaining buttons, freeing them, and plunged his hands inside, then swept them up Francis's back. Yes. He arched under his hands. Francis needed this too, needed to feel him close, needed to lose himself in Vitari.

He leaned back, and Vitari's hot mouth scorched his neck, sucking, teeth nipping. Francis moaned, and Vitari's left hand dropped, scooping around to clutch Francis's ass and squeeze. "How do you want it?" Vitari growled. "Fast or slow?"

He wanted it *all ways*, and almost whimpered with need.

"You have to tell me, or I'm going to bend you over that couch and fuck you so hard, Francis, neither of us will be the same again."

He breathed fast through his nose, *wanting* that—wanting Vitari's cock punishing him—but his damn leg had already begun to ache, and he wasn't sure his thigh would take the pounding Vitari's hungry eyes promised he'd give. "Yes, but... not yet, my leg..."

Vitari dropped and in one swift movement swept Francis off his feet. Francis yelped, held on, and laughed. "Wait! I can walk!"

"I've got this." Vitari carried him through the kitchen. "Although," he grunted, "you're heavier than you look." His grip shifted,

Francis clutched on. "Don't drop me!"

"I might," he huffed, staggering down the corridor. They reached the door, and Vitari kicked it open, then toppled against the wall, still cradling Francis. "This went a lot smoother in my head."

Francis snorted. "Put me down."

"Almost there." Vitari staggered in, tripped, and

dumped Francis on the bed, tumbling with him. Vitari snorted, and Francis laughed.

"Panama food agrees with you," Vitari said, straddling his hips, and kneeling over him.

"Wow."

"Padre." Vitari smirked in that deliciously wicked way of his, then fell forward, pinning Francis to the bed. "I'd still love you if you were the size of a cow."

"Oh my God." Francis laughed.

"Or skinny as a rake too, or ugly. It just so happens you're not any of that, but if you were, I'd fuckin' love it all. Love you, amore mio." He nuzzled Francis's neck and stroked his chest, then cupped his head and sucked on his ear. Francis's laughter fell away as lust made his veins blaze. *Love.* It didn't seem real, that Vitari would say it and mean it. There had been that one time, a drunken confession over the phone, but this was different.

"You're overthinking, Padre," Vitari crooned, then shifted upright on his knees again and whipped off his shirt.

By the Lord God, every time Francis witnessed Vitari shirtless it stopped all his thoughts, emptying them right out of his head, so there was nothing—no noise, no guilt, no shame, just a beautiful man, currently pinning Francis down with wicked promises in his eyes.

"Do not worry, vita mia, stay right there." Vitari stroked Francis's chest and came to rest at his hips. Francis held his gaze, and Vitari skimmed his knuckles across the bulge in Francis's trousers, spilling a riot of tiny shivers through him. "I'm about to fuck you up in the best possible way." Vitari leaned down and swept his tongue along the hollow of his ribs.

Francis scrunched his fists in the sheets. The sweet, wet probing of Vitari's wicked tongue promised so much more, and it was that anticipation that had him near moaning. "I missed you."

"I know," Vitari said sadly, then shifted up and flicked his tongue over Francis's left nipple.

Francis let out a startled bark of laughter and Vitari slammed his mouth over the sound, drinking him down. Francis grabbed him and clung on, holding him down, never wanting to let him go again as he kissed with his whole body, rocking into him, his mouth and tongue a teasing dance Francis matched in his own desperation. He needed to breathe but needed to feel him more, needed him to know that without Vitari, there was no Francis. "If you make me get on that plane without you"—he gasped between kisses, mouth messy, teeth nipping—"I will *never* forgive you."

Vitari's dark, lust-drunk eyes widened. "Won't you let me save you?"

Francis thrust his hand into Vitari's hair and twisted his fingers, holding him still. "I don't need saving."

A glimmer of fear sharpened Vitari's eyes, there and gone again, wiped away by his cocky smile. "You're so fucking hot when you're mad."

He was scared. Francis had seen it. This wasn't about saving him; it was Vitari thinking he didn't deserve him, as though he'd put Francis on an impossible pedestal, forever out of his reach, when the truth was nothing like that.

Vitari eased lower, and Francis freed his grip on his hair, letting him kiss all the way down his chest. His fingers worked at his fly, and almost too quickly, his tight, wet mouth sealed over Francis's cock, taking him deep with fierce strokes. The rush of savage lust swept all thought away. Old fears tried to muscle in, feelings of shame for enjoying thrusting his dick down a man's throat, but not just any man, the man of many sins, the man he loved, L' Angelo della Morte.

Vitari pulled off and wiped his mouth on the back of his hand. "No shame, Padre," Vitari growled. He grasped Francis's glistening, hard dick and pumped, but it was when his finger slid behind his balls and pushed inside that Francis dropped his head back and surrendered. It was too good, but so bad, everything he needed but was forbidden to have, and the conflict spiraled, tightening inside him, like an elastic about to snap. The hate was there too, probably always would be, and that made Vitari's touch exquisite.

"Your face when you come..." Vitari smirked, but there was more to that smile now, more to his gaze. "Hold it, Francis, not yet. Yeah, you feel that, feel how tight my fist is, how close you are."

Francis's breaths stuttered. He was falling, falling fast, he wouldn't be able to stop it.

Vitari stopped pumping but kept his grip tight, then pumped once, twice, and stopped. Francis moaned. More, he needed more, needed to chase the edge until it was right there, until he fell over it.

Vitari's finger shifted inside him, stroking, milking. A tremor spilled through Francis, his dick so hard, and so sensitive, he had to bite his lip to keep from coming.

"Will you take my confession, Father?"

Francis held his stare. "Now?" he croaked.

Vitari swept the tip of his tongue across his lips. "I wanted to fuck you since we met, bend you over a pew, lift your cassock and pound your tight ass."

Vitari continued to stroke inside him, each tease another step closer to coming, and with his words now adding to the cacophony of lust and madness, there was no holding back.

"You like that idea?"

He forgot how to speak and moaned, but Vitari already knew the answer.

"I see you do." Vitari's expression turned all kinds of mischievous, and he let go of Francis's dick, letting it drop against his navel, leaking pre-cum. "I'd hold you there, spread your cheeks, bury my dick deep inside you—"

He couldn't take any more. He was going to come without his cock being touched, brought to climax by Vitari's finger unleashing wave after wave of electric lust until the waves blurred into one long stream of pleasure, and he came, cock twitching, spattering cum over his hip.

"I don't know what's better," Vitari purred, "watching your face or dick when you come."

Francis thrust his head back, gasping, blushing, his heart a hammer against his ribs. He just needed a few seconds to come back down.

"That's a lie, it's always your face, amore mio." Vitari kissed him on the corner of the mouth and settled on the bed, tucked alongside him. Francis reached for the bulge in his trousers but Vitari caught his hand. "I'm good just basking in your afterglow."

"You don't... want to?"

"Always, but right now, I prefer this. It doesn't always have to be about shooting your load, yah know?"

He wasn't sure he had known, until this very moment. Francis touched Vitari's face, skimmed his whiskered chin and that crooked smile. He was too beautiful, too perfect, and so precious. He'd made himself into a man of violence so he had control, but that wasn't all Vitari was. Vitari Angelini was so much more than the small, jagged piece of himself. He was fierce, full of love, brave, and righteous—in his own way. He fought for the innocent and for those who could not fight for themselves.

"You should rest," Vitari said. "Heal up. I'm here. I won't leave you, Francis."

Francis's eyelids drooped, the afterglow trying to drag him into a warm, cathartic sleep. The fear of losing Vitari hadn't gone, but it had been pushed into the corners of his mind. "Promise?"

"For so long," Vitari whispered, as though beginning a fairy tale, "I belonged nowhere, had nothing. My father saved me, made me Family, but more than that, the Mafia became my life, my religion, my purpose, the reason I breathed. I should have told you, so I'm telling you now. Francis..." He intertwined their hands. "You are my family. You are my religion. I will *never* leave you, unless you want me to. I give you my word, my heart, amore mio."

Vitari's whispers followed him into his dreams, where they wrapped around him, keeping him safe from all the hurt in the world. His angel would never leave him.

CHAPTER EIGHT

Father Francis Scott was not supposed to love him, and as Vitari watched him doze, mouth open, snoring lightly, he didn't know what to do with that love. He still expected Francis would wake up, come to his senses, and walk away. Like he had in Rome.

Love.

Actual fucking *love*.

Not some messed up, twisted version of it. Love like you get in fairy tales, like that stupid ancient movie Francis had watched with Michael Douglas and his crocodile boots.

Vitari chuckled and rolled out from under Francis's arm. Francis wasn't going anywhere, and Vitari wasn't sleeping, not with his head full of *everything*.

He showered, made coffee, and settled at the table with his phone to search for more news from Europe.

A quick scan of the results around Montague's disappearance revealed rumors of historic sexual abuse claims, but the reporters hadn't mentioned details. It could have been nothing, just gossip to sell clicks, or it could have been Stanmore rearing its ugly head behind the scenes and the church crushing those rumors to dust.

Vitari scoured the various news articles for the Battaglia, but considering how thoroughly he'd fucked the family, there wasn't much news. Even the details of his father's arrest were sparse. He'd been arrested for tax evasion. Of all the viciously wicked things he'd done, tax evasion was the least of them.

Vitari wasn't sure what he'd expected. Giancarlo should have been behind bars, or even dead, considering everything Vitari had given Sasha.

Something didn't feel right.

He was missing something. Neo had survived, and he'd have told Giancarlo about Vitari taking Francis, assuming Neo was still pretending to be loyal to the Battaglia.

Neo might even be closer to Giancarlo now, in Vitari's absence.

And then there was Sasha, who'd gone out of his way to get all the information on the trafficking operation, an operation similar to Stanmore. He'd used some of it to ensure Giancarlo was arrested but hadn't acted on it, or the Stanmore photos—damning photos of all the shit that went on at Stanmore. Perhaps he'd drop that bombshell later?

But why wait?

Or Sasha hadn't done anything with the evidence because Stanmore was *his* operation?

Could it be that he'd just wanted to know how much Vitari remembered?

Francis believed it.

And Francis was smart. Mostly.

Vitari glanced at the snoring priest and smiled. "Fucking love, man," he muttered.

He had it bad. He'd known it for a long time. Francis probably didn't love him back the same way, but maybe it was enough?

What if Vitari did go to Belize with him? They could vanish with the money they had, settle down... Shit, what was Vitari supposed to do for the rest of his days? Fuck Francis every day and live to be a hundred years old?

What did normal people do with their lives?

Vitari ambled to the balcony. The sun was climbing over the ocean. Small waves lapped at the house stilts, and a few parrots screeched in nearby leaning palm trees.

Maybe Francis could tame him? Would it be so bad to be a kept man? He'd thought so once, laughed at the sheep of the world... Could a wolf ever be tamed?

The things he'd done—killed mercilessly and without remorse, beaten countless men and women, bullied, extorted, ruined lives... He didn't deserve a happy ending, but he'd fucking fight for Francis to get his.

He sauntered back inside, found a pen, and scribbled a note:

Hey, Francis.

I'm taking a walk.

I'll grab your meds from the doctor.

Should he write *love you* at the end? That seemed like a whole lot of mushiness he wasn't used to. Would it come off as too much? They'd shied away from text messages and voicemails, since any evidence of their love would be used against them. But what harm could it do here, in the ass-end of Panama?

He signed it *V. A.*, then screwed his nose up. Leaving initials was pretty dry.

"Fuck it." He added *amore mio, x*. It felt right, and it wasn't as though he hadn't already told him he loved him a thousand times, just not in English. Until last night—last night he'd laid his heart bare.

He wedged the note under the phone on the table, tucked his gun against his lower back, concealing it under his shirt, and headed out. The resort guests hadn't yet woken. The beach houses were quiet. Local fishing boats moved about the bay, heading out to catch the day's haul.

Vitari walked the beachfront, losing himself to his thoughts. He hadn't ever, not once, thought he'd have a chance at something bigger than him, at something good. Shit like relationships hadn't featured in his plans. And now there was Francis, a priest of all things, who had turned Vitari's life upside down. Now he was thinking about things like *having* a future, like sharing his life with another person, sharing his heart. He had no idea what to do with that. Although, if anyone could make it happen, it would be Francis.

Father Francis Scott didn't know when to quit. He didn't give up, even when he should. If he believed in something, he stuck with it. *"Just because something is broken doesn't mean I give up on it"*, he'd said in Rome. That *something* was Vitari. He'd been talking about Vitari. He smiled to himself again, remembering Rome, remembering Venezuela—the good times, not the bad.

Vitari circled back through the town, and as he passed the church, he glanced around, checking he was alone, then ducked under the raised foundations where he'd stashed the cash. Still there. He ducked out again and sauntered on toward the resort parking lot, where he'd left the Jeep overnight.

A bunch of parrots squawked at his arrival. He stopped

beneath a bent palm and watched the colorful birds jump from frond to frond, wings flapping. What was a collection of parrots called? Francis knew weird, random shit like that.

Boots crunched on gravel. Vitari turned and eyed the man headed across the parking lot toward him. Early thirties, tattered sneakers, faded T-shirt. He seemed to be alone, and as he drew closer, he dropped his right hand and reached behind him.

Vitari placed his own hand on his gun at his back.

Parrots shrieked louder.

The rough stranger brought his hand back around—holding a gun.

Vitari cocked his weapon and jerked his chin. He opened his mouth to warn the prick who he was about to mug—

A bag swung down over his head from behind him. Plastic handles cut into his skin. Fingers grasped his neck. Vitari gasped, sucking in air, but the bag glued itself to his face, blocking his nose and mouth. He whipped the gun behind him—the weapon was snatched away.

Panic clutched at his heart. He bent double, trying to heave his attacker over his head, but the bag stayed on. He staggered, fighting to stay upright, to breathe, to think. The stranger's blur still came for him—parrots screeched louder—and his every gasp failed, lighting his chest on fire.

His sight throbbed, ears ringing, darkness pushing in.

The bag—if he could just get the bag off! He tried to dig his fingers under the hold around his neck, but the thudding in his head spread to his chest, where his lungs screamed, desperate for air.

His knees hit the dirt.

Too fast—

He just needed—

The bag vanished.

Air rushed down his throat. He choked, wheezed.

"Come with us," a Spanish-accented voice said.

Hands hauled him to his feet.

Vitari bucked, or tried to, but his body still burned, his head throbbed, and his vision swam. A fist landed in his gut. Pain roared. Vitari hit the ground, clawing at the dirt. Hands grabbed him again, hauled him to his feet.

A pickup truck pulled in, and his attackers flung Vitari against its side.

"Fight and you get the bag," the brute holding him warned.

"Fuck... you." Vitari slammed his head back, colliding with the satisfying crunch of a nose.

The brute swore in Spanish, and down came the bag, plastered to Vitari's face again, blinding him, choking him. *Fuck, fuck, fuck...* He struggled, shoving, bucking, pushing. He couldn't let them take him, he couldn't leave Francis fucking alone. Another punch hit him in the kidney. He heaved, choked, and drowned in darkness.

The roar of an outboard engine and thumping jolts of the speedboat carving through waves dragged him awake. He coughed, tasting blood and dust. On his side, he blinked into bright sunlight and sea spray. He'd been dumped in a boat alongside the guy wearing those tattered sneakers. Shifting, he found his hands had been bound behind his back, making sitting up a struggle, especially with the brutal seesaw motion of the boat. But he managed to lift his head high enough to see San Blas's beach shrink into the distance.

He huffed through his nose.

A single man piloted the boat, two more sat up front, facing ahead, and Sneakers sat next to him.

"Where we going?" he croaked at Sneakers.

"Boss wants to talk," he replied in Spanish.

"Which boss?"

His answer was a side-eye that made it clear Vitari had no friends here. This close to Colombia, any number of cartels might want to get their hands on L' Angelo della Morte. Colombia wasn't Venezuela; the Battaglia had no foothold here. Even if it had, Vitari was persona non grata *everywhere*.

At least they hadn't killed him. Although his insides felt as though they'd been yanked out, rearranged, and shoved back behind his ribs.

If they hoped to ransom him, they were about to discover Giancarlo would prefer him dead rather than have him back on Italian soil.

He watched the San Blas coastline fade away until there was nothing but the relentless sun and a whole lot of Caribbean Sea between him and Francis.

He'd be all right, he was Francis... But this time, Vitari was the one facing uncertainty, and now that he had something to live for, fear of losing it all crawled under his skin.

Don't do anything stupid, Francis.

Vitari would get out of this, and he'd get back to him. All Francis had to do was stay put. How hard could that be?

CHAPTER NINE

Francis sat at the table and reread the note. Vitari hadn't returned from his walk.

Francis had woken late, found the note, showered, gotten dressed, and warmed up the coffee Vitari had made, but as the minutes had ticked into hours, an uneasy feeling crept into his gut.

Perhaps Vitari had gotten delayed at the doctor's?

Francis couldn't sit and wait a moment longer. He left the cabana, hurrying from the resort and down the street toward Doctor Mia's house. His leg throbbed—the painkillers had worn off during the night. But that was fine, he'd probably find Vitari chatting with Mia, and then once he'd taken the meds, they'd go find somewhere to have breakfast together. Over breakfast, they'd discuss *everything*. After last night, things had changed for the better. They were finally talking, like they should have done weeks ago.

"Your friend Vitari?" Mia asked, meeting Francis on her porch. "I haven't seen him. But I can give you the medication. How do you feel? Any side effects from the painkillers you had yesterday?"

He thanked her and waited for her return with the tablets and squinted at the church across the road. If Vitari had been returning to the resort, Francis would have seen him on the walk over. Perhaps he'd taken a stroll farther down the beach?

"Here you are," Mia said. "Take two three times a day with food."

He thanked her again, told her he'd check in later, then headed to the beach, where he dry-swallowed the tablets and limped along the sand. He scanned under each parasol for Vitari's distinctive figure, but he wasn't on the beach. He wasn't with the Jeep either, and he wasn't back at the beach house.

Vitari wasn't anywhere.

Standing back on the street in front of the church, baking under the sun, Francis checked the note again.

Hey, Francis.

I'm taking a walk.

I'll grab your meds from the doctor.

V.A.

Amore mio, x

It had been hours.

And he hadn't made it to Doctor Mia's.

Something had happened to him between the resort and town. Francis could feel it *inside*, could feel Vitari's absence.

"You're looking better."

Francis squinted up the church steps at the grey-haired man smiling back at him. The tab of white at his throat was both familiar and on a lesser level, alarming, as though this priest would instantly know all the sins Francis had committed in the past few weeks and months. Of course he couldn't know who or what Francis was, could he? "Oh, yes, Father. I uh... Have you seen the man I arrived with?"

"Not since yesterday." He came slowly down the steps. "I'm Father Federico. You're Francis?"

How did he know his name? That was bad, wasn't it? They weren't supposed to use their real names. Vitari must have told him, but when and why?

"Don't worry." Father Federico tapped his nose. "I'm in the business of keeping secrets."

Francis almost laughed. Few people knew how to keep secrets as well as priests. Federico seemed nice, and he'd helped yesterday, but Father Davis had seemed nice too, befriending Francis right before hand-delivering him to Giancarlo.

Francis absently rubbed at the scar on his palm. He had no intention of making the same mistake twice.

"Mia told me your name, if you're wondering," Federico added.

That made sense, he supposed. "I uh... My friend was due to meet me, and it's been awhile now."

"I'm sure he's around," Federico said, unhelpfully. It wasn't his fault. Why would Vitari be in danger? This priest had no idea who they were, what they'd been through, and everything they were running from. "Did you check the beach?" Federico asked, his kindly eyes smiling too.

"I've looked everywhere." Francis didn't want to sound whiny or desperate, but he was beginning to feel both. He couldn't call Vitari—he'd left the phone behind to pin down the note—and couldn't call the police.

He was alone.

"He'll be along." Federico tried to reassure him, then must have seen the panic on Francis's face. "Unless there's a reason he might be in danger?"

There were a thousand reasons why Vitari might be in danger, but none he could tell Father Federico. "I'm sure it's nothing." He flashed a smile. "You're right, he's probably around somewhere." Francis thanked him and wandered back toward the hotel. He'd checked the Jeep once already, but as he approached it a second time, something metal sparkled underneath it. He knelt and fished the heavy metal thing out.

A gun.

He almost dropped it, then remembered his fingerprints were already plastered all over it and clutched it close. Nobody was in the parking lot; nobody had seen him pick up the gun.

Was it Vitari's gun? He cradled it in both hands. It *looked* like Vitari's gun.

Why would it be under their Jeep?

He scanned the parking lot, spotted some tourists, and discreetly tucked the gun under his shirt. The dirt and dust beside the Jeep did seem to be scuffed about, with long scrapes and arcs in the gravel. Signs of a struggle? A few dark spots caught his eye. He knelt and poked at them.

Blood.

"Oh no."

Vitari *had* been taken.

It was obvious, wasn't it? The note, his absence, the gun. He'd gone for a walk, and he wasn't back, and the discarded gun was proof someone had taken hm, someone who had overpowered him, someone capable. Not just one... One person wouldn't be able to bring down Vitari. More than one. And they had a few hours head start.

What was he supposed to do? He had no idea where to look or who to speak to, nobody to call—certainly not the local authorities. The police would probably arrest him, if they even cared at all.

Francis needed help.

He turned on his heel, jogged back to the church, pushed through the big door, and found Father Federico laying out rows of prayer candles. "So... uh... I need some assistance in a... difficult matter," Francis panted out.

"Ah, Francis, back again so soon." Federico waved him over. "Is this about your friend?"

"Yes, Father. It's just..." The old priest gave Francis the same patient, mildly intrigued face that Francis often gave his own parishioners, probably expecting a menial ask or a spiritual query. "He really is missing. He's been taken."

Federico's hands stilled over the candles. He turned and met Francis's gaze, finally taking him seriously. "Taken? You are sure?"

"Certain."

"Perhaps, the policía—"

"No, no police." Francis stared back.

Francis stood in the middle of the little town church, empty pews on either side, with the kindly eyed priest studying him, and he wasn't sure if he belonged, or if he had any right to ask a man of God for help. But his church, the church he'd tried to serve, had been a sanctuary for all. Especially those in need. "It's a really, *really* long story, but he's in trouble, and I have to find him."

"But you can't ask the police?" Federico asked. Some of the lighthearted warmth had cooled in his eyes.

"No. Definitely not. It's... complicated."

Federico nodded. "Is this something to do with your gunshot wound?"

Francis winced. "Yes?"

The old priest sighed and placed the rest of the candles down on a side table. "Your friend came to me, we talked. So, forgive me for asking, but could he have decided to leave?"

"What? No." Regardless of everything that had happened last night, Francis had his gun, and Vitari never would have been so careless as to drop it. But he couldn't tell Federico that, not without revealing they were criminals.

"It's just that, yesterday, he was... troubled."

Francis took a step back. "Yesterday?" He blinked. "He was troubled?" Vitari hadn't said.

"About you."

Francis eyed the pews, the church, the candles. Vitari had come here when Francis had been out cold and feverish. He'd come for solace, when Francis hadn't been there for him. What had he told Federico about being troubled?

It didn't matter what was said. Francis *knew* Vitari. "He wouldn't leave, not like this." He pulled the note from his pocket and handed it over. It was a risk, given how Vitari had written *amore mio,* but it also proved he'd had every intention of returning after his walk.

The priest's eyebrows pinched together, but Francis couldn't be sure if that concern was for Vitari's whereabouts, or if he was about to receive a lecture in sin. He hated this, hated standing under the eyes of God, feeling small and wrong and shameful. "I know he's been taken," Francis said, more forcefully. "Will you help me or not?"

Federico lifted his gaze and handed the note back. "I will help. Wait here." Federico strode down the aisle and out of the door.

Wait here?

Waiting didn't seem like the best idea, since he had no idea if he could trust Father Federico. What if he had left to fetch the police? Francis followed just a few strides behind him. They crossed the road and entered Mia's house. Federico wasted no time in speaking to Mia in her make-do waiting room, which was at least currently empty of patients. They spoke Spanish, with Mia occasionally glancing over. Her friendly smiles faded too.

She'd been kind, she'd helped him, but he didn't know either of them, and trust wasn't something that came easily, not anymore. What would Vitari think of Francis asking these two strangers for help?

He paced a little, checked the window, hoping he'd see Vitari saunter down the street.

What if he was dead?

No, no, Francis wasn't thinking that. There was no reason to think Vitari had been killed. He'd been *taken*.

The gun poked Francis in the back. He shuffled it around. He should probably have left it somewhere, not brought it with him, but there hadn't been time.

"You think he was taken?" Mia asked in English. Federico stood stoic beside her.

"I do."

"Any proof?"

"Proof?" He frowned. "What proof? Isn't my word enough? He was taken, I know it."

"There's someone I can ask, but he's not someone you go to unless it's important."

"Vitari was *taken*," Francis said again. "This *is* important."

"You didn't have any kind of argument?"

An argument? What did they think had happened, that Vitari had stormed off because of a lovers' tiff? "You want proof? Fine." He grabbed the gun and then realized what a terrible idea that was when Mia and Federico recoiled as though Francis was some kind of gun-happy madman about to shoot them both. "Oh, no." He raised his hands, and the gun. "I'm not going to use it! I found it." He laughed nervously. "It's not mine. It's uh..."

Wide eyed, Mia waved a hand. "Maybe point it away?!"

He lowered the gun to his side. "It's Vitari's, and I found it under our car. Someone must have kicked it there. He would never do that. He's careful with guns."

"Like you're not?"

"Well, I... I don't have much experience..." He tried to put the gun down on a nearby table but Mia shook her head, making it clear she wanted nothing to do with the weapon.

He tucked it back under his shirt again, half hating it there but needing it too. "I know this is... unconventional, but I wouldn't be asking for help if I didn't need it. You're a priest, you're a doctor. I have nowhere else to go. Please, can you help me find him?"

Mia and Federico exchanged glances, until Mia muttered, "I knew he was trouble." She shook her head but managed a smile that eased some of the tension between them. "I will take you to Miguel Sanchez. If Vitari has been taken, Miguel will know who has him."

"Thank you." He glanced at Federico, who appeared to be more concerned by the minute. "Gracias, Padre. Will you please light a candle for us?"

"I already did." He opened the door and left, muttering a prayer under his breath.

Francis would take all the prayers he could get. The words might have more weight not coming from him.

"Francis, let's go," Mia said, grabbing a bunch of keys and heading out the back.

Francis hurried after her. She climbed behind the wheel of an old pickup, and Francis climbed into the cab beside her. He clicked on the belt. "Who is Miguel?"

She smiled. "You'll see."

They drove a little ways down a rough track, bouncing and jarring into and out of potholes, and then, after it seemed as though they'd traveled miles, Mia pulled up outside a dilapidated cabin. Francis left the pickup and eyed the cabin's timber walls and palm frond roof. He couldn't tell whether the place was in the process of falling down or if it was supposed to blend in with the jungle around it. A few tattered deck chairs had been placed around a cold firepit.

"Miguel?" Mia called, approaching the cabin. She added a few words in Spanish too.

The screen door clanged, and a huge man emerged from the gloom. His sweat-stained shirt clung to a round belly and gaped at his neck. Miguel—Francis assumed he was him—had muscles like Sasha Zhukov. He had big, broad limbs, white whiskers dusted his dark, wrinkled face, and a scar continued from the right corner of his mouth, through his cheek, and toward his eye, giving him a permanent smile.

Francis's gaze dropped to the curved, rusted machete in his grip.

Miguel grunted at Mia, and as his shrewd eyes took in Francis, he said something in Spanish.

"Sorry, I don't speak much Spanish," Francis said, ungluing his stare from the machete to look the man in the eyes. He had deep-set eyes—two dark holes, eager to swallow hapless tourists, like Francis. "Some, a little. But..."

Mia tilted her head and arched an eyebrow. "Francis, this is Miguel Sanchez. Miguel said he knows you."

"Really?" That seemed unlikely. He couldn't imagine where they'd met before and would surely remember him.

Miguel stomped down the steps, then sat on the final step and shoved the machete tip-first into the dirt. "Padre Blanco." He chuckled.

Mia arched an eyebrow and studied Francis with a little more intent. "Father White?"

He had no idea where to even begin explaining how he'd gotten that name or how Miguel could possibly know him. "It's complicated." How did this man, living in a nowhere shack, know Padre Blanco?

"I'll bet," Mia drawled. "That gunshot is not looking like such a freak accident now."

He'd never actually said it had been an accident.

Miguel took a cigarette from his pocket and Mia was quick to offer a lighter from hers. He lit the end and handed the lighter back. "What can I do for you, Padre?" Miguel said in a deep, rich combination of smoker's drawl and South American Spanish.

Mia nodded Francis on.

"A friend of mine has been taken, and uh... Mia said you might know about that?"

"'Taken'." He didn't say it like a question, more as an assessment, and took a drag on his cigarette. The smiling scar tightened his cheek. "Nombre?

It seemed as though the truth might take him further here than lies, and Miguel already knew of Padre Blanco, so... "Vitari Angelini."

Miguel narrowed his eyes.

"Angelo della Morte," Francis added, and recognition sparked in Miguel's eyes. "You know him?"

"I know of him, the Battaglia's vicious attack dog. I know who has him."

Mia muttered something that sounded very much like swearing.

"They take your friend to Cartagena," Miguel explained, drawing on his cigarette and flicking the ash to the ground, as though he had all the time in the world.

"What? Why?" How was Francis supposed to get him back or get to Cartagena?

"Ransom."

"Ransom, I..." Kidnapped and sold to the highest bidder... This was bad. He didn't know what to do, where to go, or how to save Vitari. "Who?"

"Very bad man."

Of course it was. Francis could feel the hysterical laughter bubbling up his throat. No *good* man was going to kidnap Vitari and demand a ransom. He was beginning to wonder if there were any good men left in the world.

His heart raced, panic trying to push him into demanding these people do something. "How do I get to him?"

"Go to Cartagena."

He said it as though such a thing was even possible. "I don't know how. I don't know..." He threw his hands up, then sighed and focused on breathing. He needed to think. What did he have? What could he use? There had to be a way... He was alone, but he wasn't without resources. "I have money, and I can get more. I'll pay the ransom?"

"How much?" Miguel drawled.

He had no idea how much Vitari had stashed under the church. What was a good kidnapping amount? Tens of thousands? A hundred thousand? More? "Enough. How do I reach this bad man, what's his name?"

"Serpiente Diablo."

"What?" Francis said automatically, even though he

knew its meaning. "Devil Snake?" What kind of name was that?

Miguel nodded. "Bad man."

"Serpiente is a local cartel boss. He controls the drops," Mia added. "And much of San Blas."

"'Drops'?" Francis asked. Maybe it was a language thing because he had no idea what any of this meant.

Miguel glanced at Mia and frowned, they shared a few words, and Mia snuffed, looking up. "Drugs, Padre."

"Oh." Serpiente was a drug dealer. So, if he was a drugs man, all he wanted was money? This wasn't revenge or a hit. It wasn't personal. It was business, as Vitari liked to say. Which meant Francis could get Vitari back. "I want to talk to him, how do I do that?"

"You're going to get yourself killed, Francis," Mia said.

"No, it's fine, I just need to talk to this Serpiente man and explain I can pay." His thoughts spilled out of him as words. "He has to bring Vitari back. I'll pay the ransom. Whatever it takes. I know people, bad people. He can't just... take Vitari. Vitari is... He's L' Angelo della Morte. This Serpiente man has no idea who he is dealing with."

Miguel smiled, then chuckled and said something that sounded derogatory at Francis's expense.

Francis stopped pacing and dug his heels in the soft jungle floor. "You think this is funny?"

"You are amusing," the old man agreed. "Serpiente will kill you, take your money, and ransom Angel to Battaglia, yes?"

"I'm not that easy to kill." He had a gun. He meant it. If they wanted to come for him, let them. He'd killed before, and he'd do it again. Nobody here understood the lengths he'd go to—he maybe didn't even understand it himself.

Vitari had *nobody*. But he had Francis, and Francis would *never* abandon him.

"Padre Blanco." Miguel chuckled. "You should leave, while you can. Go back to England."

"Go?"

"Leave Panama, go north? Get away. This business is not for you."

Just like that? Just walk away? No. That wasn't an option. "You don't know me."

"I know *you*, Padre, do not want to be here. This not your fight. Your Angel will survive, or not. But a gringo like you will not—"

Francis pulled the gun, cocked the hammer, and aimed at Miguel's chest. He saw, in his mind, how he'd pulled the trigger and blown Luca Espinosa away. He saw, in his memory, how he'd held the gun on Montague and would have killed him too, eventually. He'd do the same to this man. "Call this Serpiente, tell him I want to speak with Vitari, tell him I will get his money and buy Vitari back."

"Francis—" Mia stepped forward, then stopped as he skewered her under his glare. She raised her hands.

"Do not *Francis* me. I'm not what you think. I'm not what any of you think. I've been pushed from one crisis to another, shot at, kidnapped, abused, beaten, betrayed, and I am *done*. I am not going to stand back and let you people tell me what I can and cannot do. Vitari is mine. I am getting him back. Call Serpiente."

Miguel held Francis's stare. Those dark, sharklike eyes pierced Francis's soul.

He wasn't backing down. Everything was at stake. Miguel could laugh at him all he liked, but Francis wasn't laughing. These people had no idea the depths of darkness he'd plunder to save Vitari.

Miguel stubbed his cigarette out on the step.

Francis eyed him down the gun sights. The panic faded, his racing heart slowed, and his manic thoughts calmed. It was simple. All this man had to do was make a call, and the gun in Francis's hand would ensure that happened.

If he did not make the call, then Francis just might shoot him. He would not be laughing then.

"I underestimated you," Miguel said. He rose slowly, and Francis raised the gun with him. "Mia, you have a phone?"

"You don't own a phone?" Francis asked him.

"I left the world behind long ago, Padre." He gestured at the smiling scar from his mouth to his cheek as though that explained everything.

Who *was* he, that he lived out here in a hut, without a phone, and answered the door carrying a machete? It didn't matter. He was going to help.

Mia handed Miguel her phone. He dialed a number and raised it to his ear.

Francis lowered the gun but kept it visible at his side. He swallowed, trying to moisten his dry throat. He hadn't wanted to aim a gun at anyone, but what choice did he have? Mia was eyeing him as though she didn't know him, which, he supposed, she didn't. He wasn't even sure he recognized himself. But it didn't matter because they were getting Vitari back.

Miguel spoke rapidly into the phone. Francis caught his own name and enough Spanish to know whoever he spoke to wasn't this Serpiente man, but it was someone who was going to help.

Miguel ended the call and handed the phone back to Mia.

"Well?" Francis asked when he couldn't stand Miguel's deliberate silence a second longer.

"They will come. They are meeting off the coast. We wait."

"Wait?"

"Yes, wait. Some advice, Padre Blanco?" Miguel asked, thick eyebrows lifting.

"Advice?"

"Better hide your emotions. If they know how much you want your man, the price increases."

That was probably good advice, but he'd never been very good at mind games. "I'm going to meet Serpiente? He'll come?"

"Yes."

He tucked the gun away and dropped into one of the plastic chairs by the firepit. Everything was going to be all right. He had to believe that.

"Beer?"

"I don't drink," he mumbled, although that wasn't true. He did drink now, and he waved guns around, and threatened mean-looking men with machetes in jungle shacks. Who even was he anymore?

"Sorry about the gun," Francis said.

Miguel's laugh rumbled. "I like you, Padre Blanco."

CHAPTER TEN

The speedboat bumped against the rear of a three-deck luxury yacht. The driver tied it off while Sneakers grabbed Vitari and hauled him onto the lower deck. Whoever said crime didn't pay hadn't seen the mega yachts moored in Cartagena, because this one was a beauty and made the Battaglia's yacht look like a poor man's dingy.

Crime paid bigger and louder in Colombia.

"Sit your ass there." Sneakers shoved Vitari onto the wraparound bank of couches and sauntered off, probably to get whoever owned the floating palace.

Vitari had his suspicions for who was behind his kidnapping, especially now he'd seen the yacht. He'd hoped to have been in and out of San Blas without pinging the Serpent's radar. He shouldn't have cared that Vitari was just passing through. Apparently, Vitari had underestimated the waves his arrival had made. It seemed as though the whole fucking criminal underworld knew he was alive, and every chancer, cartel boss, low-life criminal piece of shit wanted a slice of L' Angelo della Morte.

At least they all wanted him alive.

He hadn't been sure after the bag-over-the-head move.

"Angelo della Morte." The man who jogged down the internal spiral staircase was in his late fifties, with golden skin, long black hair tied up, shrewd, sharp eyes, and a thin, narrow face. He moved fast for an older guy and swept through the living area to drop onto the couch opposite Vitari. Vitari knew of him, although they'd never met.

Cisco Roman, also known as Serpiente Diablo.

He studied Vitari without blinking. "Not sure what I was expecting, but you aren't it. You look like a daddy's boy, like you got big boots to fill, like you've coasted along on Papa's coattails all your life and now he's tired of you, you're all at sea. That you, Angel?"

Vitari snorted and adjusted his bound hands behind his back to keep them from digging into his spine. "You don't know shit about me."

"I know your father wants you back alive, but only so he can kill you in front of the family, teach them a lesson. Rough childhood, huh?" Cisco snorted. "Cry me a fuckin' river."

Vitari kept his smile, even as the words cut deep. He'd known Giancarlo would hate him for the betrayal, but hearing it spoken by this Colombian nobody made it real, and made the shit he was in real too.

Cisco leaned forward and studied Vitari with his dull brown eyes. "Did you think you could scurry through my town like the rat you are and I wouldn't notice?"

"I don't care what you think."

"You fucked up, kid. Really fucked up. Of all the places you could go, why San Blas?"

Vitari didn't have to say a damn word to this guy. "Why am I not already on a flight back to Italy?"

"Yeah, you see, I don't think much of the Battaglia, or the DeSica, and I don't care how Daddy wants you back so bad he'll pay a few million for the pleasure. I'm just here to take the cash and get you far away from my operation. You're like a bad fucking omen, L' Angelo della Morte. Death follows you."

Then he was waiting for the highest bidder. DeSica or Battaglia, Sasha or Giancarlo. Either way, Vitari was screwed. "If I'm bad luck, let me go."

Cisco laughed again, then cut himself off. "Who is Francis?"

Vitari arched an eyebrow and ignored how his heart dropped through the floor. "Who?"

"You don't know a Padre Blanco then?" Cisco smirked. "Father White."

"Never heard of him." Fucking Francis, what had he done now?

"Huh. You see, that's real strange. An old friend of mine called me up. He says a gringo—Padre Blanco—shows up at his door, waving a gun around, demanding to speak to me, says he has money. Wants to pay your ransom. And you've never heard of him?"

Fuck. "Just some crazy white guy." If Francis got on this boat, they'd shoot him and dump his body overboard. There was no way Francis could touch any of this. Why hadn't he taken the money and run? How did he always get his hands on a gun?

"You know what I heard?" Cisco added.

"I'm sure you're about to tell me."

"Padre Blanco is a Mafia priest. Rumor is he killed a Mafia man in Venezuela, one of your own?"

"I don't know anything about that." *Fuck.*

"Other rumors credit him for a village massacre, as though this priest and his angel of death herald a whole lot of bad mojo. Is Padre Blanco going to be a problem?"

Fucking Francis. Vitari's smile grew, mostly from disbelief, but Cisco saw it and narrowed his eyes.

Francis's reputation might help them. Cisco was concerned about Padre Blanco, the gun-wielding priest who did not hesitate to kill notorious psychos like Luca Espinosa. Vitari could get behind the image. "Depends if, like you said, you want a quiet life, or a whole lot of trouble?" Vitari glanced at their opulent surroundings. "Seems like you don't need a few more million, and maybe Padre Blanco is a curse you can do without?"

Cisco leaned back, losing all his smiles. "Fucking Europeans and your drama."

Shit. Cisco was actually thinking about backing off.

"Does Giancarlo know I'm here?" Vitari asked, leaning forward. He saw from the twitch of Cisco's face that he did. "Then he'll send people for me. The money won't matter. They'll fuck it all up to get to me. If you don't want my trouble to find you, let me go. The longer I'm here, the worse it will be. Not a threat, just facts. The Battaglia have already sent their priest..."

"This is a whole lot of shit I do not need..." Cisco mused aloud. "You know how I got here? Stability. No fuckups. You and your Mafia bullshit are not welcome in my Colombia."

"I understand that. I don't want to be here either. You seem reasonable. Let's do a deal. Hand me over to Padre Blanco and walk away."

Cisco seemed to be considering it. "All this fuss for some rich kid with daddy issues. Russians, Italians, even the fucking Catholic Church. They're all fighting for a piece of *you*."

The Church? Did he mean Francis? It didn't matter. Vitari was getting through to him. Cisco just might decide he was too much trouble and let him go.

Cisco clicked his fingers and Sneakers made his way over. "Bring Padre Blanco to me. Let's meet this infamous priest."

Shit, that wasn't the plan. If they saw Francis, they'd know he wasn't the big bad Mafia priest the rumors had made him out to be—he was Francis, the love of Vitari's life. If Francis got on this yacht, he wouldn't leave it alive.

"Take me back to him, huh? Saves time you may not have." Maybe if he could get back to San Blas, he'd find a way to escape them, but out here, on this yacht, even if he could get out of the restraints there was nowhere to run. If Francis came to them, they'd both be screwed.

Cisco considered it and nodded. "You so eager to see your priest, Angel?"

A few hours later, as the sun began to set over the idyllic San Blas Bay, Vitari watched the little speedboat bounce over small waves, growing larger as it headed toward the yacht. Francis's mop of sandy hair gleamed in the dying daylight, and as the boat drew closer, he could make out the deep lines of determination on his stoic face. Francis couldn't swim, but there was no sign of any fear.

Padre Blanco.

Vitari's heart swelled. They might be able to pull this off.

Not only had Francis stuck around when he should

have taken the money and run, he'd somehow made it known Padre Blanco was not to be fucked with, and he was coming for Angel.

When this was over, Vitari was going to strip him down and fuck him breathless, fuck him so hard there would be no room for doubt or fear in that amazing head of his.

Vitari waited by the bank of couches, flanked by two guards. Two more were in the boat with Francis, another piloted the yacht, and then there was Cisco, somewhere nearby. All of them were armed. Vitari and Francis were grossly outnumbered.

They just had to get through this alive. And much of that relied on Francis playing his part.

Don't smile, Francis, don't smile, don't smile. Francis looked over as they tied up the boat, and as soon as he spotted Vitari, a broad, brilliant grin broke out across his face. Vitari didn't even care, that grin was *everything*. He hadn't realized how scared he'd been that he'd never see Francis again, until that big, stupid grin.

A few seconds later, Francis wiped the smile off his face so nobody saw and climbed from the rocking speedboat onto the deck. He tripped, earning a few raised eyebrows, but straightened and brushed it all off like a fucking pro.

"Padre Blanco!" Cisco announced, crossing the deck from the living area, arms out, as though meeting an old friend.

Francis didn't smile, and instead eyed Cisco as though he didn't trust him as far as he could throw him. *That's it, Francis. Be that man I know you can be, the smart, blood-thirsty bastard who will fuck anyone up if they get in his way.* He'd always been in there, ruthless, cold, and now Francis needed to own that side of him and use it.

"He had this on him," Sneakers said, handing Cisco Vitari's lost gun.

Cisco raised an eyebrow. "Not very Christian of you, Padre."

"Catholic," Francis corrected in that thin, emotionless voice he used when he was trying very hard not to explode.

"To-may-toes, to-mah-toes." Cisco set the gun down on the coffee table, a few strides from Vitari. With bound hands, Vitari wasn't going to be able to use it unless he could writhe out of the plastic ties. He'd been working on rubbing them loose, but he had no way of knowing if they were close to coming undone.

"So, you have money?" Cisco asked.

"I do."

"How much?"

"Enough."

Francis was adamant he never lied, which was almost a shame because he was fucking good at it.

Vitari forced his expression to stay blank and continued to rub at the ties around his wrists.

"The two of you are a problem," Cisco began, glancing between them. "Angel has made it clear any bidding war is likely to be a stalling tactic. With that in mind, you're already here, Padre, and we all want the same thing—both of you a long way from me and my Colombia."

"Who wants him?" Francis asked.

"Russians, Mafia, a great many bounty hunters." Cisco laughed. "I'm beginning to wonder why I don't just shoot the both of you and be done with it."

"No." Francis stepped forward. "If Angel is killed, his father's vengeance will destroy everything you have here." He paused, took a breath, and said clearly, "As will mine."

Cisco met and held Francis's dead-eyed glare. "You threatening me, Padre?"

"Just stating facts. The way I see it, there's only one way out of this that doesn't see you suffer. Let us go. Kill us, harm us, or try and ransom us, and you will find Giancarlo and the Battaglia relentless in their pursuit to bring you down."

Fuck, since when had Francis gotten so good at this? Vitari had always known he'd had it in him, seen glimpses of it, but this was another level.

Cisco glanced over at Vitari. "Giancarlo is old blood, on his way out. Someone is going to take his crown and soon," he told Vitari. "What's your plan, kid? Outlive his reign? See if the next boss will take you in? Lions kill the male cubs."

"That's my problem, not yours." The ties holding his wrists behind his back snapped and fell away. Nobody saw; they were all too busy trying to get a read on Francis. The gun was on the table, no more than a lunge away. He'd get one, maybe two shots off before the guards reacted, but when they did, they'd spray the whole deck with automatic fire. Now was not the right time. He had to wait for an opportunity.

"Where's the money?" Cisco asked Francis.

"In town. I'll take you to it. But Angel comes too. We trade, and you let us leave?"

Vitari expected Cisco to argue, talk numbers, maybe even play a few games with Francis, try to figure out who he really was behind the myth. But Cisco gave it little thought and nodded. "You got yourself a deal."

Vitari didn't trust any of the men here, and he trusted Cisco least of all. Like Aikin, Cisco would take the money and try to gun them down. He'd have preferred to kill them on the yacht—no witnesses. But Francis had thought of that and left the money in San Blas. Good move.

The guards bundled Vitari into the speedboat—not noticing his freed hands, since he kept his wrists together. and Francis climbed in too—keeping his gaze off the water. Cisco and Sneakers rode in the middle, facing ahead. Vitari glanced at Francis—a quick flick—and caught Francis's secret smile. Vitari couldn't reach out, not when he was pretending to still be restrained, but the smile was enough.

Vitari had to look away to keep from grinning. Every fucking day, Francis surprised him. This Father Francis Scott in a drug runner's boat was a long way from the Father Francis Scott from a quaint rural English church. Vitari couldn't even claim to be the one who had corrupted him. Francis had always had it in him. The sinning saint...

"What's that?" Francis asked, raising his voice over the outboard engine.

Another speedboat carved down the bay toward them, parallel to the beach. It wasn't police, the boat was too small, but it was coming right for them.

Cisco had seen it too and pulled a 9mm gun from under his shirt. Rival cartels, or worse?

The other boat grew louder, engine roaring. A man stood at its bow and raised an automatic rifle.

"Down!" Cisco barked.

Vitari grabbed Francis, shoved him down, and ducked alongside him. Gunfire popped. Cisco fired back. The man working the outboard motor pulled on the steering bar, lurching their boat sideways. Water washed over the side. More gunfire barked. Vitari covered Francis and heard his muttered prayer—probably begging for his God to keep the boat afloat.

At a break in the chaos, Vitari lifted his head.

The other speedboat slowed, no more men pointing guns—the kill switch had been triggered.

"What the fuck was that?" Sneakers barked.

This was it, the opportunity to escape. Vitari lunged, plowed into Cisco, who stumbled, dropping his gun. Vitari grabbed it, pointed at Sneakers, and pulled the trigger. *That's for the plastic bag, asshole.* Hit, Sneakers toppled over the side. Vitari swung and aimed between Cisco's eyes but held off as Cisco flung his hands up. "Can snakes swim?"

Vitari didn't wait for the answer, swung the fist not holding the gun, knocking Cisco back, then kicked his unbalanced wobble over the side.

The guy at the motor remained, but while Vitari had been scrabbling for the gun, Francis had thought ahead and snatched the guy's rifle and had it pointed at him like the fucking badass he was.

"Turn us around, head back to the yacht," Vitari ordered the pilot.

"What?" Francis glanced behind him. "Aren't we going back to shore?"

"There's nothing back there but more men with guns."

The pilot swung the speedboat back toward the yacht. With any luck, the guards left on board wouldn't have heard the gunfire over the engines.

"What about the money?" Francis asked, still pointing the rifle at the pilot. "Are we going to leave it behind?"

"It's safe." Vitari checked the clip. He had enough rounds to finish off the rest, assuming he got the drop on them.

Ten minutes later, they pulled alongside the back of the yacht. A guard appeared from inside. Francis shouldered the rifle. "Don't move!"

Vitari grinned at his priest getting his sass on, then waved Cisco's gun at the pilot. "Out."

The man began to climb toward the yacht.

"Other way, overboard. Now. Go. Yes, swim or fucking die. Choose in the next three seconds."

He jumped.

Vitari climbed aboard and scooped up his original gun from the table. With Cisco's gun in his left hand, and his own in his right, he nodded at Francis.

"What?" Francis asked, still aiming the rifle at the guard. Then he caught Vitari's meaning. "Oh, I..."

"Lean into it, Padre Blanco."

Francis's conflicted expression was all kinds of adorable. He eyed the guard. "Sorry. It's not personal."

Vitari wasn't going to make him shoot to kill, not like this.

He raised his own weapon at the guard. "Drop the gun." After he'd obeyed, he told him to head to the back of the yacht, and like his friend, gave him a choice. He chose to jump.

"I'm going to sweep the rest of the yacht, make sure there aren't any more," Vitari told Francis. "Stay out here. If anyone shows up in a boat, shoot them."

"All right. But uh... Okay."

In a maddening urge to crush Francis in his arms, Vitari kissed him quickly on the lips instead, then looked him in those beautiful hazel eyes so he knew they'd fuck later, and soon, because it turned out Vitari might have a gun kink too, if Francis was wielding it. But then Francis lunged, slammed a rough-edged kiss on Vitari's mouth, and thrust his tongue, coming at Vitari like a man possessed. Vitari almost dropped the guns and ravaged him right there on the deck.

Francis's hand—the one not holding the rifle—plunged into Vitari's hair and knotted, gripping hard. "Are we safe?"

"Almost." Vitari's ragged breath betrayed the raw need to strip him down and lick his every inch, fuck his every hole. "Stay here, and if someone comes, you don't have to kill them, just wave the gun like you mean it."

Francis swallowed hard and nodded, and Vitari climbed the steps onto the upper deck.

The pilot in the control room went for his gun and died from a shot between the eyes before he made it.

Francis didn't ask after the reason for the gunshot, probably because he already knew the answer, and Vitari swept the lower sleeping decks. "All right, we're alone. You okay?"

"Yes." Francis set the assault rifle down by the table and wiped his hands on his trousers as though he might wipe the sin off.

"I'm going to disable the yacht's tracker and get us the fuck out of here. You sure you're okay?"

"Yes, I think so. I'm all right." He even managed to smile. "Good, actually. I feel pretty good."

Vitari smiled back. "Let's get out of here." He started to climb the stairs, but Francis's soft, "Vitari?" stopped him halfway up. The strange muddle of relief and fear on his face killed Vitari right there on the steps.

He rushed back down, crossed the floor, and grasped his face. "You fucking came for me, Francis."

"Of course I did." His lips ticked up at one corner. "I won't ever leave you. Unless you want me to?"

"Want you to? Jesus, I fucking love you." He kissed him hard again, only easing off when Francis molded himself close. He wanted to do more, ached to unravel him right there, but he needed to make sure they couldn't be followed, and then they'd be safe.

He forced himself to let go, then eyed the delicious blushing face of the priest who had just rescued him. "As soon as we're away from the coast, I'm coming back to this."

"Can I come up there with you, to the cabin, the control room—whatever it's called?"

"The bridge. And you can, but there's a dead guy up there."

Francis nodded. "It's okay. Well, it's not okay for him, but I need to be with you."

On the bridge, Francis found the horizon fascinating while Vitari dragged the body back down to the main deck and dumped it over the side. Returning for a second time, Vitari dismantled the control panel and disconnected the tracker.

"Where did you learn to do that?" Francis asked.

"Fucking about on yachts with Sal. His papa had one, smaller than this but same design. Sal and me stole it for a wild weekend around Sicily. Little Toni threatened to kill me after that, but it was worth it." Vitari fired up the monstrous engines and pointed the yacht out into the Caribbean Sea.

"Will Serpiente come looking for us?" Francis asked, staring at a whole lot of ocean behind them.

"Cisco? Yeah. Which is why we need to move *now*."

The yacht vibrated pleasantly as it raced across the ocean. No bouncing over the waves—this beauty carved right through them. Vitari could get used to this. "We've got a few hours before we get anywhere near Cartagena."

"Is every criminal in South America trying to kill us?" Francis asked. He didn't seem scared, just... tired.

It was worse than that. Vitari had been tasked with hunting down runners in the past, and he hadn't stopped until the job was done. The Mafia didn't give second chances. The South American cartels might give up hunting them eventually, but the Battaglia would never stop. Worrying about it wouldn't change a fucking thing. "Hey, why don't you go below and see what treasures you can find? I'll put her on autopilot and join you in a few minutes." Vitari watched Francis walk through the bridge deck and disappear down the stairs to the main deck, then swung his gaze back to the horizon, looking for answers.

Because, he had no fucking idea what to do.

CHAPTER ELEVEN

Francis

The yacht had three floors—*decks*, he supposed they were called. The top deck, with its wraparound windows, where the controls were. The main deck, where the luxurious living spaces were, including a bar. And a lower deck, with the bedrooms and bathrooms. The bar was stocked with all kinds of bottles of foreign alcohol he couldn't hope to pronounce, and the fridge held an array of wine. He stared at the choices, his thoughts slow to catch up since he was still coming down from the adrenaline kick. They'd done it, they'd survived—almost died too, but survived—and he wasn't thinking about what could have happened, what had *nearly* happened. No, he couldn't think about any of that. But he could pick a wine.

Francis grabbed the thick green bottle. *Champagne* was written in cursive on its neck.

"What do you have?" Vitari asked, joining him at the curved bar.

"I found this." He showed him the bottle.

Vitari's eyes lit up. "No shit, that's a ten-thousand-dollar bottle of champagne. Grab some glasses, let's celebrate."

"Ten thousand dollars?" Wine was *that* expensive? Francis found the glasses as Vitari popped the cork, then brimmed each one.

"To surviving," Vitari said, that classic glint of mischief in his eyes.

"To surviving." They chinked glasses, and Francis sipped the wine. Vitari downed his entire glass in a gulp.

Francis blinked. "Did you even taste it?"

"Tastes like victory. Another, Padre."

Francis poured another. "Is there a law about drinking while being in charge of a yacht this big?"

"International waters, there are no laws out here. There's nobody here to stop me. Unless you're going to stop me, Padre?"

His teasing tone fluttered Francis's racing heart. "I might."

"Oh?" Vitari dangled the glass in his fingers and leaned on the bar. "*How* are you going to stop me? Hold me down? Fuck me up?"

"I haven't decided." His heart pounded, sensing this was heading toward wild and wonderful sex in a stolen yacht in the middle of the Caribbean, after being shot at and almost losing Vitari all over again. Sex he could do, especially as it distracted him from the dark, terrifying reality happening all around them.

If he stopped to think, he might break down, so he wasn't going to stop, or think. He was going to drink the ridiculously expensive champagne, catch Vitari's eye, and imagine all the wicked things Vitari was thinking about right now that undoubtedly involved Francis spreading his legs. His heart thumped. Heat pooled in his groin.

"You know what we should do?" Vitari grabbed the wine bottle by its neck and gulped straight from it.

Francis watched his throat undulate. Soon, he'd kiss him there. He could already taste him. Smell him. God, it was animal-like, this attraction. This *need*.

Vitari backed up and spread his arms. "Fuck in every room. Over there, on your knees. There, against the couch. I'll kneel for *you*. There, by the TV, spread your legs and I'll fuck you from behind. This yacht is ours, we're free!" He laughed and his brilliant eyes sparkled, asking permission, seeing how far Francis would go.

And he'd go all the way. "Don't I get a say in where?" he replied coyly.

"Then say it. Where do you want to *ride my cock*, Francis?"

Francis cradled the glass and scanned the plush interior, pretending to consider the options when he already had a vivid idea of what was going to happen where, and when. "Right here."

"Oh?" Vitari sauntered back to the bar. "You have something specific in mind, Padre?" He drank again from the bottle, and Francis upended his glass and gulped down the expensive wine.

"I do, actually." He held out his hand and Vitari handed over the champagne. "Come here."

"Fuck, I love it when you're mad at me." Vitari came around the bar and cocked a hip against the mahogany bar top, then folded his arms, playing hard to get.

"Take off your shirt." Francis already breathed too fast, trying to keep his racing heart pumping, or maybe all that blood had gone to his cock, now painfully hard.

Vitari undid a few buttons and pulled off his shirt, then flung it aside with no care for where it landed. "You going to demand I drop to my knees and suck your dick, Padre?"

He had been about to say exactly that, but he couldn't let Vitari think it had been his idea. He needed a new plan of attack.

"Turn around."

Vitari tilted his head, no longer as certain he knew where this was going. "All right...?" He turned his back, and for a moment, Francis lost every single thought in how Vitari's bare muscles moved in the soft ambient lighting. He wasn't even sure what to do, until he was doing it, gently dribbling cold champagne down Vitari's spine. Vitari swore, then fell quiet as Francis pressed his lips to the liquid and kissed upward. It almost felt wrong, to relish in such things, but good too, good *because* it had been wrong before. Not anymore.

Francis tore off his own shirt and after dribbling some wine on Vitari's shoulder, he leaned in and licked and sucked his warm skin clean. He brushed his chest against Vitari's back, absorbing his every stuttered breath and needful moan. Francis spilled more wine and lapped it up. He swept his left hand around Vitari's hip, then dove downward, teasing his fingertips along his waistband. They both knew where his hand would end up, but not yet. He wanted to make him moan some more, maybe even make him beg on his knees.

Vitari was always so powerful, so in control. This was a side to him nobody saw, nobody but Francis. And he knew it belonged to him, and only him.

"Give me the wine," Vitari growled.

Francis took a gulp and handed it over. Vitari swallowed some too, then set it aside and turned on the spot, bringing him face-to-face with Francis. He'd had something wicked on his mind, but as their gazes met, that glee faded, and his face turned serious. "You're so fucking perfect."

"You're drunk."

"Not yet. I'm clearheaded enough to know a miracle when I see it."

"I'm no miracle." Heat warmed his face, and he tried to turn his head away, to hide it. Vitari was the miracle, coming back from the dead, saving Francis over and over.

Vitari hooked his chin and made him face him. "You are to me."

He bowed his head, the praise uncomfortable, then caught sight of Vitari's jutting erection trapped in his pants and had the perfect distraction. Quickly, he unzipped Vitari's fly, then shuffled the trousers down and freed his fine length of dick. It deserved admiration, and perhaps he was a little drunk, because Vitari's cock had rarely looked finer.

Vitari grabbed the expensive champagne and tilted it, spilling a dribble down the shaft, avoiding the head. "Lick it off, Francis."

His fingers dove into Francis's hair and guided him down. Although Francis needed no encouragement. He licked up the thick shaft, tasting sweet wine and Vitari. "You going to take it, amore mio? Swallow my cock, Padre."

He wanted that, wanted to swallow his cock and make him lose his mind. Francis tilted his head, peering up the glorious length of Vitari's fine body, and swallowed his dick deep.

"You're so fuckin' perfect." Vitari tugged on his hair and thrust, clearly trying not to and failing. The thick width of Vitari's dick filled his throat. Francis gagged and pulled off to catch his breath but kept stroking. *Power*. He was the one on his knees, but Vitari was at his mercy.

"Fuck, looking at you down there, your sweet mouth... My dick between your lips. You're going to make me come too soon." Vitari eased Francis off, then hauled him upright and thrust a kiss on his lips. Francis devoured him back, trying and failing to go slow. Vitari pinned him against the bar, leaned him back, and dribbled champagne across his left pec. The cool liquid tickled its way down his chest, and then Vitari's mouth and tongue followed—teasing, kissing— as he looked up through his lashes, his eyes like two dark pools of sin.

"I want to make this last, but I also really need to fuck you into this bar." Vitari tugged at Francis's trousers, jerking them down.

With a smirk, Francis finished off the wine, glugging it down, then warm, tight lips sealed around his dick, and with his head spinning, he leaned back, surrendering to Vitari's sinful mouth. The wine was definitely going to his head, probably helped along by the painkillers, because this was bliss.

Vitari fucked him with his mouth and hand. Francis could feel himself falling, feel the pleasure tightening.

"Not yet, Padre," Vitari said, lifting off and gently turning Francis around. Vitari's hand pressed between his shoulder blades, pinning him down. He heard Vitari spit into his palm, then his fingers dove between his ass cheeks and pushed inside. He didn't care what Vitari did, just that he did more of it. He clutched at the bar, dick trapped under him, as Vitari stretched him, slickened his hole, then pressed his warm, firm cock to him and eased in, filling him.

"God," Francis spluttered. If there was any more of it, he'd be tasting it.

"You've got the tightest fucking hole, Francis." Vitari's fingers dug into his back, applying downward pressure as his dick pushed in. "And you're all mine." His words brushed Francis's spine, then his tongue and teeth worked their magic, sweeping and biting at Francis's shoulder as his hips began to rock, dick pumping. "Fuck, you feel too good. Tell me how you want it."

He wasn't sure he could speak, let alone form a coherent order. Vitari always had a way with words. Francis just... "Just fuck me."

"Love it when you swear. Say fuck again." Vitari thrust hard, slamming Francis against the bar.

"Fuck!" His wounded leg barked in pain, then faded behind the ecstasy running through him. He'd be feeling that tomorrow.

Vitari's hands gripped his hips. "Oh yes, Padre." He thrust again, deeper, harder, and again. "Take it, fucking take my dick, Padre."

"Oh God." Electric shivers raced up his spine, and as Vitari sped up, pumping ruthlessly, the lines between pain and pleasure blurred, mixing into a glorious high. Then Vitari pulled him upright, hugging Francis's back to his chest, adjusting the angle. Francis let out a low moan. Vitari dropped his hand and grasped Francis's dick, kissing his neck and slow-fucking his ass; it all became a riot of feeling from head to toe. "I can't..." He was going to come, the precipice was right there, he couldn't hold back, and as Vitari's hand pumped, Francis let go with a shout, spilling over Vitari's fingers.

"Fuck, I never want this to end." Vitari slammed him forward, gripped his hips again, grunted, and fucked, pounding faster, skin slapping skin. He choked on a cry, came hard, and slumped forward, hips stuttering.

Vitari's gentle kisses rained down Francis's back. "You are the blood in my veins, Francis. The heart in my chest. If I loved you more, it would kill me."

Sparking twinges traveled up his ass. He'd have liked to have said similarly romantic things, but also, his body needed a reprieve. "I'm not sure I can do that again."

"Padre." Vitari chuckled, clutched Francis's hips, and pulled out. "That was just the beginning. Give me a minute, then I'm getting a gun."

"Oh." Yes, yes he wanted that. Maybe he could take another pounding after all.

"You wanna get dirty with me and a gun, Francis?" Vitari whispered against this ear.

Clearly, Francis was getting fucked all night, and he'd never craved it more.

Vitari grabbed his chin, turned Francis's head, and owned his mouth in a demanding kiss that left Francis breathless. "Grab another bottle of wine. I'll be right back."

Francis watched the thought-stoppingly naked Vitari saunter from the bar—semi-erect cock hanging low, ass like a peach—and forgot what he'd been asked to do. He blinked back to himself and looked around him at the sparkling luxury bar, on a drug lord's stolen yacht, in the middle of the Caribbean with temptation personified in Vitari, probably about to use a gun in a way guns were not designed to be used.

This was a dream, wasn't it? A little laugh fell out of him. Was he drunk? He didn't feel drunk.

They'd done it—*he'd* done it. He'd found Vitari, he'd talked to Serpiente as though he belonged among the criminal kind, and he had saved Vitari from the bad men, and now they were here, drinking wine and devouring each

other like animals. He felt lightheaded, elated. He felt...
free.

Vitari returned carrying his gun and set it down on the
bar like a promise of all the wicked things he planned to do
with it later. It sat there, gleaming.

"The wine?" Vitari asked.

Oh yes, he'd forgotten he was supposed to get more
wine. He opened the cupboards, gazed at countless bottles,
and had no idea where to start. Vitari leaned in beside him,
grabbed a few bottles of something dark and potent, and
winked. "Enough to lift any inhibitions that might be linger-
ing, Padre."

"What are you going to do to me?"

"I meant for me." Vitari laughed, popped the cork on a
bottle of red, and refilled their earlier glasses. "You're not
the only one with hang-ups."

He knew there was one thing Vitari *couldn't* do. "I don't
want to do anything you don't want to do."

"Let's see where we go," he said, raising his glass to his
lips.

When Vitari drew closer, Francis couldn't resist
pressing close, answering his body's call. The full-length
naked feel of Vitari was poetry made flesh. Their thighs
touching, soft hairs brushing, cocks nudging, hands stroking.
He'd never tire of exploring Vitari's body, of reveling in the
feel of *male* without shame and guilt assaulting him from all
sides.

"You're the only man who's been mine," Vitari whispered, bowing their heads together, like a confession. "I
was... confused, for a long time. Not sure if I was broken,
because I got hard for men, because of... that place. My
whole life I've hidden who I am, what I want. Numb inside,

you know?" His fingers laced with Francis's. "But not here, not with you."

Francis swallowed hard. "I know."

"Yeah. I guess you do, you beautiful fucking Saint of Disaster."

"Well, I'm definitely no saint—"

Vitari leaned in to capture his mouth in a kiss. Francis teased away, lips skimming.

"You've no idea how much you save me, Francis, every day."

Francis rested his arms over Vitari's shoulders and bumped noses. He didn't have the right words, not like Vitari, didn't know how to tell him his heart beat for him, so he brushed their lips together, as though he could say it with a kiss. Soft, at first, careful. Learning, like they had learned to be with each other in the beginning. Then, he deepened, pushing in, teasing Vitari's mouth harder, tasting him, beginning to know him like no other ever had. And when Vitari kissed him back, he felt the love on his lips.

It wasn't just sex; what they had together transcended need, it felt... divine.

Vitari pulled away first but stayed so close his dazzling eyes and smile were all Francis could see. He'd once thought this man was a devil. He never could have known Vitari would be his savior.

The cold, hard press of the gun's barrel dug into his chin, lifting his head. Vitari grinned. "Let's get creative."

"Is it loaded?" Francis asked between his teeth.

"Padre, it's *always* loaded."

Lust sparked down his back and pooled in his groin, bringing his cock back to life. This was probably a terrible thing to be doing, and despite Vitari's insistence he could do no wrong, wanting Vitari to hold the gun on him, to stroke him with it, felt like taboo, making him hunger *more* for it.

"Get over by the couch," Vitari ordered and eased off, allowing Francis out from under him. Vitari backed him up, toward the couch. This was going to get visceral, and Francis already panted hard for it.

"You want this?" Vitari asked, taking a step back, showing him the gun at ease in his fingers. Then he jerked the slide, making Francis jump.

"Oh, fuck me, Padre. The look on your face is priceless."

Francis bit his bottom lip. Vitari was naked, and hard, and holding a gun. Francis was naked, and hard, and might be about to combust on the spot.

Vitari's grin slid sideways. He circled the gun. "Turn around."

Francis turned.

"Get on your knees."

He placed his knees on the couch, hands on the back cushion, and bowed his head... waiting. Vitari's warm fingers touched his thighs, then eased off. His right hand vanished, and cool, hard metal pushed against the nape of Francis's neck. He'd wondered where it might go, but there it was, and down his spine, it stroked. His cock jumped, seeking friction. With his head bowed between his arms, he saw how his dick hung low. Cum leaked. He didn't care.

This was most certainly *not* in the Bible.

The gun's muzzle spread his ass and stroked down, skimming over his hole, then continued on and nudged his balls.

Francis panted like a dog, and his dick ached, full and heavy. He wanted to touch himself, wanted Vitari to touch him, but not yet.

Would Vitari's cock touch his hole, or would it be the gun?

Then Vitari's left hand spread his left cheek, and a soft, wet flick of the tongue passed over his hole, setting him ablaze. He choked on a moan. Could a man come from barely being touched, just from anticipation? Vitari's dark chuckle tightened Francis's balls, and his probing tongue flicked and teased. Then, Vitari's hot mouth was replaced by the cold, firm press of metal. There it was.

A rush of lust tangled with a mess of right and wrong resulted in Francis's thoughts abandoning him altogether, leaving him to *feel*. His breath stuttered. His balls contracted, dick pulsing. He gripped the back of the couch, knuckles whitening, and Vitari began to stroke the gun in and out.

He might have lost his mind in those moments, only finding it again when Vitari's fingers grasped his dick and pumped. He fought not to come, but half of him was already falling.

Then the gun was gone, Vitari's hand vanished, and with a tight grip on Francis's hips, Vitari turned him, shoved him ass-first into the couch, spread his knees, and swallowed his dick, balls to chin. Francis was done. Ruined. Scorched alive. He cried out and came so hard down Vitari's forgiving throat that the rush branded Francis's soul.

Left panting and spent, he swallowed hard and watched Vitari rising from his knees, wiping his mouth. "Sin has never tasted so good," Vitari said.

They made love again later, on the deck outside in the warm Caribbean air, under the stars, slower, with Vitari reeling off strings of beautiful Italian as he worshipped every inch of Francis's body. Later, they came together again, on their knees, the lines between them blurred, lost and found. They made love in the shower, washing off cum and sticky champagne, and fell into bed, tangled as one, cocks hard, bodies ready but exhausted and sore.

Francis lay awake as the sun rose, Vitari's hand on his cock, gently stroking, bringing that part of him to life again, even if he was too exhausted to act on it.

"How did you find me?" Vitari asked, his voice rough from lack of sleep, or from swallowing Francis's deep.

The events of the previous day, when he'd woken to find Vitari gone, seemed like a lifetime ago. He told Vitari about Mia's help, then meeting the formidable Miguel character in the jungle.

On hearing Miguel's name, Vitari jolted onto an elbow, eyes wide. "Miguel Sanchez?"

Francis nodded. "Big man, had a scar at the corner of his mouth—"

"That's him. Miguel helped you?"

Francis studied Vitari's face. "After I pointed your gun at him."

Vitari blinked, perhaps even paled a little. "You did what?" He swallowed. "Francis, you have no idea who he was, do you?"

"Not really. He knew you though."

Vitari grinned. "Miguel Sanchez is—was the king of the Colombian drug trade, you know, as big and brutal as Escobar."

"Escobar?"

Vitari snorted. "Fuck, you're adorable. You really threatened him?"

It seemed as though this Miguel Sanchez was more

dangerous than he'd appeared to be, and he hadn't exactly been all sweetness and light during their meeting either. "It was a stressful situation. I had the gun, and nobody was listening to me."

"Funny isn't it, how people start listening when you point a gun at them." Vitari rolled onto his back, absolutely naked, hard, and unashamedly on display. "He could easily have killed you."

"But he didn't." Francis shrugged. "He was... reasonable."

"The fucker's probably bored. Old blood don't retire. Natural selection, you know? Most get killed off. I bet he's going out of his mind hidden away in a shack like that. He wasn't expecting you. Padre Blanco." Vitari chuckled, but then his face turned pensive. "You got lucky."

Francis wasn't sure it was luck. He'd threatened a drug lord. And he'd have pulled the trigger to save Vitari. He dropped his head back and blinked at the cabin's ceiling. "What is old blood?"

"Like my father. That generation, when shit was done differently. Half the business now is balancing spreadsheets and doctoring shipping manifests. Giancarlo, Little Toni, half the capos, they're a dying breed. Sasha got that right..." Vitari said softly, as though to himself.

Since he'd brought up his father, now might be a good time to mention how Francis had been in touch with Giancarlo, and how not everything was as lost as Vitari believed it to be. He'd been putting it off, because when it came to his father, Vitari was volatile, but after he got angry, he'd see the good behind Francis's intentions. He just needed to know not all the Mafia were out to get him. Maybe.

Francis rolled onto his side and laid his arm over Vitari's chest, then teased around a nipple and watched goose bumps scatter across Vitari's skin. He propped his chin on his chest. "Don't get mad…"

Vitari looked down and arched an eyebrow. "Why am I not getting mad?"

"I did something… a while ago now, and it probably doesn't change much."

"Fuck. What is it?"

"It's not… bad." He'd begun to explain, so now he had to finish. It was time anyway. It hadn't felt right, not telling Vitari. "When we first arrived in Panama, after leaving England, there was a lot going on, remember?"

Vitari scooted back and sat up against the headboard, making Francis sit up. "Just say it."

"I called Giancarlo."

Vitari's smile twitched. "You what?"

"It was real quick, just a few minutes. There wasn't much time, my phone battery died—"

"Wait." Vitari flung up his hands. "Fuck. Stop. You *called* my father when we were in the safe house?"

His voice was thin, that same kind of thin he got when he was trying very hard not to explode. Francis's heart contracted and he puffed a soft, nervous laugh. "It's not a problem. It's a good thing."

Vitari smiled, almost laughed too, but the sinking feeling in Francis's gut turned into a roller-coaster *whoosh*. "How is calling my father, the man I betrayed, the fuckin' Mafia don who wants to kill me, *a good fucking thing*, Francis?"

"All right, you're angry." Vitari would listen, once he'd gotten over the shock. Francis just needed to explain. "I just said that maybe you hadn't known all the facts when you went to Sasha, and that he shouldn't be so hard on you, that you'd made a mistake."

Vitari jerked his chin up. "You fucking what?"

"It's true. You helped Sasha, but you didn't know—"

Vitari shot from the bed, thrust his hands into his hair, and paced, naked in the ambient light pouring in through the cabin's windows. "Fuck! You told my father I went to Sasha. Are you fuckin' with me right, now? Because I don't understand why you'd do that."

When he put it like that, it did, admittedly, sound terrible. "He had a right to know."

Vitari choked on a shallow laugh. "How the... How..." He paced harder and cast a scathing glare toward Francis.

Francis turned his hand over, and there was the circular scar. Giancarlo was, without doubt, a horrible person, but Francis didn't believe he'd hurt Vitari. After everything Charles Montague had said, it almost seemed as though Giancarlo had been trying to protect Vitari. He'd saved Vitari from Stanmore. He'd gotten him out. That meant something. It meant he cared about his son.

"Wait, wait..." Vitari licked his lips and breathed. "Shit, you called him from Panama?"

"Yes, just briefly—"

"Fuck!" Vitari braced a hand over his face and muttered something in Italian. "Where's your phone now?" he asked, voice flat, cold, hard.

Francis glanced around the room for his trousers. "There. In the pocket. I only called him once—"

"Once is all it takes—" Vitari's thin laugh trailed off. "Giancarlo is a sly bastard. He plays the old man act, like he doesn't use phones, but he's a goddamned tech-savvy sonofabitch." Vitari scooped up the pants, pulled out the phone, and stared at it resting in his hand.

Francis pulled his knees to his chest, hating how guilt made him sick. "I thought—"

"Sweet fuck, Francis." He dragged his hand down his face. "How are you so fucking smart *and* stupid?"

Francis's insides curdled. Nausea wet his mouth. "What's wrong?"

"Fuck." Vitari paced again. "It's my fault, I should have told you to ditch your phone in England. With everything that happened, I didn't think. What's wrong? My father knows we're in Central America. You've had this phone on you this whole time, which means he knew we were in San Blas yesterday. The only reason he doesn't know we're here, right now, is there's no signal out here. Fuck!" Vitari flung open the bedroom door and stormed out.

Francis grabbed his trousers, tugged them on, and stumbled after Vitari. He hadn't known phones could be tracked from a call. He hadn't meant to hurt Vitari. If he'd listen... let him explain...

He found him on deck in time to see Vitari pitch the phone into the ocean.

"Wait!" He stopped at the edge of the deck beside Vitari and stared at the waves. "That was *my* phone."

Vitari faced him, and there was nothing in his eyes but cold, hard ice. "You lied to me for weeks."

"I didn't lie, I just didn't say anything—"

"Don't give me that shit. You knew exactly what you were doing."

"But it's good, isn't it? It means he knows the truth, and he doesn't want you dead. He might actually just want you back, he might listen to us—"

"*Listen?*" Vitari laughed again and marched back inside. "He's the same man who burned your hand, Francis. He fucking threatened to cut off my tongue if I sucked dick again. When I was sixteen, he put a gun in my hand and told me to kill some asshole who had wronged him or shoot myself if I couldn't do it. That was my choice. What do you think he's going to do now he knows we've been living together in Panama and stealing his guns *after* I betrayed him? You think he's going to welcome me back with open arms or hang me by my balls from a bridge?" Vitari shook his head. "The fuck, Francis!? I can't—" He cut himself off and sighed. "Jesus. I can't believe you did this to me."

"I think you're underestimating your father. I'm not saying he's—"

Vitari dropped his hands. "*You* don't fucking know him!" he shouted.

Francis blinked. "You're wrong, Vitari. I'm sorry, but you're not seeing things clearly. He wants Sasha destroyed. He got you out of Stanmore, remember? All the threats, all the posturing, it's just his way of trying to protect you."

"What the fuck do you think this is, fucking happy families? He didn't do any of that because he's *protecting* me. He did it because of shame, not because of some heroic fatherly duty. He fucking hates me. Don't you get it? He *blames* me for the love of his life dying. I'm the root of all his fucking problems. Jesus... I can't do this with you..." He took the spiral stairs below deck.

"Vitari?" Francis hurried after him.

The bedroom door slammed, and Francis stared at it. Torn. He'd messed up, but he hadn't been wrong. He firmly believed that. Vitari was too close to everything to see clearly.

The photos of Vitari and Francis in Spain, the mess that was Venezuela, even threatening Francis to back off Stanmore—Luca had said it in Venezuela, it was bigger than just them—*everything* was about Vitari, not because Giancarlo hated him, but because he was *protecting him*. Francis was so damn sure of it, he'd hang their love on it.

A *thwomp-thwomp* sounded outside, somewhere nearby. A new, different sound to that of the yacht's engines. And it was getting louder.

Francis climbed onto the main deck again, shielded his eyes from the early morning sun, and stared toward the horizon. A black dot hovered in the azure sky.

The yacht's engines growled to life, and with a lurch, it plowed forward, churning water in its wake. Francis hurried up the steps to the bridge deck and found Vitari back at the yacht's controls, dressed in a rough pair of grey cargo pants and loose white T-shirt he must have found among Cisco's things.

"There's something coming," Francis said, glancing behind them. The black dot had grown bigger.

"Yeah, helicopter," Vitari said. "Let's hope they're looking for someone else, not this yacht, because there's not a whole lot of places to hide out there."

Francis leaned against the bridge controls console. Vitari wasn't looking at him, didn't glance over at all. He stared ahead, face determined. The chasm was back between them, bigger than ever. And that was Francis's fault. He should have told him before, or at the least talked to him before calling Giancarlo, but he'd have said no, and Francis wasn't wrong.

"Is it still following?" Vitari asked.

Francis took up position at the wraparound windows. "Yes."

"Shit."

"Can we outrun it?"

"No. The only thing we can do is head out into the ocean and hope they get low on fuel before reaching us."

"Who is it?"

"Cisco, Aikin, fucking Battaglia—who the fuck knows?

It could be Miguel-fucking-Sanchez since you went all gangsta on his ass."

Francis winced and tracked the helicopter, hating the sting in Vitari's words. He knew Vitari could be vicious, he'd seen him lash out at others, but Francis had never felt that viciousness directed at him, and it burned. Even when Vitari had kidnapped him after they'd first met, he hadn't been cruel, or perhaps Francis hadn't cared what he'd thought back then. He cared now and could feel the love they'd had slipping like water between his fingers.

The chopper had gotten so big, he could see its rotors now. If it was police, then it was unmarked.

"They're gaining."

"Shit. Get a gun."

Francis hesitated. If he picked up a gun, he might have to use it. And if he was holding a gun, then he'd probably be shot at. Which meant he'd definitely have to use it.

"Now is not the time to be a puppy-loving pacifist. If you don't shoot them, they will shoot you. Get the guns, Francis."

"All right. Okay." He hurried down to the main deck, found the 9mm handgun—the same he'd gotten very personal with during the night—and an assault rifle left over from Cisco's men, then hesitated as the noise of the helicopter vibrated the windows. He looked up. The helicopter came in low, keeping up with the yacht, then overshot them and banked, circling to come at them head-on.

Francis made it halfway up the steps to the control deck when gunfire peppered the yacht, pinging off the hull. Windows shattered, the engines roared, and Vitari turned the yacht so hard, Francis was forced to cling to the stair rail to keep from falling.

When it leveled out, he dashed up the remaining steps.

"Shoot them!" Vitari yelled.

The helicopter buzzed above, hovering back and forth. Popping gunfire strafed the yacht again.

"Get down!" Vitari yelled.

Francis dropped, hugged his knees to his chest, and buried his head under his arms, making himself small. Rounds pinged too close. Vitari dashed beside him, grabbed the assault rifle, shouldered it, and lunged toward the back of the bridge deck, in full view of the helicopter. Its door opened and a man leaned out, pointing a rifle right at them.

They were going to die. There was nowhere to hide, no cover. Those men would keep shooting until the yacht caught fire. Surrender was their only option.

"Vitari, stop!"

Maybe he hadn't heard over the noise of the yacht and helicopter. He tucked himself in behind one of the yacht's upright pillars, aimed at the helicopter, and let loose a rattle of gunfire. It seemed to work. The helicopter pulled up, but then swooped around again, nose pointed parallel to the yacht. The gunman leaned out the door, rifle aimed at Vitari.

Francis lunged for the yacht controls. He yanked the throttle down, killing the engine revs, abruptly diving the yacht's nose forward. The yacht rocked, and the helicopter overshot.

It would swing around again in seconds.

This had to end. They were sitting ducks.

Francis dashed for Vitari and skidded to his knees beside him. "Surrender."

"What?" Vitari pressed his back to the fiberglass wall, already peppered with splintered bullet holes.

"We can't win this."

"They'll kill us."

"We don't know that."

"Pointing guns and firing generally means they want us dead."

"Vitari, please. Don't aim at them when they come back around."

"Some of us don't have God on our side, Padre. You think they came all this way to talk? I betrayed the Battaglia. I sold my father out to his enemy. There's only one way this ends—"

"Angel!" a voice blared through a megaphone, then reeled off a string of Italian. Francis only heard one word that mattered: *Battaglia.*

All the fight and rage deflated from Vitari. He slid down the pillar and thumped his head back against it. "Fuck."

"What did they say?"

Vitari blinked at him, swallowed, and closed his eyes. "We're done."

CHAPTER TWELVE

He dropped the rifle and kicked it out onto the deck, then raised his hands. A rope spilled from the helicopter's open door. Three black-clad men abseiled onto the main deck.

They were Battaglia elite, sent by his father. They'd probably been on their tails since they'd fled Panama.

One of the men found Francis inside and dragged him to his feet, another stayed with Vitari, and the third headed to the bridge, where he gunned the motors and adjusted their course. The yacht engines roared anew, now under Battaglia control.

"Where are they taking us?" Francis asked.

"Cartagena."

"Is that bad?"

He couldn't answer him, didn't want to look at him. All of this was fucking bad, not least the fact the man he loved, the man whom he'd given his heart, had betrayed him to his father.

The elite pros sat them at opposite ends of the couch and barked orders in Italian not to move. Vitari didn't feel much like moving anyway, ever since Francis had told him he'd fucked him. Why had he done it, why had he told his father how he'd gone to Sasha? Neo would have told Giancarlo Vitari was alive, that wasn't the issue, but Giancarlo hadn't *known* how deep the betrayal went. Now he knew everything, every step Vitari had taken, and not just because he'd been tracking Francis's phone.

Francis had *told* him.

Had Francis done it to protect himself, to trade Vitari for some kind of loyalty to Giancarlo? What exactly had happened between them when Giancarlo had burned his hand? What the fuck had been going through Francis's head to make him fuck over Vitari so thoroughly?

He knew Francis was hurting. It felt good to hurt him, because the hole in Vitari's chest where Francis had torn out his heart wasn't going away anytime soon.

Even the best case, if Giancarlo was everything Francis believed, and he was trying to bring down Sasha, it didn't change the fact his own fucking son had betrayed him to his enemy. His father had no choice but to kill him. The capos would demand it. Little Toni would demand it. The whole Battaglia would be baying for his blood.

At least Giancarlo wouldn't be in Cartagena. Out on bail, he couldn't leave Italy. But that just meant he'd have someone else deal out the punishment, someone like Vitari had been. Someone like L' Angelo della Morte.

They cruised into Club de Pesca marina early in the evening and moored alongside other enormous yachts. Vitari was unceremoniously marched off the deck, with Francis bullied along behind him, to a waiting car, its back windows blacked out.

"Where are they taking us?" Francis asked once they were underway. He'd gone pale.

Vitari tried asking the two bastards in the front, but they ignored him. "Best guess, to a private airfield."

"We're going back to Italy?"

"I'm sure my father can't wait to see you, now you're friends."

Francis's face fell. "Vitari—"

He glared out of the window at the ancient city of Cartagena passing by. Vitari hated hurting him, hated how his words cut him, but it felt good too, because every cut he dealt came back on him, and Vitari deserved the pain. They both did. They could have fucking had something. Vitari might have been coming around to the idea of a normal life. But how could he ever trust Francis again?

Vitari snuck a look over. Francis's pale reflection hovered in the privacy glass, his face turned away, watching the world go by, probably wondering how he was going to survive it all. Since he had been in contact with Giancarlo there was a chance he might let Francis go after all this, but not Vitari.

He'd killed Battaglia betrayers for lesser indiscretions against the family.

"We could have had something," Francis whispered, so quietly he probably hadn't intended Vitari to hear.

"No, we couldn't," Vitari snarled, denying it even though he'd thought the same. Francis turned his head and met Vitari's glare. He looked ruined, looked fucking gutted. Good. "*You* fucked us over before we'd begun."

The pain on his face crushed Vitari's heart and he hated himself all over again. He almost apologized, almost took the words back, but Francis's shock turned to a sneer.

"If you hadn't sold those guns we'd have been fine!"

Francis seethed, searing hatred back in his eyes, just like when they'd met, when Francis had thought Vitari no better than the dirt on his shoe.

"Right. Because your waiting tables at the resort was going to save us? Be real, Francis."

"At least it was honest."

"Fucking *honest*?" Vitari laughed. "If you wanted honest and wholesome, what the fuck were you doing with me?"

"I'm beginning to wonder that myself," he snapped back.

"I know why. You thought you could save me, like a charity case. Make up for all that sinning you did? It was never going to happen, Padre."

Francis gazed down at his cupped hands in his lap and the scar given to him by Giancarlo. "I see that now."

Vitari cast his gaze out of the window again, hiding the hurt like he always did. He squeezed his eyes closed, forcing their burn away. Why had he fooled himself into thinking he could have Francis? It was a stupid dream. Dirty secrets like him didn't deserve love—not a father's love, not the love of a good man. Stanmore broke him. It would be better, from now on, if he went back to not caring and back to being L' Angelo della Morte.

It was the only damn way his heart might survive.

The Battaglia men ushered him and Francis into an empty warehouse with holes in its tin roof, flapping plastic sheeting, and broken windows. They were far outside the city, in an industrial area that had ceased any trading long ago, where it would be easy to disappear a person. Or two.

Three more men awaited their arrival. Two armed guards, and between them, Neo.

Vitari bucked against the hands holding him. "You *fuck!*" He'd been right, Giancarlo had sent Vitari's replacement. Fucking Neo. "He's DeSica!" he told the men, bucking in their grip again, but the guard's didn't let up. "You all know that, right? He's a fucking traitor!"

Neo smiled, so calm, so confident. He even looked like Vitari, well-dressed, casually classy, not a speck of dust on his black shoes. He'd climbed the ranks and taken Vitari's place in the Battaglia, right where Luca Espinosa had once dreamed he'd be.

Neo tugged on his shirt cuffs and rolled his shoulders. "That's rich, coming from you, Angel." He arched an eyebrow, and his pointed stare placed all the blame at Vitari's feet.

Hate scorched Vitari's soul and made him sick. He twisted, almost writhing free, but one of the guards kicked his leg out. He dropped, pain cracked up his knee, and then Neo loomed. The punch swung in too fast to block and landed hard, whipping his head around. Coppery blood filled his mouth and dribbled between his lips. He spat.

"Don't!" Francis's bark echoed through the warehouse.

"Oh, that's right." Neo straightened. Backing up, he shook out his bruised knuckles. "You're sucking each other's cocks." He grimaced and spat at the ground too, disgusted.

Now was not the time for Francis to get loud. He needed to stay back, stay out of this, and keep quiet, and then maybe he'd be all right. "You lying pig, Neo. You piece of DeSica shit. You have no right!"

Neo spun on his heel and marched toward Vitari purposefully. Another punch was coming—Vitari had taken enough knocks to know Neo's look of violence—but at least Neo's fists were flying at Vitari and not Francis.

But instead of landing the blow, one of the guards handed Neo a 9mm gun, and Neo studied it in the ambient lighting. "Maybe I should just end you now?"

"Don't touch him!" Francis said.

"Or what?" Neo eyed Vitari down the gun barrel but his words were all for Francis. "You goin' to execute me, Padre Blanco, like you did Luca Espinosa?" He laughed.

Vitari braced and skipped his gaze behind Neo, to where the guards held Francis. His eyes were wide, his face white. He blinked, and their gazes briefly touched. After everything they'd been through, everything they'd seen and done, even knowing Francis had betrayed him, Vitari would take a thousand punches for him, he'd fucking die for him, and he saw in Francis's narrowing eyes and tight-lipped snarl how he'd kill for Vitari. Righteous conviction burned in his priestly glare. He'd kill Neo, like he'd executed Luca. It was love, Vitari realized. Francis would kill *for love.*

"This your gun?" Neo asked, waving the gun about in his hand, then examining it.

"Mine?" Vitari blinked. Wait, was that the gun from the yacht? *The* gun he'd used with Francis? A smile tugged at the corners of Vitari's mouth. "Yeah, that's my gun, you prick." If he knew where it had been he wouldn't be admiring it like he was now.

"I should kill you with it, no? Like some kind of karma?"

Vitari's smile grew. "That gun's special, you know? Personal."

Neo smirked, thinking he'd taken something precious from Vitari, but then he saw Vitari's smile, and his smug grin faded behind a snarl. He clicked his fingers at his men. "Get the priest out of here."

Vitari shifted and propped his ass on his heels. "Wait." The guards hauled Francis backwards. Francis let out some defiant demands. "Where are you taking him?!"

"Don't worry." Neo peered down his nose. "I'm not interested in the padre."

Francis's guards manhandled him toward a side door, and Vitari's heart plunged through the floor. If Francis vanished through that door, he'd never see him again. This wasn't a hostage situation, it wasn't even a ransom. Neo would kill Francis because he could.

Francis bucked and tripped, desperate to get free.

They'd take him away and kill him.

No more Francis.

No, fuck no, that couldn't happen. This wasn't right. Francis was protected.

"Wait! Sasha said Francis would be safe! Sasha gave his fucking word," Vitari said, hating how weak he sounded, how pathetic, but it was all true. If they took Francis from him, if they killed him, there was nothing left in this life worth living for. He didn't want to live a single day without him. "Neo, don't do this," he begged.

Neo's smug smile grew. "You didn't really believe Sasha would save your priest, did you?"

He hadn't, not really. But he'd *hoped*, stupidly. He held Neo's glare. "What the fuck do you want? Huh? Name it, I'll do it, anything. Just... don't hurt Francis."

Neo snorted. "Shit, you really have it bad for the priest." He lunged, grabbed Vitari's face, thrust the gun under his chin, and sneered, then spat. Globules of spittle dashed Vitari's lips. "Vaffanculo a chi t'è morto."

Vitari didn't even care how the words burned, cutting too close to old wounds, he only had eyes for Francis. They'd take him somewhere out of sight, force him to his knees, and shoot him in the back of the head. The whole thing would take a few minutes. Problem solved. No more priest. Vitari could fucking *see* it. He'd done the same hundreds of times. Killed men as though they were inconveniences. It was wrong. The whole fucking world was twisted and fucked up, and he'd been a part of that, but not to Francis, not like this. "Neo, please, I—"

"Vitari!?" Francis cried. He knew too, knew it was his end, could sense it.

Vitari couldn't stand the fear in his voice. "Fuck, Neo, stop. Please! Don't fucking do this. Whatever you want, I'll get it for you. I can make you a fucking king!"

"Stop," Neo ordered, then he nodded at the men holding Vitari, and the grips on his arms vanished. The men backed off. But it was Francis Vitari cared for, and those men who held him had stopped by the side door. Francis stood firm between them, chin up, eyes determined. But Vitari knew him, and that determined expression was the same one he'd worn as a priest just to get through the day. He was terrified, and so was Vitari.

Neo crouched and stared into Vitari eyes. "You see how easy it is to hurt you? How weak you are, Angel? No wonder your own father hates you."

"I have hundreds of thousands in cash. It's yours. Tell Giancarlo you killed us. We'll vanish. Nobody has to know."

"Oh, no, no, no." Neo chuckled and pointed the gun at Vitari, platinum rings glinting on his fingers around the grip. "This isn't about money, it's personal." He reached out and adjusted Vitari's shirt collar. "Here is the deal. Are you ready to listen, now you know what's on the line? Sasha wants you to return to Italy and put a bullet in Giancarlo's head." Neo tilted the gun. "Boom."

What kind of fucked-up plan to take out Giancarlo was that? It didn't make any sense. Giancarlo was already on his way out. He'd see right through any attempt for Vitari to get close to him. "You're in with my father. If you wanted him dead, you could have done it already."

"Angel." Neo sighed. "You don't fucking see it do you? He doesn't trust me like he does you. Has his men around him day and night. And since you fucked him in the ass, he hides in his fucking villa. I can't get close to him, not like *you* can."

"I sold him out. I fucking ruined him. He'll kill me as soon as he sees me."

Neo shrugged. "Then you'd better act fast. Everything else is in place. We just need you to finish him off."

"Jesus, this is fucked. He's already going to jail. What the fuck does my killing him do?"

"There's no judge in all of Europe who will sentence Giancarlo. You know this. He'll be released without charge, he always is. The old blood have their ways, right?" Neo sniffed, losing some of his smirk. "There's no better justice than a bullet to the brain, we all know it."

"And if I don't?"

Neo glanced over at Francis. "After what I just saw, you'll do it, and you'll do it with a fucking smile on your face, or the priest dies. It'll be easy. I fly you back to Italy for your father, you don't say a word about our deal to anyone, shoot him between the eyes, and Sasha will let you run. You get to live your happy ending with a priest, however the fuck that works."

If Vitari could pull the trigger on his father, he'd have done it long ago. Plus, Sasha wasn't going to let him saunter off a free man. But those were tomorrow's problems. Right now, he just needed Francis next to him, where he belonged. Everything else they'd figure out together. "All right, fine. I'll do it."

"Good. I knew you'd see sense." Neo whipped the gun across Vitari's temple so fast he didn't even feel the floor rush up to meet him.

Francis

After Neo hit Vitari with the gun, Vitari fell face down like a doll tossed to the ground.

"No!" Francis thrashed in the arms of the two men holding him. He bucked and kicked, but their grip crushed harder. "Get off me!" He had to get to Vitari!

They dragged him through the door. No, this couldn't happen, why were they taking him away? "Neo! I'll tell them what you are, I'll tell them everything!"

Neo grinned and showed Francis his middle finger. "Better start praying, cocksucker."

"You can't do this!"

"Shut the fuck up," one of the guards growled.

A hand slammed over his mouth, almost smothering his nose too. He panted through his nostrils and frantically looked around the warehouse yard for a way out. Nobody else was nearby, just the car they'd been brought in. Were they going to kill him? Was Neo about to kill Vitari? They'd been talking, so maybe Neo hadn't wanted Vitari dead, but then Neo had hit him, and now Vitari was unconscious... This was bad. Worse than their typical bad.

But these armed men could have killed them on the yacht if murder had been the only thing on Neo's mind. So Neo needed them, or needed Vitari. What could he need Francis for?

Maybe he didn't need Francis, maybe he was done with him?

Or maybe he was leverage, to make Vitari do something...

They'd made it obvious to everyone around them how much they cared for each other. Everyone in the warehouse knew they were lovers, but more than that, they knew if Francis was threatened, Vitari would go to his knees and beg.

Neo was going to make Vitari do something... Something terrible, and Francis was the stick to beat him with.

Oh God.

He hadn't meant to argue with Vitari, hadn't wanted to say those horrible things, but Vitari had lashed out, and Francis had lashed back, and now they were pulled apart, used against each other. What if he never saw Vitari again? What if Neo was about to kill him? What if those angry words were the last he said to him?

The men forced him into the back of the car and slammed the door.

Francis grabbed at the handle, but it clicked uselessly. Panic clawed at his thoughts. He had to get out. He had to help Vitari. There had to be a way, like there had been a way with Miguel Sanchez. "You who are a Holy warrior," he prayed. "You who are the Saint of the afflicted, You who are the Saint of the desperate, You who are the Saint of urgent causes, protect me, help me, give me strength, courage and serenity. Hear my plea, oh Lord, give me the strength to endure and find a way back to my love. Help me, oh Lord."

The guard behind the car's wheel gave a dismissive snort. "There's no God here, Padre."

His companion laughed from the passenger seat.

They were both armed. He'd seen their holstered guns. They'd been part of the group who had ambushed them on the yacht. Capable, dangerous men. Where they took him next determined if he'd survive to see the sunrise.

"Who do you work for?" Francis asked.

They didn't reply.

The car rumbled from the industrial area into thinning traffic along the old streets of Cartagena. "Where are you taking me?"

No reply.

"Do you work for Giancarlo? You're Battaglia men, honorable men, not DeSica men?"

Nothing.

He sat back and watched the old city give way to tumbledown shacks and shantytowns, then even those flimsy structures began to thin out, giving way to overgrown lands and unkempt palms. Darkness was setting in too. How long had they been traveling now? Hours?

This road did not bode well.

Francis rubbed his thumb across the burn on his palm. *"Every time you pray, you'll think of me, and of how you will never cross the Battaglia,"* Giancarlo had said when he'd put that burn there. Francis could still smell his burning flesh. Nobody crossed the Battaglia, crossed Giancarlo.

Neo must have done some kind of deal with Vitari, promising to keep Francis safe, but whatever the deed was,

Vitari had no choice. They could kill Francis and not tell Vitari, then finish Vitari off too. That was how these men worked. They used people and discarded them.

But there was another way...

Darkness had blanketed the land when the driver pulled the car off the road, then down a gravel track. The wheels bumped through deep ruts.

"Here," the driver's companion said.

The driver stopped the car and both men climbed out.

Headlights highlighted stark, motionless palm trees.

They were going to kill him. Right here. In the middle of nowhere. Nobody would find him for days, weeks even. "Thy kingdom come. Thy will be done, on Earth as it is in Heaven. God, help me."

An angel wasn't coming to save him this time. He was on his own.

The rear door opened, and the bigger of the two men reached in, grabbed Francis by the arm, and hauled him out, almost dropping him to the ground beside some kind of drainage ditch. He rightened himself on his feet. "Wait—"

The big man shoved him in the back, lurching him forward. "Move."

"Wait, don't do this!" He stumbled along the uneven ground toward where the headlights pierced the gloom. "I'm the Battaglia priest. Giancarlo wants me alive." He tasted his heart in his throat. A few more steps, and they'd shoot him in the back.

He turned around and saw cold, hard, detached determination on both their faces.

The big man drew his gun.

Francis wet his lips. "Neo is lying to you, to Giancarlo. He works for Sasha Zhokov, the Russian. Sasha is behind all of this." It sounded like insanity, like the desperate, ranting words of a man about to die. He sounded like Charles Montague during his last few seconds alive.

The big man gestured with the gun. "On your knees, Padre."

"Oh God." Francis dropped to his knees and interlocked his hands behind his head. His vision swam, his head and chest thumping. "I helped Giancarlo. Call him, tell him I want to talk."

"Padre, the kill order came from the don," the big man grumbled, clearly bored.

No, that couldn't be true. Francis choked on a sob. Oh Lord, he was going to die, and his last words to Vitari had been awful. It couldn't end like this, not like this. There had to be something he could do, something he could say. "Please, don't..." It wasn't enough. He knew that. And he knew these men wouldn't listen to begging. How many others had they killed like this? Francis was just another mess to clean up.

"I'm sorry," he whispered. Sorry for all he'd done, for all the mistakes he'd made, for not being good enough. If he'd been a better man, a better priest, he could have stopped this. Perhaps this was all he deserved. But he'd been so sure there was more to it. Why would God send him his angel just for it to end like this? What was the fucking point in saving him only to have him die in a ditch?

There had to be something, some vital piece of information, something that would save him...

"Did you speak to Giancarlo directly or did"—his voice cracked—"or did Neo relay the order?"

Neither of them reacted, just stared, like two cold, hard statues.

"Did the order come from his lips?" Francis asked with more force. "You heard him order me dead? Tell me that."

The driver looked over at the big man. "The kill order came from don Giancarlo, right?"

"No, man. Neo's running this op."

There! See, they had to listen! Francis swallowed a sob. "Neo is DeSica—"

The big man waved the gun. "Shut up, priest. Let me think."

Francis ducked his head and prayed.

"Fucking call Giancarlo. Now," the smaller of the two demanded.

Francis slumped and breathed through the urge to throw up. He gripped his thighs and clung on, praying hard, praying as hard as when he'd sat next to Vitari in a hospital bed, desperate to keep him alive. Darkness throbbed around the edges of his vision. He prayed Giancarlo answered the phone, prayed the Mafia don would listen, and prayed he believed Francis, if they let him speak with their boss.

If he passed out, none of that would happen.

Don't pass out. Don't pass out.

He swayed, and breathed, and prayed. His ears rang.

"Here." The big man held out the phone.

Francis blinked up at him.

"Take the fucking phone, Padre."

He reached up with trembling fingers and pressed the phone to his ear. "Hello?"

"Father Scott," Giancarlo said. "Tell me everything."

CHAPTER FOURTEEN

Vitari

He had the honor of sharing a private jet back to Italy with Neo, who smirked through his champagne and kicked his shoes up on white leather seats, like a fucking king.

Vitari spent the entire first half of the flight staring out of the window, watching the clouds pass beneath them, wishing he could reach out to Francis and tell him he was sorry for everything—sorry for being a dick, for being stupid, for being the opposite of what Francis deserved, for not being good enough. He'd said some shitty things to him, blaming him when he'd known Francis had only meant to help. His own stupid hang-ups about his father had made him deaf to everything Francis had been telling him. Whether he was right or not, didn't matter. He should have listened. He hadn't, and so Francis had made the call. Literally. A call Vitari should have made himself.

There was nothing he could do now but hope Neo would stick to his word—a word that was worthless.

Francis might already be dead.

He couldn't think it, couldn't allow that thought to creep under his armor, or he'd lose his mind. He'd already fantasized about taking that gun at Neo's hip, shooting him in the head, then the guards, then himself. But he couldn't. Not while there was even a slim chance Francis was alive.

But if they fucking killed Francis, he'd lay waste to every fucker who had ever stood in his way, ever looked down on him, everyone who had ever hurt or betrayed him, and he'd crucify his fucking father.

Once Vitari was painted in blood, Francis's god would have to fucking listen then and know that love was worth every drop. He'd meet Francis again in Hell, if that was what it took to be with him.

Although, even with murder under his belt, Francis wasn't going to Hell. There was never a man more worthy of Heaven than Father Francis Scott. Vitari would spend eternity on his knees, peering at him through those pearly gates. That would be his own personal Hell.

Fuck, how had it come to this?

He'd go to his father, kill him, and then what?

Little Toni would take over the Battaglia reins.

Which meant Sal would be the one to shoot Vitari in the head. Toni would order it.

This was what Sasha wanted. To destroy it all. Because he could.

Vitari never should have made a deal with him. That mistake had been his downfall.

"Looking forward to going home, Angel?" Neo asked. "Back into your papa's loving embrace?"

Vitari ignored him, but the anger simmered, then boiled, until silence was no longer possible. "You could have had everything you want, Neo. Money, status. If you'd come to us the right way. The Battaglia embraces honor and integrity, not like Sasha."

"*Honor and integrity*," Neo mocked. "The Battaglia is last century. The whole fucking Italian Mafia is on its way out. Organized crime got sophisticated while you Italians are stuck in the past. Honor, integrity, throw in some respect too, right?" He laughed. "It's bullshit, fra. Nobody cares about family anymore."

"The Mafia has survived this long *because* of family, and respect. The DeSica has none. Sasha will turn on all of you. None of you mean shit to him. You can't follow someone like that."

"Oh, so you honor and respect your father?"

Vitari bared his teeth in a meaningless smile. "Whatever I think of my father, I respect don Giancarlo and the Battaglia. *You* have no respect."

"So that's why you betrayed him, huh? Out of respect?"

He should never have bothered speaking to Neo. He'd never understand.

"Or was it because of Stanmore?" Neo asked.

Vitari's heart turned to ice. "What the fuck do you know about Stanmore?" He couldn't know anything. Neo was just a grunt. Sasha wouldn't have told him about Stanmore, especially if the Russian was behind it all, as Francis believed.

Neo's smirk turned cruel. "I know it's where you got assfucked by a string of horny men—"

Vitari didn't even register leaving his seat and only knew he'd moved when a blast of fire surged through his knuckles and up his arm from the brutal punch he'd landed in Neo's face. Neo's guards hauled him off, but he'd done enough. For now.

"Fucking cuff him!" Neo screamed, his face red and his jaw flushed where Vitari's knuckles had landed.

Vitari was slammed back into the leather seat and cuffed there, chained like the rabid dog he was.

"Guess Stanmore's where you caught being gay, huh?" Neo laughed, then winced through his pain. He dabbed a napkin to his lip, and it came away stained with blood.

Vitari shouldn't have reacted. His rage gave Neo power. But he didn't have it in him to let some things go, and Stanmore was one of them. "What else did Sasha tell you?" he asked through gritted teeth.

"You know, I couldn't figure out why Sasha didn't just kill you. It took me a while to get it out of him. He took you from Giancarlo because Giancarlo was weak for some bitch, even back then. Sasha could have done anything with you, could have killed you, but he saved you instead, put you in that kid's home, just in case he'd need you later, you know... leverage." Neo said it all as though he were commenting on another sob story, like it was a joke. But that cruel joke was Vitari's life.

Sasha *saved* him? Vitari laughed. That was some impressive spin. Sasha's idea of saving him took a little boy in the faded Voltron T-shirt and put him in the hands of systemic pedophiles.

"*Did* he use me as leverage?" Vitari asked, hating how quiet his voice had gotten.

"How long were you there for?" Neo asked.

"Too fuckin' long."

"Then I guess not, or Giancarlo didn't rise to the bait. Whatever. It's some twisted shit, anyway." Neo looked away; even he was disturbed.

Not as disturbed as Vitari. He wasn't sure what was worse,

being ridiculed by Neo or pitied by him. But he'd learned one thing: Archbishop Montague's final confession to Francis had been the truth. Neo had now confirmed how Sasha had taken Vitari, put him in Stanmore, and left him there to rot. Montague's involvement had been more by chance than design. Montague had known Vitari's mother, helped her, and recognized Vitari when he'd gone searching for boys to fuck.

Although, Sasha had said some things when he'd lied to Vitari, back in his home that night. Things about religion and crime being intertwined. Vitari had assumed he'd been talking about the Battaglia, but he'd had it the wrong way around this whole time. Sasha had been talking about the DeSica, and he'd lied when Vitari had been trying to probe him for information on Stanmore. All of it was lies. He should have expected it, and now he knew the kind of man Sasha was—the kind to sell a child to the sex trade—he'd been a fool to ever believe a word that had passed the Russian's lips.

Should he be grateful Montague had found him? If he hadn't, Vitari would probably have died in Stanmore, like the rest of the boys from the back room.

He'd cut off his own balls before being grateful for anything that sick fuck had given him.

Shame made his guts churn.

He'd fucked up in the past, but never like this.

He should have been the one to call Giancarlo, not Francis. He should have confessed it all to his father, and then maybe he'd have had a chance to make some of it right. Somehow. He should have listened to Francis.

Now he had to kill Giancarlo to save Francis, because Neo had slithered his way into the Battaglia gaps Vitari had left wide open.

And behind Neo, Sasha encircled them all, waiting to strike.

He dozed during the flight, waking when the rough edges of nightmares grated against old memories of dark rooms and bruised knees.

They landed at a familiar airfield in southern Italy, and Vitari climbed from the jet, blinking into the sunlight. He had no idea what day of the week it was, or if he'd live to see tomorrow, but at least he was back on home soil. His soul shuffled and settled. *Italy*. Despite the circumstances, it was good to be back. The Calabrian sun blazed. Azure skies stretched from east to west.

Neo removed the cuffs, for appearances, but warned him not to try any stupid shit or Francis would pay with a beating.

Neo had been right. Francis was Vitari's weakness. But what nobody understood was how Francis was also his strength. Vitari would be dead without him. Dead in Venezuela, dead at the bottom of a bottle, dead from a drug binge, dead in heart and soul. So, what was a little patricide in the name of love?

They climbed into the family cars and headed toward the coast.

"You need a gun?" Neo asked from the front seat.

"Sure. Give me yours, right now." So he could blow him away.

Neo rolled his eyes. "Whatever, man. I'm trying to help."

Vitari sneered and wished it was over already. "If you want to help, you pezzo di merda, let me speak to Francis," he said, keeping the conversation vague since the driver was a new face.

"After."

"Fuck after. Now."

"Fuckin' after! Or not at all. Jesus. You don't make the demands here, Angel, I do."

Was Neo getting twitchy now he was in Italy? Home of the Mafia, kingdom of the Battaglia, where he was the fucking rat. "What sewer did Sasha fish you out of? How did you even get tangled up with him and the DeSica? He only hires psychos and whores, so which one are you?"

Neo laughed. "You got a mouth on you, Angel."

The driver, a low-ranking Battaglia man, gave them both a hard side-eye. Drivers were paid not to comment and not gossip. Anyone who talked got a pair of concrete shoes and a long walk off a short pier.

There wasn't a single soul in Calabria who would believe Vitari now that he was the traitor. Except maybe Sal? "Is Sal at the villa?" Vitari asked.

"Maybe. You fuck him too?"

"Jesus, were you born an asshole or did you practice your whole fucking life?"

Sal would have thought him dead, like everyone else. He'd be pissed, and in no mood to help him after that stunt, but he'd listen. If Vitari could find him before coming face-to-face with his father. "Is Giancarlo there?"

"I guess we'll find out."

"You goin' to babysit me, Neo? Are you sure you want to stay in the same room as me? You aren't afraid you might catch being gay?"

"I'm as straight as a fuckin' arrow, man."

Vitari sensed the typical macho bullshit that always bubbled to the surface when anyone mentioned *gays*. It riled him, had made him hate himself in the past, but right now it was a chink in Neo's armor. "I've seen the way you look at me. You wear the same clothes, followed me like a lost dog. Are you sure you haven't wondered, huh? You look like the type who just might like some dick up your ass—"

"Shut up. How long until we get there?" Neo asked the driver.

"Fifteen minutes."

Vitari grinned. "What's the problem? You gettin' hard, Neo?"

"I fuck women."

"No shame, man. I'll help you with that bi-awakening, since we've got some time to kill."

"Fuck you, and fuck off with the bi shit."

Vitari chuckled, but as they turned onto a familiar road that hugged the turquoise coast, his heart sank. Almost home, where fate awaited.

He'd killed for Francis without hesitating, and he'd kill his father for him too, even knowing Stanmore hadn't been his fault. But what happened after, Vitari had no control over.

If he prayed, would God even listen to a wicked person like him? Francis had said He would, that people like Vitari were who God heard the most. But he didn't believe it. If God existed, why the fuck had He let a bunch of innocent kids grow up in a pedophile ring?

The driver cruised the car through the waterside village and up the long, winding road toward the family home on the hill. He didn't get the same kind of settled-soul feeling as they arrived at the sprawling stone villa like he had when touching down on Italian soil. This Calabrian slice of paradise didn't feel like home. He wasn't sure it ever had. Giancarlo had always made it clear he was the outsider, like he didn't deserve the house, the business, the life. And all Vitari had ever done was try to be good enough, be brutal enough, be loyal enough. He'd killed for Giancarlo, butchered for him, waved the fucking Battaglia flag as though his life depended on it—because Giancarlo had made it clear. It did.

Neo climbed from the car first and gave him another warning about not fucking up, but this time he muttered it under his breath. Francis's survival hinged on Vitari following this through.

They walked through the gardens, then up over the veranda, through the arches, and into the house. House-keepers stared as they sauntered by. They'd probably all mourned Vitari, as much as they could someone they hardly knew and mostly feared.

Giancarlo and Sal weren't home, Neo said, after asking one of the staff. But Giancarlo was due back by the evening.

Vitari stood in the sprawling split-level living room feeling like a tumor feeding on the Battaglia veins. He rubbed a hand down his whisker-rough, filthy face, trying to sweep away the churn of emotion. To do this, he'd have to be L' Angelo della Morte. He couldn't be Vitari, son of Giancarlo, son of Stefania. He couldn't *feel*.

The problem was, since meeting Francis, all he'd fucking done was *feel*.

"So uh... I can't be here," Neo said, glancing around, eager to get away. "Plausible deniability. But I won't be far, and if you fucking leave this house, I'll know, and—"

"You'll make Francis pay. I get it." Vitari gestured rudely. "Vaffanculo already Neo, you piece of shit."

"Do this, and you know... he'll be safe." He shrugged as he said it and headed for the door.

Vitari had been wrong, Neo wasn't a snake. He was a

worm. Vitari watched him leave, heard the car engine burble to life and fade away, then stood alone in the living room again. A small shard of fear poked at his resolve. What if Francis was already dead, his body rotting somewhere in the jungle?

He closed his eyes and dropped his head back. "Madre di Dio, prega per noi peccatori, adesso e nell'ora della nostra morte. Amen."

Francis wasn't dead. He had God on his side. Someone had tried to execute him on the steps of St. Peter's, and he'd survived. He'd survived DeSica hitmen, survived the massacre at El Cristo. He'd survive a fucking apocalypse. He *was* alive. Vitari *had* to believe it. And to keep him alive, Vitari had to kill Giancarlo.

He showered, dressed in some of his finer clothes, since this moment would define the rest of what remained of his life, and removed a lockbox from among his rack of hand-made shoes. The gleaming gun inside had been given to him by Giancarlo—after Vitari had executed his first man—as a welcome to the Battaglia gift.

The Italian-made Chiappa 1911-22 gun sported a custom engraved grip. A work of art. It gleamed in his hands.

He loaded the clip with a satisfying mechanical *click*. He'd never used it, probably because right after he'd killed for his father, he'd spent the rest of the night on his knees throwing up.

The house was all but empty; even the housekeepers had vanished. He went straight to the study. It wasn't locked. Nobody dared enter without permission. Not here, in Giancarlo's castle.

Vitari drifted inside, numb, hiding under the skin of L' Angelo della Morte. His gaze skimmed the black-and-white pictures featuring all the things important to the boss of the largest, most notorious organized crime syndicate in Europe. Cars, dogs, guns. Not a single picture of his son.

He found himself at the desk and reclined in his father's well-worn leather chair. Giancarlo had told him all of this could be his—the empire, the throne. But that future had been a dream, not for the likes of him.

He didn't want it anyway.

What he wanted was a little farm with a well out back, a whole lot of nothing around him, and Francis. *That* was fucking paradise. Not whatever this place was, built on a foundation of blood.

Fucking hell, holier-than-thou Father Francis Scott really had rubbed off on him.

Rummaging through the desk drawers produced a bottle of whiskey, unopened. Vitari cracked the seal, poured himself a glass, then a second for Francis. "To surviving, amore mio." He downed his, wincing at the burn, but left the second glass untouched.

Inside the open drawer, a small thumb-sized USB drive caught his eye. A sticker wrapped around it read: *Vitari*. He picked it up and teased the drive between his fingers. Why would his father keep a flash drive with his name on it? Was it filled with more horrible pictures like the other drive he'd found?

It didn't matter. Whatever was on it wouldn't change what had to happen.

A car engine disturbed the crickets chirping outside.

He tossed the drive onto the desk, flicked the safety off the gun, and waited.

Car doors slammed, voices murmured. The housekeepers would tell his father he was home. But it didn't matter how his son had come back from the dead—Giancarlo always visited his study first.

The voices faded. Shoes clipped the tiled floor, coming closer.

Vitari breathed in, lifted his chin, and in the gloom, watched the door.

The handle turned, the door swung open, and Giancarlo's broad profile filled the doorway, lit from behind. He hesitated, and Vitari felt the weight of his judgmental gaze fall on him, as it always had. Always there, always watching, judging, even from afar.

"My boy." He reached for the light switch.

"Leave it."

That hesitation, that moment of knowing... Giancarlo lowered his hand, stepped inside, and closed the door behind him, sealing away the world outside the study. Now it was just them, father and son.

"I always knew it would come to this."

Vitari huffed a sour laugh. "Is this the part where you claim you've only done what's best for me? You had to be cruel to be kind?"

"My son." He moved into the light cast from the window.

He looked older. More lines had gathered around his eyes and mouth, which was always fixed in a grimace. He wore a grey suit, similar to the black one Vitari wore.

"I'm only your son when it suits you." Vitari heard him swallow. He was afraid. Good. He should be. "My whole life, you let me believe I was nothing, but it wasn't about me, was it? It was about my mother and your cowardice? Sasha Zhokov murdered her and took me from you, from your own front yard, and you were too weak to stop him. You weren't ashamed of me, you were ashamed of *you*, of your own weakness. Because you did nothing." He tasted the rage again, like the whiskey burning inside. "Nothing!" Vitari swallowed the knot in his throat. "I rotted in Stanmore *for years* and *you did nothing.*"

"You have every right to be angry—"

"*Angry* doesn't touch the surface, *Father.*"

Giancarlo took another step, and Vitari raised the gun from under the desk. Giancarlo must have known it was there, but now he saw it—saw the exact gun it was. His eyes widened, but not in fear. He nodded and met Vitari's gaze again.

"Was she a whore?"

Giancarlo spread his hands and breathed in, filling his lungs. "I loved your mother more than life."

He hadn't expected those words to mean anything. He couldn't remember his mother, didn't know her, but hearing the quiver in his father's voice told him he *would* have loved her too. He'd been robbed of that. Giancarlo had taken the truth from him. Had he known he'd been the product of love, things might have turned out differently.

"Why *did* you hide it?" Vitari whispered. He'd have yelled, but his voice wouldn't have held.

"I was ashamed, son. I couldn't look at you without seeing her. I blamed you. I failed her, failed you in the worst ways." His voice cracked. His hands trembled at his sides.

Vitari steeled himself, slamming down barriers. He wasn't here for this. This wasn't a cathedral in England, and he didn't care for Giancarlo's confession. He was here to save the love of his life, to do what Giancarlo couldn't. He wouldn't fail Francis like Giancarlo had failed Stefania.

All he had to do was pull the trigger.

"Do it," Giancarlo said. "Do it, son."

Vitari smiled. Even now, in his final moments, his father

barked orders at him like a dog. He would kill him, but he wanted more, he wanted a fucking apology. Giancarlo still hadn't given him one.

"Know this, I am proud of you, Vitari."

His smile froze, pinned in place. *Proud?*

"You are stronger than I have ever been. When I learned of all the things that had been done to you... Son, I... I was sick, sick for days. I did not want that. And to go through it and become who you are? You are the man I wished I was. You are worthy."

The knot was back in his throat, choking him. His smile twitched, and the more he clung to it, the more it cracked and fell away. "You don't get to say these things now, when it's too fucking late!"

Giancarlo turned his palms up, pleading. "Forgive me." His face was wet, but that wasn't possible. Giancarlo didn't do emotion, just stone-cold viciousness.

He'd never seen his father cry before.

Vitari's aim wavered, his hand trembling, like his snarl trembled. This had to be done! Giancarlo had to die! Vitari stood, knocking the chair back, and aimed the gun between his father's haunted eyes.

Damn him, it was too late to be proud, too late to talk of being worthy. He'd needed that fifteen years go.

He had to end this, if there was even the smallest glimmer of hope in seeing Francis again.

"I'm sorry, Papa."

Giancarlo nodded, smiling as the tears fell from his face. "So am I."

CHAPTER FIFTEEN

Francis

Something was wrong.

He waited in the car outside the pretty Italian villa, just as Giancarlo had told him—the only words he'd said since collecting Francis from the private airfield.

The porch light glowed, and all around was quiet. Maybe too quiet?

Everything had felt wrong since he'd spilled the whole truth to the Mafia don over the phone, on his knees, on a muddy track somewhere outside Cartagena. He still wasn't sure what, if anything, Giancarlo believed. After the call, the Battaglia men had bundled him onto a plane, and nine hours later, here he was, on the other side of the world again, somewhere in picturesque Italy. But the wrongness was getting worse. It felt slippery and oily, like guilt, for leaving Vitari in Colombia, even though he hadn't had a choice.

He had to be here. Giancarlo was the single person who

had the connections and power to stop everything, and while Francis was under no illusions that the man was as wicked as they come, his gut told him *this* was the only way.

And now his gut was telling him Giancarlo had been gone too long.

He peered out of the passenger window and saw a lone man walk up the driveway. Something glinted in his hand, something shaped very much like a gun. Was that normal? Did people carry openly in these parts? He glanced around, but nobody was about. No staff, no guards, even their driver had disappeared.

Was this how a Mafia don did things in his own home?

Back in Rome, Giancarlo had guards nearby.

There were no guards here now. Unless that man walking toward the villa was a guard?

The figure stepped onto the porch, and Francis saw his face.

Neo.

Oh dear.

Francis had told Giancarlo *everything* about Neo, and if he believed him, then he knew Neo was an imposter, put among the Battaglia to disrupt it and supply Sasha with any and all information he required.

Should Francis do something? Should he warn Giancarlo?

Neo entered the villa, leaving the front door ajar behind him.

He had to do *something*.

He climbed from the car and searched the nearby grounds for someone to pass on the warning, but there wasn't anyone... This *wasn't* right. He had to go inside. He stepped onto the porch, passing under the light, and eased through the open front door.

"You don't get to say these things now, when it's too fucking late!"

The shout resounded through the house. Was that... *Vitari?*

It was. He'd know his voice in a crowd of a thousand, know its accent anywhere, and its rage. Francis dashed along the short entrance hall and stepped into a large open-plan living area. He stopped and listened. Vitari was here—not in Colombia—and by the sounds of it, he needed help. Maybe if Francis called out, he'd reply?

Hard iron poked against the back of his head.

"You just won't stay dead, will you, Padre?"

He'd found Neo.

Francis raised his hands as ice spilled into his veins. "Vitari is here?"

"Yes, he is. And you're going to sit tight while he does what he's told, or I will paint that nice white wall over there with your brain matter."

"What's going on?" As he asked, events fell into place around him. Giancarlo was here. Vitari was here. Neo was here. Neo, who had made Vitari agree to something in Cartagena, to keep Francis safe, while all the while he'd planned to have Francis executed.

Did Vitari think Francis was dead?

Vitari was going to kill Giancarlo for Sasha. Of course he was. The final, ultimate betrayal, and the catalyst that would bring down the Battaglia, leaving it in ashes at Sasha's feet.

But that wasn't going to happen because Francis wasn't dead. He'd called Giancarlo, and Giancarlo had brought him *here.* Exactly where Vitari needed Francis to be.

Was it God's work? Fate?

It didn't matter. Francis had to act.

"Vitari!" Francis yelled.

"You dumb fuck!"

The gun cracked against his head. Pain blasted down the back of his neck. Francis reeled, stumbling against the wall, but as his vision blurred, he saw Neo run toward another door.

He had to get to Vitari, had to help him. "Vitari, I'm alive!" He shoved off the wall and stumbled forward. "I'm here."

CHAPTER SIXTEEN

Vitari

Giancarlo muttered a prayer, and Vitari blinked useless tears from his eyes so he could see his father's end in all its horrifying glory.

"Vitari!"

The moment stalled, reality slamming back in, tearing down all Vitari's defenses.

"Francis?"

How...

Vitari swayed and clutched the edge of the desk. Francis was here, just outside... But that didn't make any sense. Unless...

Giancarlo smiled, but it wasn't the snarling smile of a man who loathed his son. Not anymore. It was a soft smile, a smile of understanding, a smile the likes of which Vitari had never seen on his father's face. A smile that said it was all right, a smile of *understanding*.

The study door flew open.

Giancarlo began to turn.

A gun barked.

A dash of warm wetness rain over Vitari's face, and Giancarlo fell.

Neo stood in the doorway, gun raised. "You weren't ever going to do it."

Vitari aimed down his gun's sights at Neo's face and tugged the trigger. The gun kicked, a neat hole opened up in Neo's cheek, and his whole body jerked, as though tugged on strings. Neo collapsed and lay twitching on the floor.

Vitari stole a breath, trying to make his heart and lungs work again. His mouth tasted coppery, like blood. *Not my blood.* His papa lay on the floor, crumpled like a frail old man. Dead.

"Vitari..." Francis stumbled into the doorway, still in his scruffy Panama clothes, his hair wild and eyes wilder. He reached for the doorframe and looked down at Neo, then over at Giancarlo. "Oh no."

Oh no.

Vitari tried to hold the pieces of himself together, he really did, but the more he clutched at the stoic version of himself—L' Angelo della Morte—the more it turned to dust between his fingers. He was falling, coming apart at the seams. A sound fell out of him, a strange, keening moan, and then he was back in the chair, fighting to keep all the tiny pieces of himself in one place before they shattered forever.

"Francis?" he whispered, prayed, dreamed.

"I'm here."

And he was. He collected Vitari, hauled him into his arms, and it was there where Vitari finally stopped trying to hold himself together. He sobbed and clutched at Francis, needing to know he was real, and here, and solid, and everything. He smelled of earth, sweat, and Francis, and Vitari crushed him close, clinging to him, desperate and destroyed from the inside out.

"I've got you," Francis whispered.

He sobbed so hard it hurt, as though each sob scooped out another piece of him. He didn't want to cry, but he couldn't stop. All the hate and fear and countless feelings flooded out of him. His papa was dead, he'd killed the man who'd murdered him, and Francis was here.

His papa had brought his love home.

"I'm here, amore mio," Francis said, hugging him close. "I'm here, I've got you. We're together." He said the words over and over, in different ways, but also the same, and slowly, carefully, Vitari picked up the broken bits of himself and put them back where they belonged, so he could breathe, and think, and function.

Francis eased back. His warm hands cupped Vitari's face, and his big hazel eyes were bright and glassy and all Vitari wanted to see because everything around him was too much. A dribble of red blood stood out starkly on Franci's pale neck. *Someone had hurt him.*

Vitari almost lost it again.

"Breathe." Francis bumped their foreheads together.

Breathe. Yes. Breathe and live. And survive. Like always. Like he'd been doing since he'd been trapped in Hell as a boy. Had he ever escaped? Was he still there?

"All right?" Francis asked.

Vitari blinked, shedding the last of his tears, and nodded. He licked his lips, tasting salt now, not blood. Sitting back, he picked up the whiskey and poured another glass. "That one's for you," he croaked, flicking his finger at the glass he'd poured for Francis before the world had shifted on its axis.

"Oh."

"You're going to need it."

Francis picked up the glass and gulped it back in one. He coughed, wheezed, and smiled, and Vitari's heart cracked wide open for him. His love. Here. Somehow.

Francis's smile faded, though, when he looked across the room and saw the two dead men.

This was... going to change everything.

"Uhm... should we run?" Francis asked.

He could see why he'd ask it. They'd always run before. But there was nowhere left to run to, no sanctuary where the Battaglia wouldn't find them.

"No." There was no running from this.

"All right," Francis said, not missing a beat.

And that was why Vitari loved him, among many, many reasons. Father Francis Scott would stand by him forever, no matter what.

Vitari stood, breathed out, and crossed the floor. He dug Giancarlo's phone from his pocket and used his thumb to unlock it, mentally disassociating himself from the horror of manhandling his dead father. "But we're going to need help."

He scrolled the phone's caller list and hit the number for Sal. He picked up on the third ring. "Ciao, boss."

"Sal, it's me."

"...Angel?"

"Yeah."

A long, weighted pause sailed down the line. Sal might hang up, might rage at him, might call him a traitor. "I never thought I'd hear your voice again, fra."

No anger, just relief. It was good to hear Sal's voice too. "I need your help. Just you. Not your papa. Can you come to the villa?"

"You're home?" Sal's big, relieved sigh said enough. He'd help them.

"Come now, fratello. Don't tell anyone."

"On my way."

Vitari ended the call and turned to see Francis's concerned expression. "Everything is about to get real, Padre Blanco. If you want to leave, go now. You can still have a life."

His gaze danced around, as though maybe he was considering it, like he should. "A life without you."

It would kill Vitari if Francis left, but he had to give him the choice. Francis had to know what this meant. There was no going back. With Vitari's father dead, the Battaglia would be in freefall unless someone gripped the reins, fast. "Yes, but still a life. Go be a priest in some sleepy English village somewhere, if that's what you want, Francis."

"I don't think I ever wanted that," he mumbled. "Not really."

"I can't save you from this after tonight," Vitari admitted. "Can't save you from me."

Their gazes met, and Francis's soft smile grew. "I'm not going anywhere."

He'd hoped he'd say that—*needed* to hear him say it. Francis had no idea how Vitari's every heartbeat was poised on a knife's edge, how his every breath pushed him closer to breaking. "How are you here?" After that prayer he'd uttered earlier, he'd begun to wonder if God really had been listening.

"Neo was going to have me killed, and I knew he'd made you do something because of me, so I uh... I..." He glanced at Giancarlo's body. "I told Giancarlo. He had those men bring me here... to you. This is probably not the time, but I think, in all this, he was trying to keep you safe the only way he knew."

"Yeah, with threats and abuse." Vitari refused to look at his father.. He'd have to do that later, when they moved the body, but for now he only wanted to drink Francis in. He was a mess. His clothes were the same he'd been wearing since they'd left Panama, all creased and filthy, as though he'd been dragged through a field. He even had grass in his hair. Vitari rested a hip against the desk, plucked the grass free, and showed it to him, making him smile. "You brought some of Colombia back with you."

"At least it's not drugs."

Laughter shot out of Vitari. "You look a little rough around the edges, Padre." He brushed his knuckles over the golden fuzz of a beard along Francis's jaw. A blush touched Francis's face.

"And you look amazing, like always." Francis wiped something from Vitari's cheek. Blood, probably.

He really, really hoped what came next didn't break them. Because it was going to be a shitshow.

Vitari sighed. His gaze fell to his father's empty chair. The crown had fallen, and he didn't want to pick it up. He wasn't ready. Didn't want it. But life had always been something that happened to him, sweeping him along, like Francis and his Church. Just once, he'd have liked a choice in it all.

And if he'd had that choice, he'd have chosen none of this. This life wasn't for him.

He'd have chosen Francis.

CHAPTER SEVENTEEN

Francis

The man who arrived an hour later was built like a wrestler, with arms as thick as his legs, cropped short black hair, and a mean Italian face. Perhaps, in other circumstances, he might have smiled, but he saw the scene in the study, swore at length in Italian, and then ranted at Vitari. Vitari fired off a retort in a similar tone, until the two of them were flinging rapid Italian back and forth like gunfire.

There was a whole lot of gesturing and what sounded like some crude name-calling. As Francis had little hope of following any of it, he poured himself another whiskey. When he set the bottle down, a USB storage device with Vitari's name on it caught his eye.

On instinct, he slipped the drive into his pocket. If it wasn't important, it wouldn't matter that he'd taken it. And if it was, then it should be kept safe. Because there were two bodies that needed to be dealt with, one of them being don

Giancarlo's, and nothing about any of this was going to be *safe*.

"So, you're the priest who's caused all the trouble, huh?" Vitari's friend, Sal, grumbled in deep, Italian-accented English.

The sudden switch to English stalled Francis's wandering thoughts. "I suppose I am."

"You killed Luca Espinosa?"

He glanced at Vitari—how much should he say?

Vitari nodded and said, "We can trust Sal."

"I did." Francis chased that confession with a gulp of whiskey.

"Then you saved Vitari in Venezuela?"

What did this man, this friend of Vitari's, want from him? "I will always save him. Like he saves me every day."

Sal narrowed his eyes, trying to get a read on him. He sensed Vitari's friend perhaps didn't like him, but Francis hadn't slept in forever and there was a lot going on, and he didn't care what this man thought. He'd told him the facts. Sal could take them or leave them.

Vitari gripped Sal's shoulder, said something in Italian, and then they got to work bundling the two bodies into the back of Sal's car. Sal made a call, and a little while later, more people arrived. They swept in and *cleaned* the study, wiping down the floor and walls, then demanded Francis and Vitari hand over their clothes. Which was fine for Vitari, as he had plenty of outfits to wear, but Francis was left—after showering—with trousers an inch too short and a shirt that hung off him. It smelled of Vitari's woody cologne though, which made all this a little less horrible.

As the sun rose on a new day and car doors slammed outside, Francis couldn't help but wonder where he fit in with all this, or even if it was real. But he'd stay with Vitari.

Vitari was the sun he orbited. He couldn't escape and didn't want to.

"Okay, so here's what's going to happen..." Vitari swept into the room, then he saw Francis on the end of the bed and hesitated. "This was so much fuckin' easier to ask in my head."

"I want to help."

"I know, I just..." He braced his hands on his hips and huffed. "There's a meet. A big one. All the capos. I just need to get through it and we'll be all right. So here's what we're going to do." He pulled a thick strip of white from his pocket. "I had someone go to the local church and uh... borrow this. I need you to be Padre Blanco."

It was a priest's collar. Francis frowned at it, a little confused. How would being a priest help them now?

"I'm sorry I have to ask," Vitari said. "It's like with the Church, it's all about the theater. If I show up at the meet with my lover, who happens to be a man, they'll butcher us. But if I show up with Padre Blanco, the priest who shot Luca Espinosa? It's a whole different thing. But it's also *not* like the Church, because if we take a wrong step, no amount of Hail Marys are going to save us from a bullet to the brain. God, do you fucking hate me for all this?"

"I'll do it. Absolutely." He took the collar and stood. "For you. For us."

"Are you sure?" Vitari winced. "It's not against your religion or vows or whatever?"

Francis swallowed his laugh. "Are you asking if using my reputation as a priest who kills people will be frowned upon by the Catholic Church? I think that ship has sailed into the horizon and been set upon by pirates."

Vitari gave a snort. "Fuck, I love you."

"Can you get a cassock?"

Vitari glanced side-on, clearly suspicious at Francis's enthusiasm. "I'll get you anything you need."

"Good, because after I've done this"—he threaded the collar in place and stepped into Vitari's personal space, right up close, so there was nothing between them but sizzling tension— "you're going to fuck me while I'm wearing it."

Vitari's sly grin ticked.

The thought alone had Francis's knees going weak and his cock hardening. To be fucked from behind while wearing a cassock was so wrong—so forbidden, blasphemy—but he needed its rawness to scorch his soul, to brand Vitari there, where the church had once been.

It wasn't often he caught Vitari speechless. Or with a touch of heat in his face. Francis hovered his mouth over Vitari's and fell into his eyes. "I'm sorry about all those things I said, and for not speaking to you first before calling Giancarlo."

"Fuck, Francis, don't apologize. I was wrong about all of it. I should have listened."

"We're going to get through today, and tomorrow, and we're going to survive, because it's what we do."

Vitari smiled against Francis's mouth and stroked up his chest, scrunching his shirt. "What if I fuck you against the wall now, or is this a buy now, pay later deal?"

Francis teased Vitari's lips apart and slid the tip of his tongue in, going so slow that it hurt to hold back. "Later."

"You're killing me, Padre." Vitari flicked his tongue over Francis's, teasing, then easing off, rocking together but hardly touching.

Maybe they could get off quickly, before the day began? The idea of having sex while dressed in his robes had been a spur of the moment thing, but since Vitari's eyes now burned with lust, that idea had lit a blaze inside Francis, searing his veins. "Can I change my mind?"

"No." Vitari chuckled and backed away, then adjusted the front of his trousers, drawing Francis's gaze to the thick line of his trapped dick. "You made your bed, now lie in it, Padre."

Francis glanced back at the bed with a heavy dose of suggestion, but Vitari laughed him off. "I am going to make *you* pay."

Vitari stalled at the door, probably waiting for his erection to wane, or mentally preparing for everything waiting for them on the other side. Francis loitered by the end of the bed. Padre Blanco was a myth created in a Venezuelan village, a way for Francis to pretend, but he didn't exist. But that was the point. Father Francis Scott hadn't been real either. Underneath it all, he was just Francis, a broken man who loved a broken angel.

"You good?" Vitari asked.

"Yes, I think I really am." He held Vitari's gaze, like he'd held him in his arms earlier, feeling every sob rack his soul. Together, they were going to be okay. "Are *you* all right?"

"Fuck, no." Vitari opened the door. "I'll get through this shit show knowing you're beside me. You ready?"

Francis was about to become part of the Mafia. How hard could it be after a lifetime raised by the Church? "Not in the least." He smiled, and Vitari mirrored the same smile. Despite what they were about to endure, Francis really did believe they'd survive. As long as they were together.

They drove into the picturesque, ancient city of Catanzaro and climbed from their line of cars outside a restaurant with tables beneath a vine-wrapped pergola, but no customers. Francis guessed the Mafia owned these parts of old southern Italy. The entire town probably knew they were here and had been told to stay away.

One of Sal's people handed Francis a cassock and directed him toward the restroom at the back of the restaurant, where he could change.

He found himself alone in the men's room, cassock folded in his arms, staring at his pale reflection.

The scar above his eye seemed more prominent under the harsh lighting. What was he doing here? He spoke only a handful of Italian. How was he going to back up Vitari without following what was about to happen?

But it *was* happening, so he'd better get himself together and act like he was Padre Blanco. He'd taught himself some basic Italian, perhaps enough to muddle through, but the accents in the south were different to the north. Although, the accents weren't going to be his main problem. Pretending he belonged would be.

Being gay in the Catholic Church didn't get you killed. Out here, in rural Italy among the Mafia, desiring another man was a death sentence. And if that man was the dead don's son?

Francis's hands trembled. He placed the cassock down, gripped the washbasin, and bowed his head. He'd lost all right to pray for guidance at a time like this, but he prayed anyway, and when he faced his reflection again, all the doubt and fear had vanished from his glare.

He'd do this for Vitari. No cost was too high.

With the cassock and white collar on, the proud, stoic priest in the mirror stared back. Padre Blanco. It was theater, and he'd been playing this role his whole life. He'd just... fine tuned it some. *Evolved* it.

He emerged from the restroom strangely calm, almost untouchable, as though God's grace made him invincible. The cassock wouldn't stop a bullet, but it felt as though it would, and when he passed by the guards dotted about the restaurant, they all looked at him differently. Some even dipped their chins. He'd forgotten how powerful religion could be, which was absurd, since he'd been submerged in it his whole life. But he'd been looking out from the ruined, twisted mess of his own mind. People *looking in* saw a priest, and one who wasn't afraid to go to Hell for what he believed in.

He might be able to do this.

The large back room had been made up to cater the group with a long oval table, decorated with fine cutlery and all the sparkling luxuries. A few men were already seated, and from the sounds of car doors slamming, more were arriving. Francis wasn't taking a seat. He needed to be visible, to be the first thing they saw. He stood beside a huge arrangement of blood-red roses, making sure everyone who entered had to look him in the eye.

His heart pounded in his throat.

Eighty percent of the men were older, over fifty, but there were some younger faces too. Vitari wasn't yet here.

Francis clasped his hands behind his back, hiding how he squeezed them into fists.

Sal arrived and nodded at Francis. As he sat, Francis spotted the bulge of a gun under his jacket. The others were likely armed as well. With the table full at almost thirty men, Vitari still hadn't arrived. But only one chair remained, the chair at the head of the table. Were these men waiting for Giancarlo to fill it? Did they know the Battaglia don was dead?

Vitari had to walk into the lion's den and preside over a

world he'd been trapped in, wear a crown he didn't want, control men who he believed despised him.

Francis breathed in, filling his chest, and stared ahead, waiting for the new don to arrive.

He'd get through it.

They both would.

They didn't have a choice.

CHAPTER EIGHTEEN

Vitari

Vitari paced.

The capos had arrived. If he walked into the meeting looking weak, they'd tear him to pieces.

Fuck.

He couldn't do this.

He had to do this.

No running, not anymore.

He refused to live his life in shame.

Stand. Fight.

You are worthy.

Fuck.

There was no use delaying it. He'd either walk out of this alive or die in a bloodbath. Fifty-fifty it could go either way.

Fuck, fuck, fuck.

He strode through the empty main restaurant floor and pushed through the doors into the dining room. The

Battaglia men all turned their gazes on him, almost knocking him back a step, but then he saw Francis standing at the back, his tall body dressed in slim-fitting black, the stamp of white at his neck, his face stoic and stern, as though he had the power to smite every single man here.

Vitari's galloping heart slowed.

He wasn't alone.

His gaze slid down the table to the lone chair. His father's chair.

If anyone was going to lose their shit and pull a gun, they'd do it now.

He stood at the end of the table but didn't sit, not yet. All eyes turned to him, some widening, as they realized the calls they'd received were true.

The king was dead. Long live the king.

"Giancarlo was murdered by the traitor, Neo. I executed Neo. This is the state of the Battaglia, and Sasha Zhokov will pay."

Chaos didn't erupt. Nobody pulled a gun. No blood was spilled. Yet.

Much of Vitari's support hinged on Little Toni, Sal's father, and when Toni had listened to all Vitari had to say about Stefania Angelini, the missing Vatican girl, about his father's feud with the Russian, about how Sasha had been working to undermine the Battaglia for years, and how Vitari had been caught up in all of it... it could have gone either way. But Toni had listened, occasionally glancing at Sal, and in the end, Toni had nodded, and that single gesture secured Vitari's throne. For now.

Of all the men here, half of them had wanted Vitari

dead *before* he'd betrayed his father. More likely wanted him killed now Giancarlo was gone. Vitari wasn't as naïve as to think he could walk into his father's shoes and become the king at a click of his fingers.

Honor had to be earned, and he hadn't earned a damn thing.

The killing blow wouldn't come here, it would come later, after these men got to talking between themselves and figured out a way to get rid of him.

But Vitari didn't need forever. He only needed to wear the crown long enough to destroy Sasha Zhokov—a sentiment everyone at the table agreed with. Sasha killed Giancarlo and had to die.

"Sasha is in Monte Carlo for a poker tournament," Little Toni said, leaving the sentence hanging in the air for Vitari to run with.

Monte Carlo, southern France. Just a short flight away. This could be over sooner than he'd expected. Sasha would never expect him to amass a Battaglia force and take the fight right to him.

"I want the Battaglia there, I want us all over him. Surround him and close in. Any rats, any traitors in your ranks, take them out now. Fucking mail their eyes to the DeSica bastard so he knows we see him, and we're coming."

"This will be all-out war," Slider said—the capo running the gun trade with the US. "Is that what you want?"

"It was war when Sasha killed my mother and took me. Giancarlo was too weak to fight back. I'm not weak. Are you weak, Slider? Are any of you weak?"

Nobody said a fucking word.

Slider's lips twitched. "There will be blood on the streets of Monte Carlo."

Vitari smiled. "Then we'll paint the fucking city red."

"L' Angelo della Morte," Sal said, raising his voice above the murmurings and catching his father's eye, as though to challenge him to deny Vitari his place. Sal had his back and always would.

Toni hesitated a beat and raised his fist. "L' Angelo della Morte!"

Others joined in, until the entire group chanted *Angelo della Morte, Angelo della Morte, Angelo della Morte!* Vitari measured his smile, keeping himself calm, even as his bruised heart soared. He'd been so fucking afraid they'd reject him because of who he was, where he'd come from, and who he loved. But right now, in this very moment, the Battaglia would follow him.

He glanced over their heads at Francis and saw his smile too.

The one smile in the room that touched his heart.

The meeting wound down. The Mafia old guard took Vitari's hand and kissed the backs of his fingers, pledging their allegiance and offering their condolences, even while they likely plotted his downfall. Several spoke with Francis, probably in his capacity as a priest, as most of the capos were religious men. He prayed with a few, Vitari saw, keeping Francis on the fringes of his radar while he did the rounds and smoothed over frayed edges. The meeting dragged into the morning hours, as they often did. Too much wine and macho bullshit flowed, loud posturing, DeSica death threats and all the creative ways they could destroy them.

Vitari kept an eye on Francis through it all. He didn't

seem distressed, but he was clearly trying to convey *something* with several frequent, pointed glances at Vitari.

Francis caught his eye again and twitched his head, signaling to step away. He headed for the restrooms, and Vitari counted down the minutes before he could leave without it seeming too obvious. He feigned getting a drink at the open bar, then slipped through a back door.

Francis waited outside the restrooms, saw Vitari coming, and opened an adjacent door. His stern expression suggested he might be about to chastise Vitari. The only thing upsetting its perfection was the tiny scar over his eye. Vitari glanced around, checking if they were being watched, then ducked into the room—a large walk-in pantry with racks of shelves along each wall—and turned to ask Francis if he was all right.

Francis's mouth slammed into his, desperate hands cupped Vitari's face, then shoved Vitari back to the shelves, rattling spice jars. A few breathless moments of shock vanished and he grabbed at Francis, wrapping him close. Vitari slid his hand up, grasped the nape of his neck, holding him firm, and kissed him as though he could taste his soul.

Francis's hands speared into his hair, then his fingers dragged down his back, hauling a needful moan up from Vitari's depths.

This was the worst possible moment for them to do this —in a storage cupboard, a room away from a collection of brutal, vicious men who would hang them both if they were caught—but fuck, Vitari needed him, craved him, was out of his mind for the touch and taste of Francis. He shoved, forcing him against the opposite shelves. Something clattered to the floor.

Vitari grabbed his thigh, lifted it as far as the priest's

gown allowed, and ground his eager dick against all the hard parts of Francis he could find.

Francis flung his head back, and Vitari attacked his neck, sucking, biting, pressing himself into Francis—needing to be inside him. But they couldn't fuck here. They had to get back before they were both missed. "Voglio scoparti. We can't," Vitari breathed, forcing himself to stop.

Francis, freckles ablaze, looked at him as though he were about to launch into a vicious tirade. "I'm naked under this gown."

The growl that tumbled out of Vitari was a whole new sound he hadn't known he could make. He hiked up the cassock's thick black fabric and ran his hand up Francis's bare, warm thigh. He *was* naked. And hot. Francis bit his lip, like the sweet innocent priest he hadn't been in a long time.

Vitari almost lost it, might still lose it. He jerked Francis's thigh higher, slamming him into the shelves again, then reached in and cupped and roughly squeezed his balls. Francis's throaty moan spilled into his ear and shivered to his soul. Vitari grasped his cock. Francis grunted, hips shifting, trying to plunge his dick through Vitari's fist.

It was mad, and rough, and brutal. He was pretty sure he'd hurt him, pushing him into the shelves. If the restaurant staff hadn't heard them, they would soon.

"I want to turn you around and sink inside you, Padre, but there's no way I can go back out there after fucking your tight ass." God, the restraint was killing him. If he didn't cool off, he'd come from dry-fucking him alone.

Francis dropped his hand, and like the wicked tease he was, he palmed Vitari through his trousers, rubbing hard.

He just might explode if Francis didn't stop.

And then he did stop. He dropped his hands, leaned

back, and smiled a smug bastard smile while Vitari gripped his dick. Two could play that game. Vitari let him go, brought his hand out from under his gown, and licked precum from his thumb, then staggered back. Francis's innocent brown eyes dropped to Vitari's crotch, probably taking in the sight of his straining cock.

Francis wanted it, wanted to be fucked, right now, and hard.

"Fuck, you're killing me." Vitari laughed. He was going to ruin Francis later and when it happened, there would be no stopping him. "Enjoying yourself, Padre?"

"You mean out there or in here?" he croaked.

"Both?"

"I am... Both. It's strange, but I like it."

He briefly looked confused. Before he could overthink it, Vitari swooped in and kissed him on the mouth. "Thank you."

Hazel eyes lifted. "What for?"

"For being here."

He reached down and twined his fingers with Vitari's. "There's nowhere else I'd rather be."

"Hiding in a pantry with a raging hard-on and blue balls?"

Francis snickered. "Are you going to be able to go back out there?"

"If you stop torturing me, yeah."

"I've stopped. For now."

He was such a tease. "I'm going to fuck you raw. You know that right? If I tell you exactly what I'm going to do to you, my dick will never calm the fuck down. But you won't be able to walk straight tomorrow. Maybe never again."

Francis's mouth twitched around a grin he tried to control, and failed. "You know, I always thought you were saying sweet, romantic things in Italian, but all this time, you've just been telling me how you want to fuck my tight arse, haven't you?"

Vitari covered his mouth, muffling his choking laugh. "Say *fuck my tight arse* again."

Francis's grin grew. "Get back out there, Don Vitari. I'll join you once I'm certain my cock isn't going to poke at this gown like a tent pole." Which was exactly what it was doing.

"Stop making me love you more." Vitari chuckled, straightened his hair, then his shirt, since Francis had wrenched around, and willed his dick to get over it.

He side-eyed Francis and caught his satisfied smirk. "You're going to be the death of me, Padre."

"Then I'll pray for you."

He had no right to be so fucking adorable while also being a savvy, cold-blooded badass.

Vitari steeled himself, took a breath, and sauntered from the pantry as though he hadn't been about to fuck a priest blind.

The end to the capo meeting couldn't come fast enough.

CHAPTER NINETEEN

Francis

It was still dark out when they left the restaurant and returned to the villa, but with a hint of red on the horizon. Francis should have been exhausted—he hadn't slept since dozing on the plane from Colombia and so much had happened—but he wasn't tired. He was *wired*. The meeting had gone better than anyone expected. Vitari had the support of the Battaglia, and Francis had even helped some of the Battaglia's most important men grieve the loss of their leader and pray for their continued success—although he doubted God was going to grant those prayers since the Battaglia's success came from the violence and extortion of others.

Vitari posted two guards at the front of the villa and two more on the grounds. Loyal men, friends of Sal, *his* friends, he'd assured. He'd told them, with a straight face, how he was going to confer with his priest, and they were not to be disturbed.

Then they'd headed inside.

"Where shall we *confer*?" Francis asked, wandering into the enormous open-plan lounge. He still had the bruise where Neo had hit him over the back of the head a day before. Was it a whole day? He couldn't remember, didn't know what day it was. Life had blurred together in one long desperate attempt to survive until tomorrow.

It would be better now, wouldn't it? Easier, now Vitari was the boss.

It had to be. He turned to Vitari to ask him if they were safe.

Vitari held up a finger as a thought occurred to him. "Wait here." He disappeared down the corridor, leaving Francis drifting between enormous luxury leather couches and over rugs that cost more than a priest's salary.

A white grand piano took up one corner, a large TV and couches another. There was also a small bar area, and large glass doors opening onto the essential pool, lit up at night. Giancarlo must have felt safe, to be so exposed to the outside world. Francis, however, did not. He found the controls for the long swath of blinds and closed them, shrinking the room, making it cozier.

Had Vitari ever found the man who had taken pictures of them through the glass doors of the Spanish villa? Probably. He'd been quite annoyed at Francis at the time, since Francis had been the one to let the would-be assassin go. How far they'd come, from Francis not knowing how to hold a rifle, to attending a Mafia meeting as the Battaglia's priest.

"What are you smiling at, Padre?"

"I was just thinking..." He trailed off as he turned to see Vitari striding across the room, his fingers working at his cuffs, rapidly unbuttoning them, with a fire in his eyes that could only be described as savage lust. "How I once threatened you with that assassin's rifle." He swallowed, trying to moisten his suddenly dry throat. "In Spain," he croaked.

"I remember." Vitari's smile almost resembled a snarl.

Francis heart skipped over its own beats. Vitari had the same determination now as when he threatened people, as though he had his target in his sights and nothing would stop him.

His own sharp little jagged spikes of lust stole half his breath as he retreated a step. Vitari had threatened earlier to make him pay, and it was clearly about to happen. He might even be a little afraid—not of Vitari, but of how much he wanted this. How he *needed* it.

"You're so fucking hot in black."

Vitari swooped in and captured Francis in a kiss so brutal it rocked him backward, almost knocking him over, but Vitari's hands were there, his arms wrapped around him, crushing him close, holding him up.

Not so long ago, it might have been too much, but right here and now, the kiss didn't touch the rising, desperate desire to have Vitari in all the right—and wrong—ways. In the next few minutes, Francis was getting fucked, and he'd never craved it more.

Breathless, Vitari pulled from the kiss. "It's killed me all night knowing you're naked under this." Vitari clutched at the robe, scrunching it in his fists. "I was hard the whole ride back."

Oh God. Francis tilted his head back, and Vitari's hot, sometimes filthy mouth branded his neck. He clutched at him too, desperate to hold on. So much had tried to tear them apart, the whole world it seemed, but he had him now, and he wasn't ever going to let him go.

"Forgive me now, for what I'm about to do," Vitari

whispered.

Francis caught his face in his hands and held him firm. His dark eyes were wild and all the more beautiful for their honesty. "You're forgiven."

Vitari's eyes softened, and his face crumpled. Francis's heart plummeted. He hadn't meant to make him sad—

Vitari dropped his hands, growled something deep and raw in Italian, clutched Francis by the hips, and spun him. He slammed a hand between Francis's shoulders, bending him over the back of the white leather couch. Francis gripped the cushions, grunting as his own hard dick got trapped under the cassock. Cooler air touched his thighs, then Vitari's hot, digging fingers clutched his bare ass.

Anticipation made him breathless, had him panting. His body blazed, his skin alive, his heart galloping. Vitari was in his head, in his veins, in his every breath, every heartbeat, and as he spread him, his lube-slickened dick touching Francis's hole—lube he'd excused himself moments ago to find—Francis moaned for more.

Vitari was talking, growling, speaking so fast in Italian that Francis had no hope of understanding, but he heard the passion behind the tone and knew Vitari craved this too. Then Vitari thrust in, and a blinding surge of pain, topped off with a flash of pleasure, surged through Francis. He gasped and arched upright. Vitari caught him, one hand thrusting up under his cassock, sweeping across his bare chest, while the other spread his ass cheeks, opening him to take Vitari's hard length inside.

He forgot how to breathe, how to think, then Vitari's mouth was at his ear, filling him with sweet Italian. It was an assault on his senses, pleasure and pain entwined, and he was wonderfully, hopelessly lost to the storm of Vitari's lust. And his own.

Shoved forward again, he reveled in every rocking thrust Vitari gave. The brutal sounds of skin slapping skin burned his desire hotter, scorching the pain away. Now there was nothing but sweet, delicious waves of pleasure rolling over him, pushed on by Vitari's masculine grunts. "Take it, Francis," Vitari growled in English. "Fuckin' take it."

His own dick ached, pinched between the couch and his hip. Each thrust in the ass rubbed his cock too, and it wouldn't take much, he was already halfway to coming, his lower back and balls tingling.

"Seeing my dick inside you. God, Francis... I can't..." Vitari gulped whatever words he'd been about to add. His thrusts stuttered, his grip on Francis's hips dug deeper, and as he pumped ruthlessly, Francis felt the tension pull through Vitari's body as though it pulled through him too, as though they were connected deep inside.

"Fuck!" Vitari sputtered. He gave three last, desperate jerks, then rammed home and stayed there, trembling, tight against Francis's backside, buried so deep he was surely a part of Francis's soul now.

Francis breathed. Was it normal to feel lightheaded after such a brutal railing?

"Francis, turn around, amore mio."

Vitari's dick slid free, and with cum running down his thighs, Francis turned, dizzy and wrecked, but in a good way. Vitari hitched up the cassock in his left hand and went down to his knees, and suddenly—almost too quickly—had Francis's dick between his lips.

Oh Lord God... Francis wasn't going to last, not even a

minute. He rocked, grunted, panted, and tried not to look down because if he saw Vitari's mischief-ridden face, saw his own cock sliding in and out from between Vitari's lips, he'd lose it. But then he did look, and Vitari's brilliant eyes fixed on Francis's with no intention of letting him go.

Vitari pulled off long enough to demand, "Fuck my throat, Padre. Fuck it hard." And then he was back on, sucking and pumping.

Madness must have gripped Francis because he didn't think, just grabbed the back of Vitari's head and did exactly as Vitari ordered. He fucked his mouth like an *animal*. And came like one too, with a shout that filled the villa.

When he came back into himself after the high, he freed Vitari's hair from his white-knuckled fist. "Oh! Did I hurt you?"

"Francis," Vitari croaked, climbing to his feet. He wiped his mouth on the back of his hand. "My mouth is yours to fuck anytime you like, just like the rest of me." He slammed a salty kiss on Francis's lips, then slumped against him with a thick, satisfied chuckle.

Francis tried to right Vitari's hair by stroking the locks sticking out at odd angles, put there by his fist, then winced when they refused to obey. "I ruined your hair."

"My hair?" Vitari snickered and nuzzled his neck. "It's my throat you ruined. I never want this to end, but I'm also dead on my feet. Come to bed. Sleep with me. Just be with me?"

An unexpected knot clogged Francis's throat, put there by everything, but mostly a surge of needing to love and care and comfort this brutally brilliant yet also vulnerable man who held Francis's whole heart in his hands.

They fell into bed, tangled together, warm skin on skin,

and Vitari planted delicate butterfly kisses all over him—on his face, his neck, his chest—and told him of all the ways he loved him in Italian. Francis knew the words now and knew what it cost Vitari to say them.

Because Francis felt the same.

CHAPTER TWENTY

Vitari

Francis snored against his shoulder, so damned adorable it was criminal. Vitari wanted to stay spooned around him forever. But the real world seeped back in, souring his thoughts. This was a long way from over. He'd started a war —a war his father should have begun long ago. A war of vengeance. But so much still didn't add up, and the more he lay and stared at Francis's blissful face, the more his heart ached, full of fear for the future.

He didn't want to think about his father. He'd spent the moments since his brutal murder *not* thinking about what had happened, or what his father had done, or his confession. Or how Neo had been right...

Vitari wouldn't have killed him. Did that make him a coward?

Staring at the ceiling wasn't helping clear his head. The questions chased each other around his head.

He shifted out from under Francis's arms and sat on the

edge of the bed. His watch read just gone 3 a.m. The plane to Monte Carlo would leave early afternoon. They had a few hours yet, and Vitari needed to think of every possible scenario in which to keep them alive.

"Ughm... don't go," Francis mumbled.

"Go back to sleep, amore."

Francis blinked sleepy, glassy eyes. "Every time we do this, you leave and something horrible happens. Stay." He reached out, grabbed Vitari's tattooed wrist, and pulled.

Vitari surrendered, flopping back down beside him. Admittedly, he hadn't put up much of a fight.

Francis's leg locked around his thigh, pinning him down. "Hm," he purred and shuffled up against Vitari, tucking all of him in close. "Venezuela," Francis muttered. "Panama... I just want one night together and to wake up with you beside me. And nobody shooting at us."

It was hard to argue with that. Hard to argue with *him*. Vitari sighed, and with his arm trapped under Francis, he stroked up and down his back. He had to admit, this—being in the moment—was good.

They stayed like that a while, calm, quiet, fingers teasing. But Francis wasn't sleeping now either. He blinked soft brown lashes and occasionally glanced at Vitari's face to see if he was still awake.

"You know, while training as a priest, we had classes on counseling, and I suspect I—we—might be using sex as a trauma response," Francis said.

Vitari snorted. "I'm okay with that if you are."

Francis smiled, and draping his arm over Vitari's chest, he danced his fingers around Vitari's left nipple, making him shiver. Sex with Francis was a trauma response, but it was also where they were both the most free. Free of the church, free of the Mafia. Was it any wonder they snatched at sex as though it might save them every damn time?

"Vitari?"

Vitari dipped his chin and met Francis's gaze. His expression had gotten serious.

"Are you all right?" Francis asked. "I mean... Everything has changed for you."

He knew what he meant. His father had been shot dead a few rooms away, a father he'd hated, but also loved. The most fucking awful father anyone could have, but Vitari had begun to accept he'd gotten some shit about Giancarlo wrong. "I don't know... If he'd just told me the truth, none of this would have happened." Vitari would still have gone after Sasha, but all of the lies and stupid threats, trying to get Francis to back off Stanmore? "He didn't have to hurt you." Vitari found Francis's burned hand and clasped it in his own. "He hated me, or I thought he did, but at the end... before Neo killed him, he brought you here, and he must have known I was waiting. Maybe he planned to use you as a shield, but... that doesn't feel right. I think he was trying to tell me something, in the end. Trying to tell me that you and me, maybe we're okay? So, I don't know what to think."

"Delle pene d'amore, si tribola e non si muore," Francis said. Then winced and added, "Did I say it right?"

Vitari raised his eyebrows. Francis had mangled some of the pronunciation, but he knew the meaning of the phrases, which boiled down to: love hurts but time heals. "I'm going to have to be more careful what I say around you, huh."

"Your father was a complicated man."

Complicated was one way of describing Giancarlo. "He was a sociopath. But he was still my father, and he got me out of Stanmore. What happened there, I'd have died... if he hadn't." After a creak in his voice, he took a few moments to steady his heart. "Listen, I... There's something... I want to tell you, want to... explain..."

Francis propped himself up on an elbow, all messy and innocent, a look he wore so well.

Vitari huffed through his nose. "I've started now, so I... have to say it."

"Tell me in Italian, if it hurts?"

"No, you need to understand this." He wet his lips and filled his lungs again. "You and me, we can do whatever the fuck you want, but... I mean, earlier, you... What we did... I can't... Fuck, this is stupid. I'm being stupid."

"Hey." Francis's goofiness faded, and now he was the severe, no-nonsense Francis, who took no shit from anyone and held up ex-cocaine drug runners in the Colombian jungle to save his male lover.

"I can't do anal, okay?" Vitari admitted. "I can't. I just.. It's..." He shrugged and avoided Francis's eyes. "I can't. Ever."

"I know, it's all right. I knew from before."

"You knew?" He swallowed and lifted his gaze. He'd been worried Francis would want that, eventually. And he'd been thinking about it, wondering if he could, but every time he'd considered it, fear had lanced his heart. Too many strangers had touched him that way. Francis wasn't like them, he knew that, but his body remembered, even when his head had begun to forget.

Francis gave a lazy smile. "I don't want that. I like the way we are."

"What the fuck did I do to get someone as good as you?"

He batted his light lashes, all innocent. "Technically, you kidnapped me—"

Vitari growled, and before Francis could tense up to

defend himself, Vitari flipped him onto his back and kissed the rest of his words away.

Francis chuckled into his mouth, and when Vitari gripped his wrists, he surrendered, pinned down.

"Hm, I like you under me, Padre," Vitari mumbled against his lips.

"Do you still have that lubricant you used earlier?"

"*Lubricant?*" Vitari mocked in haughty English. "Father Francis Scott, you're a wicked tease."

Francis's laugh did wonderful things to Vitari's soul, like repair all the holes, but as Francis gazed up at him, the weight of what was to come weighed on the delight in his eyes. They couldn't stay here like this forever.

"I owe you an apology," Francis said.

"Oh?" Vitari sat up, straddling his hips. Francis's hard cock nudged against his ass, apparently oblivious to whatever had turned Francis serious again. "What did you do? Was it wicked? Tell me it was. Tell me it's dirty. Confess your filthy thoughts, Padre—"

"Vitari," he scolded, trying not to smile. "Back in Panama, I was trying to turn you into someone you're not, asking you to get a job. That was wrong of me."

"Ah, that. When you tried to tell me gangsta isn't a real job?"

"Yes. I don't ever want to change you. You are who you are, and I love you for who you are. I wasn't trying to force you to be someone else, I was... Well, I was scared, I suppose."

"Me too. Still am."

Francis nodded. "Yeah."

"You were right though."

"About?"

"A little farm somewhere, grow some grapes, make

wine. I can do that. With you, I mean. I wasn't ready to hear it, but now I am. If you'll have me?"

"A farm?" Francis whispered, eyes lighting up as though it were Christmas morning. "Like the one you took me to when we saved those people?

"With less Spanish cops and fewer trafficked kids. But, yeah. Unless it's weird? Is it weird? I'm not real good at the relationship shit."

Francis grinned. "Make wine?

"If you like."

His teeth gleamed behind a broad grin. "I'd like that."

"I figured you might." Vitari braced over him, bowed his head, and nudged noses. "Our own place that nobody will dare take from us."

Were those tears in his eyes? Vitari kissed him quick, chasing those maybe-tears away. He couldn't stand it if Francis cried over a future that would need a fucking miracle to ever come true. Maybe he'd pray for it. Francis's mouth grew demanding, his body too, and it felt like the most natural thing in the world to spread his ass and sink home, rhythmically easing in and out, going slow, making it last. He watched his face, watched his lips part, heard his tiny gasps as his heart opened.

Francis didn't take his eyes off Vitari...

A smile lifted Vitari's lips, mirrored on Francis's face too, and then a single, brilliant tear slipped from Francis's eye.

"Farei di tutto per te," Vitari whispered. *I'll do anything for you.* "Solo tu mi capisci." *Only you understand me.* "Vuoi stare con me per sempre?" *Will you stay with me forever?* His voice creaked, about to break.

"Yes," Francis replied, understanding every heartfelt word.

Breakfast, or lunch, since it was gone midday, sizzled in the pan. Vitari had thrown some ingredients together, as they were both starving. They had a couple of hours left before they'd need to head to the airstrip, but he was determined to make these final hours even better than last night—no easy thing to do, after they'd spent last night wrapped in each other's arms in the throes of passion.

Francis was semi-dressed in loose pants and a shirt and was fiddling with a radio across the room, trying to find some music. Vitari watched him on the sly, admiring his lean outline, remembering all the ways he'd had that body rocking in motion with his.

He found an old track, "Smooth" by Santana.

"Hm, leave that playing." Vitari left the pan and crossed the large kitchen. "Do you dance?"

"Dance?" Francis's eyes blew wide.

Vitari laughed, took his hand, and maneuver them both to the more open-plan breakfast area beside the sunlit window overlooking the lawns.

"Oh. I uh... No.. I don't.. erm..."

Vitari gripped his hand and slipped his free arm around Francis's waist, easing closer. "It's easy, use your hips."

"My... uh..." He looked down. His head almost bumped Vitari's chin. "Oh! I don't—I haven't..."

"The hips," Vitari said again, keeping his laugh behind his twitching smile, then began to shift his hips in time with the beat. He saw Francis's throat move and had an idea of what was running through his head. Vitari could absolutely dance. "Like this." He jerked Francis tighter to him and spread his hand on his lower back, holding him there, and then *moved*, drawing Francis with him, like they'd been close last night, consumed by a different kind of dance.

Heat rushed to Francis's face, highlighting all his freckles, but as he relaxed, he stopped fumbling and allowed himself to fall into the rhythm.

They danced, Francis's soft-eyed glare pierced Vitari's soul, and then the music ended, the presenter moved on to discussing the Mediterranean heatwave, while Francis gazed at Vitari, making *him* blush.

"Will we ever have normal?" Francis asked.

Vitari cleared his throat and separated. "Breakfast, amore?" Because the answer Francis wanted, he couldn't give.

They ate and laughed about Francis's trip through the Spanish countryside in a stolen car before the cops had picked him up, but then the topic switched to DeSica, and the mood cooled as the weight of the task ahead loomed.

"He's still selling children into the sex trade," Francis said, pushing the remains of his food around his plate. "Montague said as much."

"That's one of several reasons I'm going to kill him," Vitari said, then upended his glass and finished his wine.

Francis looked up, and for a moment, Vitari feared he'd tell him not to, and feared how he might listen to that advice. It would be a whole lot safer to walk away.

"Good," Francis said.

"There's my Padre Blanco."

With a snort, Francis leaned back in his chair, his face pensive. "It's wrong, isn't it? Wanting someone dead?"

Vitari gave it a few second's thought. "It's human. If someone hurts us enough, revenge is all we have left."

"Is it revenge?"

"Revenge is also justice."

The phone beside them on the counter rang—Giancarlo's mobile, now Vitari's. He got up from the table and snatched it up. Sal grumbled down the line, on his way over, ready to take them to the airstrip. They had to be ready in fifteen minutes.

Vitari ended the call and repeated the message.

"We can trust him?" Francis asked while clearing the plates away.

"Sal is as solid as they come. The others, not so much."

"He's a good friend?"

Vitari folded his arms and leaned against the counter. "When I first came to Italy, I didn't remember the language, didn't know anyone. Giancarlo threw me in with the wolves, other Mafia kids. Battaglia fathers raise their boys *hard*. I got the shit beaten out of me day after day. I fought back, but... You know how it is, the Mafia don't fight fair."

Francis briefly closed his eyes and muttered something like a prayer.

"It was a long time ago. They set on me, five on one, and I didn't stand a chance. But I fought anyway because fists were all I had. To this fucking day, I'm sure my father had hoped they'd kill me. And then this enormous bastard shows up. Eleven years old and already as big as a gorilla. He saw what was happening, said it wasn't fair, and took out four of them with a few right hooks. He left one, though, for me."

"Salvatore saved you?"

"Yeah. He's as vicious as he looks, but everything he does has a reason. If Sal is coming for you, you deserve it. But Sal is one of the few good ones. He's saved me from a few tight spots over the years." Francis didn't appear any more comforted, and it wasn't going to get any easier for them. This life had its claws in him too now. "We should get dressed." Vitari eyed Francis's slouched form, wishing he could devour him all over again. "The honeymoon is over."

Francis tried to hold on to his smile, but it crumbled away. "The cassock?"

"Yeah, but put something on underneath or I won't be able to think."

Vitari left him chuckling at the table to shower. When he stepped from the bathroom, the cassock was gone from over the back of the chair where it had been draped all night. Vitari adjusted his cuffs in front of the mirror, straightened his hair, and reapplied all the layers of sophistication that put distance between him and L' Angelo della Morte, mob boss's son, and now the Battaglia don. He didn't much like the man looking back at him.

A vineyard in the Italian hills couldn't happen fast enough.

He found Francis waiting in the corridor, dressed in his priestly layers, his hair smooth and eyes cold.

"So I uh... I found this and forgot to mention it. It seemed important." He held out the USB drive with Vitari's name on it. Francis must have picked it up from his father's desk. A good thing he *had* taken it; too many people had come and gone since then. Anyone could have found it.

If the contents of that drive were anything like the ones he'd found before, then he did not want Francis seeing any of it. But it was also safer with him than anywhere else. "Thanks, just... keep it for me? Don't look at it, just keep hold of it?"

He closed his fist around it. "Of course."

A car horn honked outside.

"Ready, Padre?"

"Yes." Francis straightened to his full, composed, holier-than-thou height and Vitari was reminded of the troubled priest with the haunted eyes he'd met inside a rural English church, desperately trying to keep the pieces of himself together.

What sin brought you here?

You did.

After that first meeting, he could never have imagined how they'd save each other, in so many ways.

Vitari reached up and pressed his forehead to Francis's. "Whatever happens, know how I love you with all my heart and soul, Francis. And if..." He wet his lips. "If we don't—"

Francis kissed him, silencing the rest of his words. "I know," he said, then whispered again, "I know."

CHAPTER TWENTY-ONE

Francis

Francis was embarrassed to realize Monte Carlo was in southern France, not Italy, as he'd assumed. Although there were only a few miles between the two countries. Monte Carlo was a waterfront city, resplendent alongside sparkling azure waters. Countless luxury yachts clustered in the marinas like gems in a crown, and enormous palm trees framed pretty, ancient hotels, all gathered around colonnade structures and limestone churches.

The Battaglia's obvious procession of impressive black cars pulled up outside the Hôtel de Paris, and the moment Francis entered the domed foyer, he willed himself not to react to the gleaming marble floors, sparkling chandeliers, white and cream furnishings, and breathtaking fresco that wouldn't have been out of place in the Vatican.

"We're rather.... obvious," Francis mentioned to Vitari, as their troupe of at least twenty men left their cars and entered the hotel.

Vitari flashed his L' Angelo della Morte smile. "That's the point."

They didn't stop at the reception, going straight to the elevator. Sal stepped inside, then Francis, but as Vitari approached, one of the others in their group called him back. "I'll be right up," he said, then the door closed, leaving Francis rigid beside Sal.

The floor numbers counted up slowly. Background music chimed. It might have been quicker to take the stairs.

"I have a great deal of respect for priests," Sal said. His deep baritone voice rumbled in the tiny space. "But a priest who breaks his vows? He has no honor, no integrity. He is no priest."

Since they'd met, Francis had sensed Sal didn't like him, and now, trapped in an elevator, that sense had been proven right. Of course, much of the Battaglia probably thought the same, especially if they believed he was in a relationship with Vitari. "There are vows of the head, and vows of the heart. The head can be deceived, but the heart knows the truth."

Sal ruminated on that for a few floors, then side-eyed him and asked, "What vows have you pledged from your heart, Padre?"

"Vitari is my calling, not the Church, not God." Francis met Sal's less-than-friendly glare. "I will protect him regardless of the cost or sacrifice."

Sal held his glare, scrutinizing him, and as the elevator dinged on the top floor suites and the doors opened, he said, "You may have to."

The hotel staff brought their overnight bags to the ocean-view suite, and a few guards eyeballed Francis when they thought he wasn't looking. As lovely as the enormous suite was, he'd have much preferred a smaller room on the ground floor and with more exits. On the hotel's top floor, they had nowhere to run, should they need to make a quick exit.

Perhaps that wouldn't be necessary and this trip would go as Vitari hoped.

Vitari joined him a little while later and dismissed the guards. Now they were alone again, Francis watched him stop in the middle of the lounge, take a deep breath, and drag his hand down his face, clearly trying to settle himself.

"Are we safe here?" He didn't feel safe. He hadn't felt safe since Neo had shot Giancarlo. But the villa had felt safer than this hotel, as luxurious as it was.

"Fuck, no. Let's get a drink at the bar."

"More escape routes?"

Vitari smiled. "You're learning."

"I've rather had to."

They headed back down to the hotel bar, a glitzy high-ceiling room with low-hanging enormous light features and a black marble wraparound bar. Vitari ordered their drinks in French, while Francis got settled on the stool and scanned the other patrons. All were well-dressed business men and women, their smiles as perfect as their sparkling jewelry and expensive watches. Vitari fit right in. Francis, on the other hand, in his black cassock, felt as obvious as a nun at a strip show.

Two glasses of wine arrived. "I probably shouldn't drink," Francis said.

Vitari picked up his wine and glanced around. "Nobody gives a shit if a priest is sinning here. It's Monte Carlo. The rich man's playground."

They may not *give a shit*, but they were looking over. Francis squirmed some, unaccustomed to being stared at when he wasn't at a church pulpit. "I feel like a target," he admitted, picking up the wine.

"We both are, but you're also a deterrent. Nobody is going to shoot me next to a priest. And you're untouchable, Padre. Own it."

"I am very much *not* untouchable." He'd learned that—among many, many other things—about himself during the past year. He tasted the wine, liking it, and chinked his glass with Vitari's, unable to resist his contagious smile.

"Act like you own the world, and they'll believe it," Vitari said, turning his back to the staring faces. "We're the fucking wolves here, you and me. And the sheep know it."

"Is that what you do? Act like you belong?"

"Every day since my father saved me from Stanmore, and I owned nothing. I've gotten this far on bullshit and bluster."

"No..."

"No?" Vitari laughed. "Father Scott, do enlighten me."

"You're here because you fought for every second of it."

They shared a knowing smile, unable to reach out and touch each other. They would later, Francis vowed. Between the sheets, he'd make sure Vitari knew how special he was. "You're everything Neo wanted to be, just like Luca Espinosa. It's not faking it to make it, if you've already made it."

Vitari chuckled at that too. "You know, in all this? There's a lot that doesn't add up still, right? I still can't figure out how Sasha knew my mother." He peered into his wine glass. Mention of his mother had brought the memories back, clouding his expression. Not even his grin could withstand the past.

"Are you certain he did?"

"He told me, said something about her wanting me to

have a life far away from the Mafia. When I pushed him on it, he denied it. He knew her. I'm certain. And they talked about shit like taking me away..." Vitari raised his glass and sipped.

Francis read his unspoken meaning. Sasha and his mother had likely been close. "Do you think they..." He didn't want to say it, knowing what he did about Sasha and the DeSica operation. But was Vitari's mother involved with Sasha Zhokov? A Russian mob boss and a Vatican girl. It would have been absurd, if they didn't already know Stefania and Giancarlo had been in a relationship.

"I don't know." But it clearly bothered him. "But I got to thinking, why kill her? Was it just because she was there, an easy target to hurt my father with, or was there more to it? More between Sasha and my mother at the time?" He winced and cleared his throat. "I wish I knew her."

"I'm sorry you didn't get that chance."

"Yeah, well, Sasha is going to pay for that too. When I find him. He's in town for some high-rolling poker tournament. I have people looking for him. Once I know where he's staying, I'm going to pay him a visit."

"How are you going to... do it?"

"I haven't decided. Sniper, maybe."

Francis skimmed the scar on his forehead, remembering how close a call he'd come with a sniper rifle. Nobody had ever been caught for that. Killing from a distance would allow Vitari to get away clean.

"The problem with that is he won't know it was me. And I need my face to be the last fucking thing he sees."

Vitari's talk of murder should have made Francis uneasy, but as he sipped his wine and gazed about the bar, he didn't feel anything. What was it Vitari had said? Sometimes revenge *was* justice. Stanmore had been

Sasha's operation, and while Francis had escaped lightly, others hadn't. He still had the boy's home photograph; not with him, though, since Vitari had thrown his phone into the ocean. But the original was in his office in Westminster.

They'd all been Sasha's victims.

Killing Sasha was justice. Like killing Charles Montague had been justice. Although justice was not man's remit, but God's. And he should trust that God would deliver vengeance, but too much had changed. He wasn't sure he trusted God at all anymore.

Francis's idle gaze snagged on a man leaving the bar. Something about him seemed familiar, the cut of his wide shoulders perhaps, coupled with the blond hair... The American priest he'd last seen in Rome, the priest he'd once thought to be a friend. Father Davis was here? That wasn't possible. It *couldn't* be possible. Could it?

"Did you see that?"

Vitari glanced behind him at the door. "See what?"

"Nothing, I... Hold on..." Francis hopped off the stool. Ignoring Vitari asking after him, he dashed outside, into the reception area. But there was no sign of the figure. Perhaps it hadn't been Father Davis at all, but someone who resembled him. He hadn't seen his face, just his back and shoulders. He was probably jumping at ghosts again.

Francis returned to the bar. "Sorry, I thought I saw someone."

"Someone... Who?" Vitari asked, eyes narrowing.

"It's nothing."

"Who?" Vitari asked again, glancing back over his shoulder.

"A priest from the Vatican."

"A priest?" Vitari spluttered.

"Like I said, it probably wasn't him." Francis sipped his wine, wishing it were stronger.

Vitari shifted closer. "This is not the time to dismiss your instincts," he said, keeping his voice low. "Who did you think you saw?"

"Father Davis. He worked for your father, I think—"

Vitari's eyes turned hard. "Davis? Yeah, I know him. Two-faced suck-up. He was tight with Giancarlo and I never figured out why."

"You know him?" Francis wasn't sure why that surprised him. It shouldn't have. Davis had been among Giancarlo's closest people, who Vitari would naturally know of. "You never said."

"I met him a couple of times, that's all. How do *you* know him?"

"I didn't, not really." He was embarrassed to admit how he'd fallen for Father Davis's lies, and it probably hadn't been him anyway. "I didn't see his face. It's nothing. Why would he even be here?"

Vitari glanced around them with shrewd interest. "Yeah, why would a bent priest be in Monte Carlo?"

"Did you just imply I'm bent?"

Vitari grinned. "Padre, you bend in the best way. But if that sleazy prick is here, then we have a problem."

"Why, if he's Battaglia and half the hotel is full of Battaglia?"

"Because I didn't invite him. Which means someone else did. I need to talk to Sal." Vitari pulled his phone from his pocket. "He'll be around here somewhere. Go back to the suite. I'll meet you there. Don't let anyone in, understand?"

Francis nodded and downed his wine. "You won't be long?"

"I'll be right up." He pressed the phone to his ear. "Yeah, Sal, we might have a problem, where are you? All right, I'm coming up." He ended the call. "Like you say, it's probably nothing." His hand closed around Francis's and he guided him off the stool. Francis tightened his grip, not wanting to let him go, and the seconds ticked on, hands held in full view of everyone.

"I've got this, Padre." Vitari kissed Francis on the cheek in a typical Mediterranean style. "I'll be right up," he said, holding his gaze. Vitari squeezed his hand, then let go and sauntered away as though nothing could touch him, but Francis knew *everything* touched him.

Alone now, he sighed and tried to find the composure he'd entered the bar with. He didn't want to be here—he wanted to bundle Vitari into a cab and drive away and keep on driving, like he had in the Spanish countryside, drive until they ran out of road.

People were staring, watching him stare after Vitari, as though they could see how Francis's heart beat for him.

He cleared his throat and smoothed down his cassock. He and Vitari just had to get through this night, locate and kill Sasha, and then it would be over. Vitari would leave the Mafia, and they would go find a farm in the hills somewhere, just like Vitari had said.

For the first time ever, they had a chance at a future.

"Just keep on surviving," he muttered like a prayer and headed toward the elevators.

CHAPTER TWENTY-TWO

Vitari

"Come in, fra." Sal opened the door to his modest room on the second floor, then stomped back to the bed. His suitcase lay open, with a few items of clothing flung on the bed around it.

"You good?" Vitari asked. Sal wasn't usually so chaotic.

"Yeah, yeah." He reached for the bottle of vodka on the bedside table and refilled a glass. The way his hand swayed suggested he'd already had a few.

"You sure?"

Sal sat on the edge of the bed. "What's this *problem*?"

"Father Davis, you remember him?" Vitari ambled into the middle of the room, caught sight of a gun handle poking out under a discarded shirt, and remembered he'd left his in the suite. Didn't matter, he was going there next.

"The loud cigar-loving American priest?" Sal asked, wiping a hand down his face. He wasn't as together as he typically kept himself. Vitari was the one who lost his shit on a daily basis, not Sal. Maybe he'd had an argument with his papa. Vitari knew what *that* felt like.

"Francis thinks he saw him in the bar," Vitari said. "Did you invite him? Because I know I didn't."

"Why would *he* be here? Don't we already have one priest too many?" Sal slurred.

"Sal, I know I got no right to say it, but what the fuck is going on with you? You got your head on straight? I need you. This isn't a vacation."

"I know, I know," he mumbled. "I'm good, I just—I'm good."

Vitari huffed. "Davis was close with Giancarlo, and I know everyone is smiling and shaking my hand, Sal, but I'm not a fool. Half of them want me gone. Most probably think I killed my father—"

"Did you?" He looked up, eyes too glassy for reasonable conversation.

"Come on, fra." The fact he'd asked tripped Vitari's thoughts. Sal knew him better than that. "You know I didn't."

"It's just the only living witness is a damned priest who'll say and do anything for you, so I'm just saying... You're right, half of them think you killed Giancarlo and they got good reason to. You and your papa, you were always at each other's throats."

"And you and Toni aren't?" Fuck this. What had gotten into Sal? "Do *you* think I killed him?"

"I've seen what he's done to you, shunned you, threatened you, I'm just... I'd have wanted to kill him. Shit, everyone wanted a shot at Giancarlo. It's more *likely* you killed him, is all I'm saying."

"Neo fucking killed him in front of me. I had the blood splatter on my face, Sal. You fucking saw *that*. How the fuck do his brains get on my face if I shot him? Fucking tell me that!" Vitari panted, only now realizing he'd been yelling.

Sal's expression softened but that chaotic, drunken gleam still shone in his eyes. "God damn it, Angel, I'm telling you how it is. I can't make him see you like I see you, I just can't."

Vitari waited a few beats, letting his words settle. "Make *who* see me?"

"What?"

"You said you can't make *him* see me. Who, Sal?"

"You know who." He slumped forward, elbows on his knees.

"Your father. Toni. He's giving you shit? Is that what this is?"

"Same old shit, fra. Same old shit."

"What's he saying? Huh? Did *he* invite Father Davis?"

Sal snorted, dumped his glass to the side, and got to his feet. "Papa hates that fucker, hates all priests, especially yours."

"Toni hates Francis?" That didn't make any sense; they'd never met before yesterday. Francis had never crossed Little Toni's path. They had nothing to do with each other.

"You should have let him go, fra," Sal said, wringing the words out, as though they hurt to say.

"Let who go, what are you talking about?"

"The priest, the fucking priest!" Sal snapped. "You couldn't let it go, could you? You had to keep chasing him down!"

What the fuck—where was all this coming from now? "Sal, Jesus. Your papa has a problem with Francis, fine. But now is not the time—"

Sal grabbed his gun from under the shirt and pointed its silenced muzzle at Vitari.

Vitari stumbled back a step, raised his hands, and glared past the gun at Sal's twitching, snarling face. "Sal?"

"I'm sorry, I'm so fucking sorry." Sal pushed forward.

Vitari stumbled back another step. "Sal, wait. Whatever this is—"

"I have to—I have to."

Sal didn't look like the friend he'd known for years. He looked... scared. "Sal, stop. This isn't you, I know that. Put the gun down."

His mouth twitched, but his aim steadied. "Where's the flash drive?"

"The... what?" Vitari's thoughts stumbled. Had Sal lost his mind?

"The USB drive. I saw it at the villa after you killed Giancarlo, but it's not there. We searched the place, floor to ceiling, and it's not fucking there! So where's the drive?"

"Sal." Vitari swallowed. "Your father is making you do this, I know that. Toni wants the Battaglia, right? Always has. Put the gun down, we'll work it out. Brothers. Together. You and me."

"'Brothers'?" Sal snickered, but the sound was toxic. "If we were brothers, this wouldn't ever have to happen."

"I don't... understand." Why was he doing this? Toni, it had to be. Sal's father was the only one who could make Sal do anything. But they could talk through it. "Sal, wait."

Sal was on him now, the silencer inches from his forehead. "Where's the fucking drive, fra?"

He knew the USB stick he wanted, but had no idea why. What was on that drive that could turn Sal against him like this? "Sal." Vitari wet his lips, "Listen, I don't know what drive—"

Sal swung the gun. Pain lashed through Vitari's head. He staggered, stunned, fell against a wall, and then the gun muzzle wedged under his chin, holding him up.

"Where's the fucking drive, Vitari?"

The man snarling at him, the man holding a gun under his chin—it wasn't Sal. Not the Sal he'd known and loved. He'd turned into a stranger.

"I fuckin' loved you, man."

Sal's thick fingers locked around his throat. "Does the priest have it?"

Vitari glared. "Touch him and I will fucking kill you."

Sal squeezed his eyes closed and gave his head a disgusted shake. "You should have let him go."

No. No, if Sal went to Francis, he'd butcher him. "Don't —" Vitari shoved, jerked his knee up, trying to catch Sal in the balls, but skimmed his thigh instead.

Sal smacked his forehead into Vitari's. Pain exploded across his face. The room spun. Vitari's head flew back, hit the wall, and he dropped, clinging to the edges of consciousness. *Francis...* His vision drifted, there and gone again, like a dream that faded on waking. His ears rang. He couldn't pass out. He had to stay with it. He tried to claw at the thick fingers around his wrist, dragging him. Tried to kick out. But then the room greyed, washed away by the thudding in his ears.

The metallic sound of cuffs ratcheting around his wrists brought him back into blistering reality in time to see Sal stomp away.

"Wait..." Vitari mumbled. But it was already too late. When he blinked again, Sal was gone.

Cuffs clattered—locked around water pipes.

"Fuck!" Vitari yanked, trying to rip the pipes from the wall. They rattled but didn't loosen. He writhed, trying to wriggle his wrist free, but the cuffs were too tight. He pulled anyway, pulled until his thumb bled, hoping he could yank his hand through. But it was no use.

He groped with his free hand into his pocket and removed his father's phone. But who was he going to call? There was no one he trusted more than Sal.

And Toni had gotten to him...

This was it. This was the end.

Vitari had been king of the Battaglia less than twenty-four hours. Little Toni was making his move on the crown, like they'd all known he would.

Sal would kill Francis for whatever was on that drive, for Toni.

Vitari slumped against the wall. "Don't trust him, Francis," he spoke aloud, to nobody. "Trust your instincts. Run. Please run... God, please keep him safe. Please."

The hotel reception. He could search the internet for the number. If he called the front desk, would they connect his call to the suite, to Francis?

With his free hand, Vitari opened a browser, and searched for the hotel webpage.

CHAPTER TWENTY-THREE

It probably hadn't been Father Davis. Francis was just jumpy. This whole trip, on top of witnessing a double homicide, in addition to almost being executed in Colombia, had frayed his nerves to ragged edges.

He stood at the windows overlooking the marina and wrung his hands, waiting for Vitari. Next door to the hotel, the infamous Monte Carlo casino glinted in the dark. He'd seen that facade in a movie once too. Now it felt as though he lived in one of those Saturday morning movies he'd watched at Stanmore, one of the action ones, but with more murders, graphic violence, and sex.

Did it even matter if Father Davis was here? They had countless other killers in their entourage, what was one more? Although, he didn't know for sure Father Davis was a killer, only that he'd lied. A great deal. And betrayed Francis's trust.

A knock at the door interrupted his thoughts. He

opened it to find the imposing figure of Salvatore looming in the hall.

"Vitari isn't here."

"It's you I need to speak with, Father. May I come in?

"I uh—"

"It's a confession."

He couldn't turn anyone away from confession, least of all Vitari's friend.

Sal's right hand clenched at his side. A little gesture, nothing really, but add the sheen of sweat on the man's forehead and the odd shift in his gaze? Something was off. But how could Francis refuse him without seeming rude? He didn't want to drive a wedge between Vitari and Sal, and Vitari trusted him.

"Well, Father?"

A phone rang in one of the suite's many rooms.

He glanced toward the room where the shrill sound came from, then back at Sal. "Vitari will be back soon, then we can—"

"You should probably answer that," the big man grumbled.

"Another time, perhaps? I'll just... I'll get that." He closed the door on the man's resolute face, crossed the living area, stepped up, and entered the bedroom. A light flashed on the ringing phone beside the bed. He scooped up the handset. "Hello?"

"Is this Francis Scott?" a French-accented female voice asked.

"Yes."

"I have a call for you, Father. From a Vitari Angelini? Shall I connect you?"

"Yes, thank you."

Why was Vitari calling him, why hadn't he come up to the hotel room—

Something thin and dark fell in front of his eyes, then cinched around his neck. He gasped, or tried to, but the rope at his neck cut off his airway.

"Francis! Get out of there!"

Vitari!

Francis choked. The rope cinched tighter. The phone slipped from his fingers. He grabbed at whatever was strangling him—thick leather, a belt. He dug his nails under it, to try to pry it off. His heart pounded in his ears, wedged there. He couldn't breathe. Couldn't get air. His mouth gaped, his chest burned.

Jerked backward, he stumbled.

A hand slammed between his shoulders, toppling him forward at the same time as the belt loosened. He fell face-first onto the bed and clutched at the bedsheets, gasping, spluttering, wheezing. Even with the belt still on, but now loose, his throat was clogged. Air squeezed through, but not fast enough. Every breath wheezed into screaming lungs.

Hands gripped him, flipped him over. Sal loomed. "Where's the drive, Padre?"

Francis kicked. His heel connected with Sal's crotch, and the big man grunted and doubled over.

Francis launched off the bed and bolted for the door. *Get out.*

The belt still looped around his neck snapped tight, his feet flew out from under him, and his back slammed into the floor.

He lay, looking up, stunned.

Sal circled into sight, with one end of the belt wrapped around his fist. He stepped over Francis, knelt, and pulled the belt tighter. Francis choked and gasped and gaped all over again.

"You're going to tell me where the drive is and all of this will be over."

The vodka on his breath burned Francis's eyes, squeezing out tears, or maybe those tears were due to his lungs scorching him up from the inside. He bucked, kicked, but Sal's weight pinned him to the floor. His whole body throbbed in time with his struggling heart. Darkness beat in, wave after wave.

The belt loosened. "Breathe," Sal said and patted his face. "Slowly now. You ever choked on a grape, Padre? Yeah, like that, just calmly breathe. Slow down, don't panic... There you go... Slowly, nice and slow..."

Gradually, Francis's throat opened again, and his lungs ballooned, filling back up. The thudding in his head faded. "Where's Vitari?" he wheezed.

"He's fine." Sal dangled a small key, then dropped it back into his pocket. "But he's not coming to save you. So give me the drive, and I'll let you go. For however long you've got left."

He didn't believe him. He wouldn't let him go. People like him said they would, to make their victims compliant and easier to kill. "You had... a good friend... in Vitari."

Sal's eyes betrayed his pain. He didn't want to be here either. Francis almost pitied him. Whatever was happening had cost Sal a lifetime of friendship.

"Padre"—Sal produced a gun from behind his back—"time to confess. Where's the drive?"

"What drive?" he wheezed.

"USB drive, had Vitari's name on it. You saw it, same as I did."

That drive. The one in his pocket. "I don't—"

Sal tightened the belt and the choking, horrible gut-knotting agony began again. Minutes, hours, he wasn't sure how long it was before Sal loosened the belt and consciousness seeped back into his tingling body.

"You don't want... to do... this," Francis panted.

"I don't have a choice."

"Always... a choice..."

Sal kept the gun pointed down, not yet aiming it. Perhaps not wanting to. "He loves you. I didn't think it possible, two men... But I see it, it's real."

More tears squeezed from Francis's eyes. It was love, and it wasn't right that the whole world kept trying to take it from them.

"I wish I didn't have to do this," Sal said, with real hurt in his voice. "I was with him when he learned you'd been shot in St. Peter's. My papa, he..." Sal winced away the end of that sentence. "Vitari would have razed Roma to get to you. But I will do this, Padre. I love Vitari, but I love my papa more. Give me the drive."

Whatever was on the drive, it couldn't be worth dying for. "Pocket... In my pocket."

"This gown has pockets?"

"Underneath. Let me up..."

Sal eased off, then got to his feet, but he kept hold of the belt around Francis's neck and hauled him upright too. Francis swayed, sweating hot and cold, dizzy, but he managed to lift his cassock and dig into his pocket.

He removed the drive and handed it out. "I hope it's worth Vitari's love."

Sal let go of the belt and took the drive, holding it up in his left hand between his finger and thumb, checking it was the one he needed. Then he raised the gun in his right hand and aimed at Francis's head. "This time, we won't miss."

Francis closed his eyes. "Our Father, Who art in Heaven, hallowed be Thy name; Thy kingdom come; Thy will be done on Earth as it is in Heaven. Give us this day our daily bread; and forgive us our trespasses as we forgive those who trespass against us; and lead us not into temptation, but deliver us from... evil."

As he opened his eyes again, he saw the agony on Sal's face. He did not want to do this, because of Vitari. Because of a love he knew to be real. Because he knew he'd never come back from it. "Is this the family way?" Francis asked quietly. "Can you live with yourself, once you pull the trigger?"

"Probably not, Padre," he said with great pain in his eyes.

A hooded figure rushed up behind Sal and slammed a huge vase over the back of Sal's head, dropping the big man to his knees, then the floor. Francis gaped, not recognizing the intruder in the hooded sweater and black jeans, but then he saw the man's blue eyes and square jaw.

"Father Davis?"

"Hey, you okay?" Father Davis asked.

"I just, I..."

Sal groaned face down on the floor, the drive a few inches from his hand. Francis tore off the belt from around his neck and picked up the drive. And then Sal's gun.

"C'mon, Father, we need to get you out of here," Davis said, heading toward the door.

"Vitari—we need to find Vitari."

"Who?"

Francis blinked at the American. "My friend, the one I told you about. You know what a friend is, don't you, Father Davis?"

Davis's mouth twisted down. "I deserved that. But it's not what you think."

Clearly, since Father Davis was here and knocking men unconscious. "I'm not going anywhere with you. I'm finding Vitari..." His voice croaked around the burn in his throat. Vitari... The key... Francis hurried back to Sal and rummaged through his pockets.

"What are you doing?! This place is crawling with mafioso. We have to go. Now!"

"Thank you for the... vase intervention. But I'm fine. I don't need your help."

"You mean thank you for saving your life?"

"He wasn't going to shoot, but yes. Thank you. You can go." He found the little key—handcuff keys, he guessed—and just hoped Vitari was in Sal's room, otherwise he might not find him before Sal's father did, and it seemed as though Little Toni was the one they all needed to avoid. Francis didn't know the politics of the Mafia, but the very thing Vitari had feared—a coup—was happening, and they were at the center of it. Perhaps whatever was on the drive was a big part of it.

"I can't go without you," Father Davis said. "My cover is blown. The Battaglia is about to tear itself apart. You need to leave with me, Francis. It's now or never."

"Then never. I'm finding Vitari." Who *was* this man? Was he even a priest? He'd been in the Vatican, so he had to be clergy, didn't he?

Francis hurried from the suite, called the elevator, then stepped inside. Father Davis entered beside him. "I know this is a lot—"

Francis was still holding the gun. He lifted it, then glanced at Father Davis and saw the man swallow. "Good Lord, I'm not about to shoot you."

A little bubble of nervous laughter fell out of Davis. "Sure."

"Although I should."

The elevator car counted down. Sal's room was on the second floor. He'd heard that much when Sal had been speaking with the guards. The guards who *hadn't* been outside their room. Because Sal's father had likely recalled them.

The elevator stopped on the fifth floor, the doors opened, and a young couple stepped in.

Francis hid the gun behind his back.

The woman said something in French. Francis smiled at her. Did his appearance show how he'd just been nearly choked out and was on the run? "Peace be with you," he added, hoping that his being English might help confuse matters.

"You are long way from England, Father."

"Yes, I am," he replied, his mind going blank. "A long way. But the weather is lovely here, isn't it."

"Oui, yes," the French lady agreed.

This was going well, even as he was sure she could see right through him to the gun behind his back.

Father Davis was eyeing him as though he expected Francis to use the gun at any moment. Did he think Francis was the villain? Father Davis was the villain, not him.

The elevator stopped at the second floor. Francis smiled and dipped his chin, bowing his head, then backed out of the elevator, keeping the gun hidden until the doors rumbled closed. He breathed a sigh and studied the long corridor. How was he going to find Vitari behind so many doors?

"What are we doing here?" Father Davis asked. "Someone is going to see that gun."

"You act as though you've never seen one before but you were in Giancarlo's inner circle, so don't tell me you're just a priest, *Riley*. When we both know you're much more than that."

Riley laughed. "Do you even hear yourself, Padre Blanco?"

"I'm not *like you*."

"The infamous vengeful priest with the angel of death at his side who together leave a trail of bodies in their wake? No, my mistake, Father Scott is the epitome of saintliness."

Francis rolled his eyes. He didn't have time to convince this man he was the good guy here, or time to go door to door. "Vitari?" he called. "Are you here?"

"Room twenty-three!" Vitari replied.

Francis hurried down to the right numbered door and tried to open it. It didn't budge. The key reader glowed red. "I don't have a key," he told Davis.

A door to a room farther down the hall opened and a middle-aged man emerged. Francis hid the gun at his back again and smiled innocently. "Good day—night." What time was it?

"Father," the man said in English, side-eying them.

Admittedly, they did look horribly suspicious. "You're drawing attention to us," Francis hissed at Davis.

"Me? I'm not the one in a cassock holding a gun. He's going to call the police, you know that, right?"

"Francis, are you all right? What's going on?" Vitari called from behind the door. "Who's with you?"

"I don't have a key," Francis called back.

Some colorful Italian swearing sounded from inside.

Francis stepped away from the door, aimed at the lock, and pulled the trigger. The gun bucked, the muffled shot still sounded loud, but the door clunked open.

"O Dio mio!" Vitari's eyed widened, taking in the gun, then Father Davis. "You're all right? Did he get to you, did he hurt you? What happened—*your neck*! I'm going to kill that motherfucker, or did you kill him? Francis, what happened, are you hurt?"

Francis slipped the key into the cuff's lock. Vitari flicked the handcuffs free and flung his arms around him. "Amore mio, you're all right."

He smelled so good, felt good too, solid and real and safe. Francis shivered, adrenaline wearing off, but there wasn't time for him to crumble. "I'm fine."

"Thanks to me," Father Davis said, standing back.

"Who the fuck—you're the priest. The *other* priest."

"Father Riley Davis," Francis said as he helped Vitari to his feet. He held out the gun, relieved when Vitari took it so he wasn't tempted to use it on Davis. Not that he would ever kill a man of the cloth. Probably.

"Did you—did Sal... ?" His eyes asked the rest. Had Francis killed Sal?

"No, Father Davis hit him with a vase."

"He was about to shoot Francis, I might add," Davis said.

"Fucking priests." Vitari chuckled, but soon turned serious. "Whose side are you on Father Davis?" he asked, checking the gun's chamber. The wrong answer would see Vitari point that gun at him. "Little Toni's or mine?"

"The Vatican!" He raised his hands. "I work for the Vatican! Always have."

"What?" Francis and Vitari both asked together.

"Explain," Vitari said.

Father Davis huffed and waved his hands.

"Quickly," Vitari added.

"Where to begin... Well, with three bodies in an English

church. Your church, Francis. No, actually, it began before that. With your mother, Vitari. The night Stefania Angelini disappeared."

"You're investigating my mother for the Vatican?" Vitari asked.

"Yes, among other things, such as why some of the Vatican's finances finds its way into organized crime—"

"If you're trying to solve my mother's murder, it's a bit fucking late. Sasha Zhokov pulled the trigger."

Father Davis grimaced. "I'm just trying to survive, so if we could leave and all talk about this later, that would be great?"

"Agreed." Vitari tucked the gun against his back, under his shirt. "We need to get out of here and see what's on that drive."

"Something Sal was willing to kill for," Francis added. Although, that wasn't entirely true. "Something his *father* is willing to kill for."

"Francis." Vitari stopped him by the door, gripped Francis's shoulder hard, and peered into his eyes. "Make no mistake, Sal would have killed you."

Vitari clearly believed it. His friend had turned on him. But Francis had looked in Sal's eyes, he'd seen the pain there. "I don't think so."

"Would you kill for me?"

"I... have," he said quietly. And he'd do it again in a heartbeat.

"It's the same. He loves his father. He'd have pulled the trigger. Don't forgive him. He doesn't deserve it."

"C'mon, I know where there's a back entrance," Father Davis said, checking the corridor. "You can discuss this after we're safe."

"Can we trust this priest?" Vitari asked, hurrying with Francis after Davis, toward a stairwell.

Could they trust a priest who had been working for the Vatican this entire time? Who had lied, and probably done worse, since he'd been so close to Giancarlo. Francis had assumed he was the only priest neck-deep in a crisis of faith. Now it seemed he had more in common with Father Riley Davis than he could have realized. "I have no idea."

CHAPTER TWENTY-FOUR

Vitari

They paid cash for a pay-by-the-hour room in a run-down hotel far from Monte Carlo's glitzy main drag, the least likely of places to find L' Angelo della Morte and his priest, and after ensuring they had somewhere to stay for the night, Vitari turned on the charm, asking the sweet, helpful young man behind the front desk, if they could borrow a computer.

In a back room, stacked with dusty file boxes, he plugged the USB drive into a laptop with sticky keys, opened the folder, and stared at over a hundred numbered subfolders. "Fuck." It was a lot. And without knowing what they were searching for, he had no idea where to start.

Francis leaned against the desk, while the American priest peered over Francis's shoulder. As Father Davis had saved Francis from Sal, Vitari gave the man the benefit of the doubt, for now. But if he so much as glanced at Francis sideways, he'd find himself in a shallow grave. Since Sal had turned on him, Vitari had no trust left to give.

"The file names, I've seen them before," Francis said, leaning closer to the small screen. "On the back of a Stanmore boys' home photo. Those numbers were given to the boys, and me."

"Stanmore still has secrets to give up," Davis said.

Vitari twisted in the seat and narrowed his eyes at the American. "What the fuck do you know about Stanmore?"

"Not much. It wasn't my remit. But I was aware of it, through Archbishop Montague. Do either of you know what happened to Charles Montague?"

"No." Vitari caught Francis's widening eyes. "We don't, do we Francis?"

"No. Absolutely no idea."

Davis's glare skipped between them. "Regardless, Stanmore is over."

"It's not over," Francis said. "Open that one." He pointed at a folder on the screen.

Vitari eyed the number on the file and glanced again at Francis. "You sure?"

"Yes. Open it."

Vitari double-clicked the file and opened the first document.

Male. Francis Julian Scott.

Mother: Joanna Scott. Deceased.

Remittance: 30,000 euro.

Dependent of Charles Montague.

Current address: St. Mary's Parish Church, South West England.

Thumbnail photos of a shy two-year-old boy were queued up, waiting to be opened. Vitari hovered the arrow over the first but there was no use seeing the truth, when they already knew what it meant. Francis's face was grave in the glow from the laptop.

"This links you to the boys' home," Vitari said. "And Montague. It's proof it's all connected, proof you were... bought."

"I never knew my mum's name," Francis mumbled. "My middle name is Julian? Huh."

Fuck, this was already too much. He couldn't put Francis through this. "We don't need to do this."

"Yes, we do. Keep going," Francis said. "Another file. Open it. We have to know they're all here."

Vitari closed Francis's file and opened another. He didn't recognize the boy, but from Francis's gasp, he did.

The name was marked: *Deceased.*

This entry had a dependent name associated with it too, a well-known politician. The dead kid had been bought like a cheap whore and killed when he no longer suited the man's requirements, or when he'd become a liability.

"This is everything," Vitari whispered. "It's all here, all of it. Missing kids, their names, numbers, locations, addresses before and after they were sold, who bought them." He slumped in the seat. "My father knew all this and did *nothing*?!"

Blood rushed in his ears. He needed to move and shot from the chair. He paced the small space behind Davis and kicked at some fallen papers. "He fucking kept it quiet. My name is written on a sticker on that drive. Why the fuck didn't he tell me before? Why wait?"

Francis dropped into the chair Vitari had left and resumed opening the folders. "Maybe he thought it too dangerous? The names here... The people who bought the boys. This is an international scandal."

"He could have blown the whole thing wide open years ago."

"So why didn't he?" Father Davis asked.

"Cowardice. Shame," Vitari snapped. "This would make him look weak. His own son, his wife, ruined by Sasha, and he did *nothing*."

"It's more than that," Francis said. "Sal's father, Antonio? I ran a search in this folder, and look. His name is in these files." Francis opened the folder marked with an X that had popped up.

Blurry black-and-white photos filled the screen.

"I don't know…" Francis mumbled. "What is this? What am I looking at?"

Vitari leaned over Francis's shoulder and the grainy black-and-white photos took shape, so fucking familiar it sickened him. The boys in the images, he knew their faces. They were the boys from the back room… But in these horrible pictures, they were no longer alive. "Fuck." Bile burned his throat. "These are snuff photos."

"What's that?" Francis asked, then after a few beats he exhaled hard. "Oh God. No." He cringed away from the laptop screen. "I can't… look at that."

A younger Antonio, Sal's father, featured in one of the images. And the more Vitari searched, the more he recognized Little Toni's bulk in the other pictures too.

He hadn't thought Stanmore could get worse. But it had.

The file contained photographic evidence, videos, names, addresses, everything. "This is why Toni sent Sal for the drive."

Francis looked up, his eyes so fucking wide and innocent that Vitari wanted to slam the laptop closed and toss the whole thing in the trash. "We need to get this information to the police."

"Francis, the people in these pictures—billionaires, celebrities—they will make this shit go away. It'll never see a courtroom."

"Then..." Francis glanced at Davis and back to Vitari. "What do we do?"

"The Vatican—" Davis began.

"No," Francis and Vitari echoed. "The Vatican will bury this," Vitari said. "There are priests in these files. Priests who can't keep their dicks in their cassocks—no offense, Francis."

"I mean, well..." Francis shrugged. "I'm not exactly the epitome of priesthood, am I?"

At least Davis didn't try to argue. Instead, the American stood back, arms crossed, his expression troubled. "This is disturbing. And it's still happening?"

"What about Catalina Diaz?" Francis asked, ignoring Davis.

"Yes!" Vitari grinned. "Do you know her email?"

"Erm, I think I remember it." Francis opened the email app on the computer and attached a bunch of files. "There are too many to send all at once. I'll send them in batches. It will take a while." He hit send but an error message popped up. "The files are too large. Videos, photos, they're huge. We can't email them."

"Then call her," Vitari said, pacing again. "Get her to come here."

"Me?" Francis asked.

"She has a thing for you, she'll come."

"Oh, I don't—"

"Trust me, she'll come if you ask. A flight from

Barcelona to Nice is a few hours? She could be here by morning. Here." He handed Francis his phone. "Call her."

Francis left the seat and made the call. Vitari took his place behind the laptop and searched more files, finding reference to other charities, other numbers, some of them as recent as a few weeks ago. It really was still happening. Stanmore had been its beginning… Sasha had been selling children and getting away with it for over a decade.

But when he searched for Sasha's name among the files no results came back. "Clever bastard." The charities would be run by a spiderweb of shell companies, their origins impossible to trace. But he knew it was Sasha. Knew it from the smug expression on the bastard's face when he'd handed over the first drive, thinking he was saving Francis by handing over a smoking gun.

But Sasha had known everything. He'd been toying with them both.

"She's coming," Francis said after ending the call. He handed the phone back.

Vitari slumped in the chair and pulled the USB from the computer. "This one little stick is going to fucking blow Stanmore wide open."

"Good." Francis swallowed. "It's time."

Vitari nodded and handed it back to him. "Keep it safe."

"I will." He lifted his cassock and dropped the USB into his pocket. Had they been alone, Vitari would have already wrapped him in his arms, needing him close after seeing the evidence of the horrible fate they'd both narrowly escaped as boys.

The red welts around Francis's neck were beginning to swell. Vitari was going to fucking kill Sal for hurting him. Brothers or not, *nobody* fucking touched Francis. "You know, months ago, when I kidnapped you, Francis—"

"You what?" Davis asked.

"I told you I was *taken*," Francis snapped at Davis.

"Yeah, I took him. Cable-tied his wrists, shoved him in a car, and took him to Spain. He wasn't happy about it." Vitari grinned and Francis leaned against the desk, smiling too. "Best thing I ever did."

"You're both crazy," Father Davis muttered. "This whole fiasco is insanity."

Vitari ignored the American and focused on Francis's warm smile. "When I drove you to that Spanish villa and the would-be assassin took pictures of us together? You remember?"

"Vividly. I was so angry with you, I threw a mug."

"And I used the pieces of that mug to torture that prick?"

Francis grimaced. "I also nearly shot you with his rifle."

"Foreplay." Vitari held his gaze, saying thank you without words, and watched the warmth bloom in Francis's smile. "That bastard told me Sal sent him, he admitted it, and I didn't believe him because Sal would never fucking do that."

Francis saw where this was going and sighed. "He uh... Sal said something to me. He said, *this time, we won't miss.*"

Vitari clamped his jaw shut, then squeezed his eyes closed and fought back the urge to scream. Because he knew exactly what those words meant, and it was the final nail in the coffin of his love for Sal. *We won't miss* meant one thing. Sal had been behind the hit on Francis. He'd sent the assassin who had taken a shot at Francis in St. Peter's Square, same as he'd sent the would-be assassin to the Spanish villa. He was the only one who had known where they were hiding out.

It was always Sal. His fucking friend. The one man he'd trusted, the brother he'd chosen.

"I'm sorry, Vitari..." Francis said. He stroked his neck and winced. "My files on Stanmore, the ones that were taken from my apartment in Westminster? Do you think Sal or his father took them, looking for the evidence that's on that drive?"

It fit. All this time, Sal had been watching him, working against him, for Toni. Vitari doubled over, fists clenched on his thighs, and choked on betrayal. Sal had blown up the yacht in Puerto Banus, almost killing Vitari. Because he'd believed they knew about Toni's snuff images from Stanmore and the dead boys from the back room.

Vitari would have been among those dead kids, if not for his father.

The father he'd almost killed, the father he'd hated and loved and lost when Neo had blown his brains all over Vitari's face.

"I need a minute." He left the room and jogged up the trashy hotel's cluttered, filthy staircase that smelled of mold and piss and made him want to heave his guts up. He climbed three floors, but on the third landing, the stairwell closed in around him. He reached for the wall to keep from going to his knees.

The assassin had told him months ago who was behind it.

They'd almost assassinated Francis on St. Peter's steps.

His father could have—*should* have fuckin' told him about Toni, told him everything. But he hadn't because it would have brought down the Battaglia. And Family was all. Except, it hadn't been. If Family had been all, then Giancarlo would have razed Rome to the ground for Stefania, he'd have scorched the earth to get Vitari back.

His father was weak, just like him.

Vitari swung a fist at the wall. His knuckles struck concrete, splitting open. Pain shot up his arm. He hit it again. Pain felt good, felt real. How much it hurt was the only thing he could control.

Francis's slim black outline hovered in Vitari's peripheral vision. "Don't..." Vitari braced both hands against the wall and bowed his head between his arms. "Don't touch me, Francis."

Scarlet blood dripped on the filthy floor.

Francis's hand skimmed his shoulder, landing like lightning. Vitari hissed and reeled, needing to get away. He shoved, not caring it was Francis he hurt, not caring about anything, needing to lash out, to fight, like he'd always done. Francis didn't leave though. He caught Vitari's wrist, over the razor-wire tattoo, and dragged Vitari into his arms, holding him against his chest. Vitari hated him, hated everything, tried to push him away. But he didn't want him to go, not really. He needed him, because if Francis let him go, he'd fall and never get back up.

He'd always been the broken boy in that back room.

He'd always been forgotten, alone in the dark, his knees bruised, with stranger's hands on him.

L' Angelo della Morte didn't exist, and never had. It was all a lie to keep himself from shattering. Like he was right now.

He clutched at Francis's cassock, clung on as though he could climb inside him and hide. "God, Francis, I'm so fucking scared."

"Me too." Francis's arms encircled him, making him small inside them, but building him up too, piece by piece. "We're going to beat this, you and me, Vitari. I know it." His voice, so calm, and a little rough from his bruised throat. The calm voice of reason in the hurricane of his mind.

Vitari swallowed, his own voice long gone. He was just Vitari, he'd always just been Vitari, scribbling his name on a wall, afraid his initials would be all that was left of him. *V.A.*

A little boy, clinging to hope.

He pushed from Francis's arms. "I'm uh…" he said, then slumped against the wall, head back, swallowing. "Just…" He held up a finger and swallowed more hot, wet saliva. "I might throw up."

Francis leaned a shoulder against the wall beside him. "You can throw up on me. I don't mind."

He slid his gaze sideways, fighting nausea, and caught his shy smile. "It must be love," he croaked, blinking through wet lashes.

"Yeah, must be."

He'd told him not to touch him, and like always, Francis hadn't listened. He was glad for that, for him. He needed someone who didn't listen, someone he could trust, someone who would always hold him up when he fell apart.

"You want some water?"

"I'll be all right."

"Want me to stay?"

"Per favore."

Francis nodded. "What grapes are we going to grow?"

"Huh?"

"In our vineyard?"

"Fat ones. What the fuck do I know about grapes?"

Francis laughed. "I assumed you must know something since it's your idea."

He knew he liked to drink wine. But that was the extent of his wine-making knowledge. "I tortured a wine-maker once."

"Oh dear Lord." Francis shook his head. "Did you torture how to make wine out of him?"

"Not really. It was more a... where's-the-money-you-owe-or-die conversation."

"Did you get the money?"

"I did, and a great bottle of wine."

Francis's laughter trailed off, leaving his sheepish, honest smile behind. The smile of a man who still wanted to help people, after all the horrors he'd witnessed, after everything the world had done to him.

"I fucking love you, Francis Scott."

His smile tucked into his cheek, and Vitari's heart swelled, filling his chest. "Fat grapes?"

Vitari shrugged. "The best grapes. We'll make wine, drink it, and fuck all night under the stars." It seemed like a stupid, far away dream, especially while they stood in a rank smelling concrete stairwell. But that was okay. At least he had a dream to hope for.

Francis sighed. "I suppose I can do that."

Vitari gave a snort. "You suppose?"

"Yeah, it's got to be better than gun smuggling."

"You like guns."

Francis frowned. "I don't—" His eyes widened as he caught Vitari's meaning.

"I know you like guns, Padre." Vitari laughed, his heart free. "I'd kiss you, but you know—"

"Nauseous? Yeah, no thank you. Definitely later."

"Later." Vitari ran his hand through his hair, then winced as his knuckles throbbed.

"Shall we fix that hand?" Francis asked.

Vitari flexed his fingers, regretting he'd lost it and lashed out. But it was done. He nodded, and step by step, they headed together down the stairs.

Inside the hotel room, Francis dabbed Vitari's knuckles with antiseptic wipes he'd gotten from the receptionist's first aid kit. Vitari watched him work, not really listening to his muttering about unsanitary conditions, just enjoying the sound of his voice.

"How's your neck?" Vitari asked him once his knuckles were clean and wrapped in a soft bandage.

Francis danced his fingers down his neck, afraid to touch the bruises. "Oh, you know, sore... It could have been worse."

He would have been dead if not for the Vatican's intervention in the form of Father Davis. The American stood at the window, parting the stiff drapes to check the street. Vitari wasn't sure what to make of him. But if he took the man at his word, then he'd been trying to do some good amidst all of this chaos. A little like Francis but with Vatican backing instead of flying blind.

"How long until your Inspector Diaz arrives?" Father Davis asked.

Vitari checked his watch. "A couple of hours." All they had to do was sit tight all night and wait for Catalina Diaz to call once she'd landed in Nice, a thirty-minute drive away.

The priest went back to checking the street. "I didn't know the Vatican sent priests undercover." Vitari kept his voice low, meant for Francis only.

Francis had been watching the American too, keeping him in the corner of his eye. "Neither did I."

As much as Vitari didn't trust the American, they also needed all the help they could get. Toni would have turned the entire Battaglia against him, accusing Vitari of Giancarlo's assassination. He knew they had the drive, and he'd do anything to destroy it.

"Thanks for nothing, Papa," Vitari muttered. "Leaving your shit show behind."

Keep your friends close, but your enemies closer.

Giancarlo had kept Toni close while gathering evidence, knowing the net was closing. Whatever his intentions, he'd likely known the scandal would be the end of them. But he'd waited too long.

"You should get some rest," Vitari told Francis, noticing how he fought to keep his eyes open.

Francis settled in a tattered old chair, hugged his knees to his chest, and fell asleep in minutes. Vitari remained at the flimsy fold-out table, watching him.

Sal had been too close to killing him. When Vitari had been cuffed to those pipes, when he'd made the call and Francis had answered, only for Sal to attack him... Vitari had heard it all and almost torn himself apart trying to get free off the cuffs. He'd thought... He'd thought Sal had killed him.

"The Vatican has been watching Francis since the DeSica murdered the prostitute in St. Mary's churchyard," Father Davis said, keeping his voice low so as not to wake him.

"Where do you fit in all this, huh?" Vitari asked, slumping back in the chair. "How does a priest lie his way into the Battaglia."

Davis arched an eyebrow at Francis.

"He's different, he didn't want any of this," Vitari said. "But *you* sought it out. You *wanted* in."

"Your mother, an Angelini, fifth-generation Vatican family. The Vatican failed you. I was sent to right that wrong."

At least they were acknowledging it now. "They dismissed her as a runaway, then covered it up."

"They didn't investigate," Davis corrected. "Wrongly assuming she was a runaway."

"She was gunned down less than ten miles from St. Peter's and the Vatican didn't give a shit."

"We didn't know," Davis said. "We didn't look. But her father, your grandfather, never gave up asking. Pope John Paul refused to take the matter further, but after his death, Pope Benedict looked into the case, finding nothing. Then, after *his* death, our Blessed Father Pope Francis saw the failures of the past. He is working for reform within the Catholic Church. I'm here because of him, trying to right past mistakes the Church has made."

"That's a long fucking list, Father. He'd have more luck turning an elephant into a unicorn."

Davis smiled. "He gathered a few priests with certain skill sets and put us on your mother's case, and others like it. There was a time when the Church and the Mafia were tightly intertwined. It's not something the Vatican is proud of, for obvious reasons. It's not as bad as that today, but there's work to be done."

Vatican reform. Vitari would be impressed, if he was naïve enough to believe it. "Certain skill sets?"

"I wasn't always a priest." Father Davis smiled.

"No shit." Vitari laughed, remembering Sal telling him how Father Davis did lines of coke off naked women. "Found God and changed your ways, huh?"

"I did. My wife was killed in a drive-by shooting in Phoenix." Davis held his gaze, barely hiding the veiled anguish from his eyes.

Vitari sighed. Father Davis appeared to be sincere, and

he was invested. "Francis doesn't much like you and he has good instincts." He glanced at Francis, still sleeping.

"I used him, but it was necessary. I regret it. But look at it from my perspective. A dead prostitute in his churchyard, then two dead gang members. He vanishes, taken or on the run. He reappears in Spain, apparently unharmed. The Vatican is already watching Montague closely due to his personal ties with Giancarlo. Francis is Montague's protégé. Then Francis goes missing again, and rumors are he's in Venezuela with L' Angello della Morte, Don Giancarlo's son." Davis spread his hands. "From the outside, Francis is in this up to his neck."

Vitari could see how it might have looked. But if anyone knew Francis, they'd know he wasn't a bad guy. "He didn't want any of it."

"I'm beginning to understand that. He's... not at all what I was expecting."

"No." Vitari smiled. "He's not like anyone expects."

"You love him?"

And here it came, the sneer, the disgusted snarl. As soon as anyone learned Vitari was gay, they changed. He was so damn tired of defending himself. "You got a problem with that?"

"No. Like I said, the Church is changing... The Vatican will get there, but it's like trying to turn a container ship of several thousand years of doctrine in an ocean of expectation. Takes time. I have no problem with love. Love is love."

Maybe. Vitari doubted he'd see Catholic reform in his lifetime. But the fact Davis was here, investigating his mother's death and all that went with it, was unexpected and welcome. "What do you know of Stanmore and Sasha Zhokov?"

"I know it's a defunct children's home where Father Scott met Charles Montague."

"The word you're looking for is *groomed*."

Davis closed his eyes and winced. "I wasn't... I wasn't aware it went that deep."

"Montague is gone, but there will be other priests on that drive. If that drive comes to light, it's going to get biblical. You know that, right?"

He opened his eyes and nodded. "And they will be prosecuted in a court of law. This won't be covered up, you have my word. As for the Russian, I'm only aware of him through the Battaglia and Giancarlo's visceral hate of the DeSica."

"You don't know of any connection between my mother and Sasha?"

"There's nothing in her past to suggest she had any kind of relationship with the Russian boss, no."

But the more Vitari considered it, the more he knew she must have been connected to Sasha in some way. That one line from Sasha proved it... *Like your mother wanted.* What if Vitari asked Sasha outright? He'd never expect Vitari to face him alone. Neither would the Battaglia.

But he couldn't meet Sasha with Francis at his side, the risk to Francis was too great, and Francis wouldn't let him go through with it, anyway.

No, he had to do this alone.

All he needed was proof of a link between Sasha and Stanmore. Proof that wasn't in the files, proof Sasha thought Vitari had known, then let him go after realizing Giancarlo had kept him in the dark.

That was why Giancarlo hadn't said anything. He hadn't yet connected the last piece of the puzzle. He didn't have the proof Sasha was behind it all. Without that, his father wouldn't have acted. He didn't want to bring down the Battaglia, or Toni. It had always been about ruining Sasha Zhokov.

And when the Stanmore scandal broke, if Vitari had the proof, then Sasha Zhokov would fall too.

But how to make the Russian talk?

That was the final piece, the one thing his father had been waiting for, and the last act Vitari had to perform before all this was over and they could chase that crazy dream of a vineyard in the hills. Vitari watched Francis's chest rise and fall. If something happened to him, Vitari would lose his damn mind.

But there was a way to save him.

Vitari stood. "Watch him for me?"

Father Davis straightened. "It's best we stay here, wait until your contact from the police arrives. The Battaglia will be looking for you."

Vitari picked up Sal's gun, stolen by Francis. "I need your sweater."

"My sweater?" Davis glanced down at himself, then the gun.

"Just hand it over, and when Francis wakes up, tell him... I'll be back soon."

Davis pulled his sweater over his head and handed it over. "What are you going to do?"

"Something my father should have done a long time ago."

CHAPTER TWENTY-FIVE

Vitari

As far as anyone in the Battaglia knew, Vitari had escaped with his priest and had already fled the country. Which was why Father Davis's oversized hooded top worked so well to hide L' Angelo della Morte as he sauntered back into the Hôtel de Paris, where nobody would expect him to be.

Before Toni had made his move, Vitari had received word of the hotel Sasha was staying in, but there was only one place a man of his standing would be at this late hour.

The infamous Casino de Monte-Carlo.

Unfortunately, most of the Battaglia would be there too, but nobody would expect Vitari to be there, and after he found Sasha, he just needed a moment alone. In and out. Easy.

Concealed by the hooded top, he ducked into the reception restrooms, wrapped the gun in Davis's sweater, and stuffed both in the trash. Facing the mirrors, he smoothed his hair and ditched the bandage Francis had so tenderly wrapped around his knuckles. This was no time to appear weak. His shirt was creased. He tucked it back in, then picked at a few specs of dried blood that weren't coming out. Didn't matter. Like he'd said to Francis, this whole life was all about appearances, and he knew exactly how to behave like a fucking king.

He shrugged his jacket into line, hiding the blood, and adjusted his cuffs.

L' Angelo della Morte stared back from the mirror.

One final time.

A subterranean tunnel from the hotel, used by high-rollers, took him straight to the casino's gaming floor. Security knew his face and waved him through. He eased into the crowd, perfectly camouflaged alongside the glitzy elite. Faking it until he made it.

Sasha was a poker man, in Monte Carlo for some kind of international tournament. Vitari headed toward the card tables, and there the big Russian was, as bold as brass, seated among men and women who were oblivious to the snake in their midst. He looked bigger in a suit, with the tattoos hidden. Looked refined, untouchable.

Vitari wouldn't be the only one watching him. Sasha would have his men nearby, but not too close as to ruin his evening. Skirting the fringes of the glitzy, noisy crowd, Vitari spotted a couple of alert bodyguards positioned around the room, as well as some of the Battaglia peppered among the people, getting high and drunk, having fun.

His heart leaped into his throat, trying to choke him. Coming here was insane. This was the *last* place he should be. But the best way of catching an enemy off guard was to do what they least expected.

He watched Sasha's poker game unfold, then spotted an opportunity.

Francis would kill him for this.

One of the gamers folded his cards and bowed out. Vitari moved in, dropped into his seat, and smiled. "Deal me in."

Sasha hiked a thick eyebrow. "It is small world, Angel."

"It really fuckin' is."

The dealer dealt a new round while Vitari collected the intrigued gazes of the others at the table. Then two of Sasha's men muscled their way in. Vitari leveled the pair with a cool glare. If they wanted to create a scene, he was fucked. He needed this game to stay on the down-low so he slid right under the Battaglia radar.

"You scared of a little game, Sasha?" Vitari asked.

Sasha grunted a laugh and waved his men off. If he believed Vitari a threat on his own and needed guards for a simple poker game, he made himself look weak.

"Condolences for the loss of your father," Sasha said, his bodyguards dismissed.

He'd said it with sincerity too. "I suppose I should offer you the same. Were you and Neo close?"

Sasha's broad mouth twitched in some semblance of a smirk, or a sneer. "He is a good soldier."

"Gentlemen, shall we keep our eyes on the game?" the dealer suggested in thick French-accented English.

"*Was* a good soldier," Vitari corrected. "I punched his ticket, if you catch my meaning."

The Russian's smile vanished.

They played a round. Vitari lost, but it wasn't the game he was interested in. This wasn't about poker—it wasn't about winning or losing—it was about Vitari fucking with Sasha's head enough to unbalance him, have him make mistakes.

Vitari lost the next round, won the third, won the

fourth, and with each smirk, or flick of the wrist, Sasha bristled. Vitari was ruining his evening.

"I think I'll retire." The Russian folded and moved to stand.

Vitari reached for his wrist. "A word, you and me, in private? No guards."

The Russian's dark eyes penetrated deep into Vitari. "Why would I agree?"

"Because you knew my mother, and I think you cared about her, despite what you did. That's why I'm still alive and not in some shallow grave somewhere. Isn't it? Out of respect for her." It was a long shot, but it was the only card he had left to play.

Sasha held his gaze. "Соглашаться."

They left the table together and headed for the bar, under the wary gaze of Sasha's guards and the keen-eyed glare of several Battaglia men. Vitari didn't have long before the circling vultures moved in. He'd need to make a quick exit soon. But not before he got his answers.

Settling at the bar, Sasha ordered their drinks, then told the barman to leave the Vodka bottle. "Russian vodka, the best," he said, raising his glass. "за здоровье."

Vitari echoed the sentiment, *to your health,* and downed the potent vodka, welcoming its heated kick. "My mother? Tell me about her."

"Why now? Why here?" He gestured at the huge crowd, the glitzy glamour, the extravagant opulence. Laughter bubbled around them. Sometimes cheers rose up when someone had won big.

"Because, if events play out like they're shaping up to, I won't be around to ask again. She'd want me to know."

Sasha looked him over again, trying to think around every question and understand why Vitari had put himself at such a risk by facing him. "They think you killed your father." Not a question, a statement.

"How do you know I didn't?"

The Russian smirked. "любите."

"Love?" Vitari snorted. "You mention love like we have hearts, when we both know we're just fuckin' animals underneath this pantomime." He gestured at their fine clothes, the blood on his shirt. The Russian couldn't have missed his cut up knuckles either. "Kings of blood and bone."

Sasha's deep laugh rumbled. "She was good woman, your mama. She did not want this for you."

"How the fuck do you know that?"

Sasha refilled his glass from the bottle. "Chance put your mama in my way. And love."

Vitari didn't know whether to believe him. It was all so long ago, in another life, not his. But Sasha was talking, and *that* was why Vitari was here. "You want to explain what that means?

Sasha's cheek twitched. "I was Battaglia underboss. Close to Giancarlo, close with your mama. Before Giancarlo cut me out."

Vitari couldn't hide the surprise. Yet another fact Giancarlo had kept from him. "You were Battaglia?" More than that, Sasha had been close to Giancarlo, close like Sal had been close to Vitari. Brothers in the Battaglia, if not in blood. "That's not possible."

"Giancarlo ensured nobody survived to remember, just old blood. The loyal take secrets to grave, only they know how I was"—he gestured with the glass—"excommunicado, cast out." His cheek twitched, lips tugging into a snarl.

"Were you more than friends with Stefania?" Vitari almost didn't want to know.

"No." He laughed. "Giancarlo had your mama's heart. Always."

"What happened?"

"What always happens. Vengeance."

Vitari's heart galloped. "Why did my father cut you out?"

"A project, lucrative, make much cash." He rubbed his finger and thumb together. "Make us rich. But Giancarlo refused. Too soft, too weak. Pathetic. I did it anyway."

Vitari hesitated a beat. "Stanmore? That was you?" *Say it, you bastard. Admit it to my face.*

The Russian's eyes held the answers, like they always had, keeping his secrets close. "Stanmore was convenient hiding place for you."

"Stash the don's kid in Stanmore, then use him later as a bargaining chip?"

Sasha waved a finger. "Not to sell, not you."

"Oh no, you can't lose track of leverage like that. So you just make it so he's *rented* out by the hour?"

"Stanmore was good money," Sasha said, sipping his vodka. "Easy money."

Vodka boiled in Vitari's guts. It wasn't anything he hadn't known, but hearing the man describe so flippantly how he'd been used like a possession... Worse than that— possessions were cherished. Vitari had been a piece of meat passed around at a feast for the rich, influential, and famous, and Sasha had made it happen.

"Stanmore made you rich?" Vitari asked, his voice thin.

"Stanmore built the DeSica, built a family like family Giancarlo took from me."

"Is that what you think, you were *family*?" Vitari swallowed the bitter nausea, then thought better of it. He rolled saliva around his mouth and spat. "Vaffanculo a chi t'è morto."

Sasha jerked, spittle dripped down his cheek, and someone gave a shout from nearby, one of his guards.

Vitari snarled, "You're *nothing*."

"You have five seconds." Sasha's cold, hollow eyes fixed unblinking on Vitari. "Leave or my men kill you."

Vitari eyed the vodka bottle, wishing he could smash it over Sasha's skull. He would have once, if he didn't have Francis to think of, but he sensed the wolves circling, and he was not dying here because of old family feuds that should have ended long ago. He needed to be gone already, but not before he gave the Russian a message. "I will destroy you in this life and the next for my mother's murder and the kids you killed."

He pushed from the bar and plunged into the crowd.

"Your priest will be dead by morning, Angel!" Sasha yelled.

Vitari hurried off the gaming floor, toward the tunnel. Out of sight, in one of the quieter corridors, he checked his phone and hit END. The memo was twelve minutes long and contained the confession that would destroy Sasha Zhokov. Vitari hit FORWARD and sent the memo to Catalina Diaz's number. She'd get it when she landed. He hoped it was enough. Slumped against the wall, he took a few moments to stop and breathe. It *had* to be enough.

He just had to get back to Francis, meet with Diaz when she landed, and it was over.

"Vitari!"

He looked up at Sal blocking the exit into the hotel's corridor. His eyes were clearer and fierce with purpose, now his earlier binge had worn off.

Vitari straightened and rolled his shoulders. Anger

burned his chest, but he swallowed its heat. This was not the time for a standoff with Sal. "Step aside, Sal."

"Why'd you come back, fratello?"

"Brother?" Vitari snorted. "Brothers don't fuck each other, Sal." He glanced behind him. Any second now, those doors would open and the casino security, the DeSica, and the Battaglia would charge after him. He needed to be anywhere else, not fucking around with Sal. Even if the hunger for vengeance demanded he pay Sal back for hurting Francis.

Sal drew a gun from his jacket. How the fuck he'd gotten it inside the hotel, Vitari had no idea. Paid off security, maybe. Vitari's weapon was still in the restroom trashcan.

Vitari snorted a laugh and started walking toward him. "You're going to have to shoot me."

"Don't make me." Sal spread his stance and cupped the gun.

"Make you? I'm not making you do anything. Walk away. It's easy. I was never here."

"I need that USB drive, Angel."

Sal aimed, and Vitari stared down the gun's barrel, slowing. "*You* don't need it, your father does. Did he tell you what's on it?" Knowing now how Sasha had been Battaglia made a whole lot of things make sense. Things like how Little Toni knew about Stanmore to begin with, and why he thought he'd be safe feeding his sick desires under Sasha's protection. Sasha had once been trusted as a Battaglia underboss. He and Toni might even have been close... Might still be close.

But Sal wasn't a part of that; there's no way he'd sanction the sexual exploitation of children. Sal was not his father.

"Take me to the priest," Sal growled.

Vitari stopped with the gun an inch from his chest. If he made a grab for it, there was a high chance Sal would fire. "I'll break your fucking face before I take you anywhere near Francis."

"I will kill you, Vitari, and find him anyway." Sal licked his lips. "I don't want this, but I don't have a choice."

"Yeah, you do." He stepped forward, into the hard press of steel. "We are not our fathers, you know that, right?" If Vitari told him now the kind of man Sal's father was, he wouldn't believe him. The truth wouldn't be enough. But Francis had seen something in Sal, something that made him believe he wouldn't have pulled the trigger, and Vitari thought he saw the same now too.

Sal was fair. He fought for what he believed in. He'd befriended the fucked-in-the-head boss's son from England, who didn't speak any Italian and couldn't stop getting into trouble, because he'd known, given a fair chance, Vitari would survive, thrive even.

Sal wasn't going to shoot.

Vitari laid his hand on the gun and eased its aim toward the floor. "This is where we end."

"They'll kill you," Sal said, resignation dragging his voice down.

"I know. But not before I do the right thing. Trust me, this *is* right. Probably the most fucking right thing in my whole life."

Sal's face crumpled. His lips trembled, and his mouth turned down as he fought his emotions. "It's not fair."

"No, it's not, fra." Vitari stepped close and cupped his cheek. "I know this isn't you, and I'm fucking sorry he's making you do this."

"He'll kill me, Angel. I don't know what's on the drive, but I know it's wrong. I need it, please?"

"I can't. You understand? I can't let him have it. It's bigger than all of us, you get that? It's fucking justice, and we all have to face it."

"Fuck," Sal choked. "I'm sorry, fra. I'm sorry. I didn't want this."

Sal dipped his head, and Vitari gripped his shoulders and kissed his forehead. "I know, fra. And I fucking love you, man. I wouldn't be here without you helping that fucked-up kid I was."

"You're still fucked up." Sal looked up. Tears brimmed his eyes. He knew it was over. He was going to let Vitari walk away, and his father would kill him for it. They really were brothers. Sal's huge hand grabbed at Vitari's face. "Love you, fra."

The casino door flung open and Sasha's bodyguards from the poker table poured in, each pulling 9mm handguns. They yelled in Russian.

"Run!" Sal boomed.

There was too much corridor left to run, too much hotel to flee through to reach the restrooms, and Vitari didn't have his gun. He wasn't going to make it.

"DeSica sons of bitches!" Sal roared, swinging the gun up. "It's been a fucking honor, Vitari. Like real fucking brothers! Now run!" His big arm swooped around, shoving Vitari behind him. Sal's gun barked three times.

Vitari bolted and glanced back. Sal's rounds hit the first guard in the chest, jolting him almost off his feet. But as Sal switched aim to the second, those few seconds delay gave the second guard time to aim and fire. Sal grunted and charged at the guard. He fired, missed. The round chipped off a chunk of plaster to the guard's right.

Vitari ran and slammed through the door, but as he glanced back, holding the door open, Sal dropped to his knees. But it wasn't over. Not yet. Sal raised his gun and put a round between the DeSica guard's eyes.

The far door flew open. More armed men poured in. Battaglia men.

Fuck, fuck...

Sal was down. Vitari couldn't do anything for him.

He couldn't think, thinking would freeze him. Needed to run. Get his gun. Get back to Francis. *Run!*

Vitari flew down the rest of the corridor. "Gunshots that way!" he told security, hoping he looked innocent since he wasn't armed. They ran toward the shouting, leaving Vitari to plow through another door and take the stairs three at a time.

Gunshots sounded behind him.

Vitari skidded into the foyer, drawing a few alarmed glances, then dashed into the restroom and dug the gun out of the trash can. A well-dressed middled-aged hotel guest gaped at him from one of the stalls.

Dull, muffled shots sounded somewhere in the bowels of the hotel. And the screaming started.

Vitari tugged the gun's slide, loading a round in the chamber. "Get down," he told the bystander.

The man whimpered and scurried back into his stall.

Vitari pressed his back against the wall, gun cupped in his hands, and listened for any commotion outside the restroom door that might indicate they knew where he was. The screams came in waves. The longer he waited, the worse it was going to be. Once the police showed up, he was fucked.

If he didn't get out of this in the next few minutes, he

wouldn't be getting out of it at all, and Francis would kill him.

But Vitari had done it, he'd gotten the confession. Diaz had the memo waiting on her phone. He'd done... Sal had died—his heart lurched—but he'd fucking done it. He choked on a laugh. God, he was so fucked.

If this was the last thing he did, it would be worth it.

"Vitari Angelini!" Little Toni bellowed. "Face me by choice, boy, or I will drag you out of that restroom and gut you in front of all these fine people."

Vitari held his breath. He hadn't expected it to be Toni. Sasha, yes. But the Russian was too clever for public showdowns. No, this was personal. But he hadn't thought Toni would take this public either? Shit. Then the Battaglia really had turned on him.

"You killed my fucking son!"

Vitari swallowed. "Fuck." Blood for blood, justice in vengeance. That was the Battaglia way.

Toni was going to kill him, had probably always wanted to. But Giancarlo had stood in his way. Giancarlo was gone now. Vitari was on his own, and Toni needed to kill all his secrets, as well as avenge Sal.

Vitari gripped the door handle, gun raised in his right hand. "Grazie di tutto, Francis, perdonami, amore mio." He opened the door and walked out.

CHAPTER TWENTY-SIX

FRANCIS

Francis woke wedged in the chair, his body stiff and aching from the fight with Sal.

Father Davis stood at the window, ever the sentinel. It was still dark outside. Francis hadn't been asleep for long. He searched for Vitari in the room, then noticed the gun was missing from the table.

"Where's Vitari?" he croaked, stretching his legs out.

"I told him it was bad idea—" the American began.

Oh no. Francis planted his feet, wincing around bruises. "Where's Vitari, Riley?"

"He said he'd be back soon."

"*Back soon?*" His panicked heart pounded harder. "Back from where?"

"I don't... He didn't say. He took my sweater though."

The sweater wasn't all he'd taken. "And the gun."

"Yeah, he did take that too."

"He took the gun..." Francis repeated, now his mind

was catching up with reality. That was bad. Very bad. Vitari had taken the gun because he thought he'd need it, and he hadn't woken Francis because he'd known Francis would stop him. "Oh no, no, no."

He should have known Vitari would do something outrageous, something stupid, something like try to save them. Alone.

Sirens sounded somewhere outside. Monte Carlo was a large city, and they weren't in the best parts of it. Sirens weren't unusual.

"I'm sure it's nothing." Father Davis glanced at the window, then back at Francis.

"It's *not* nothing." Francis clutched at his head, briefly dizzy. He'd gone from sleepy to terrified in a heartbeat. Vitari... He was in trouble. In the last forty-eight hours, Vitari had lost *everything*. His father, his home, his best friend, his life in the Battaglia. It had pushed him near the edge of desperation.

What had he done?

Francis hurried for the door.

"Where are you going?" Davis asked.

"To find him."

"Do you know where he is?" Riley followed him into the hall.

"Follow the sirens." He hurried down the stairs and out of the hotel door, into the humid night air.

"You don't know those are because of him," Davis said, raising his voice over loudening sirens. "He might be back at any moment—"

Francis spun on his heel, cassock whipping around his legs. "Then wait here, but I'm not waiting, I'm not. He does this, he leaves when I'm asleep because he knows I'll get mad, and something happens, something terrible. When we're together, we're safe, but like this? You don't understand. I have to find him."

"All right, then I'll wait here, should he come back. But what if you get picked up by the Mafia? What then?"

"I'm not scared of the Mafia, Father, I'm terrified of losing Vitari."

Vitari needed him, and Francis wasn't wasting another second on a morally corrupt priest who may or may not be on their side. He strode down the alley and out onto one of the main streets. If the sirens were for something else, so be it. Then he'd have gone for a midnight walk for no reason. But if they were for Vitari, he needed to be there, needed to be beside him. Whatever he'd done, Francis would always stand with him.

A police car raced by, lights flashing.

"Lord make haste." He quickened into a jog, and as he turned a corner, more police cars sped toward the direction they'd run from earlier in the evening, from the hotel.

But Vitari wouldn't go back there, he wouldn't be so stupid...

Unless he'd been maddened by rage and despair, unless he'd been so angry, and so afraid, that he'd believed he could end Sasha. Unless he was afraid and grieving and lost. Unless this was Vitari's Hail Mary...

A blacked-out armoured vehicle with giant white letters on the side roared by, chased by an ambulance.

Francis ran.

The scene outside the Hôtel de Paris and the nearby casino was like a scene from a movie, with flashing lights, fast cars, and men and women in elegant wear hugging each other.

Armed police had cordoned off the scene.

This was real. Not a movie, not a dream.

He pushed through to the front of the line, where the police held the crowd back.

Nobody came and went from the hotel. The steps out the front were vacant, empty, and the doors closed.

What was happening in there? Was Vitari inside?

Across the sealed-off square, at the front of the casino, paramedics loaded a stretcher into the back of an ambulance. A sheet covered the person from head to toe.

Because they were dead.

Vitari...

Francis's heart constricted. What if...

He didn't know what to do.

"Officer! Officer!" He thrust out a hand, catching a nearby officer's eye. The uniformed cop said something about standing back in French. "Officer, what's happening?"

"Nothing to be worried about, Father," the officer said in fluent English.

"It's just... if I say a name... can you tell me if it's related?"

"A name?" The officer studied him closer.

"Vitari Angelini?" Francis ventured, hoping this man knew the name, but also, that he didn't. Hoping that Vitari was somewhere else and this commotion was nothing to do with him.

A few people in the crowd took note of the name. If Francis was wrong, Vitari would laugh at him. And he hoped he was wrong, he really did, but the way the officer had hesitated suggested he might, in fact, be right. The officer muttered something into his radio, then said Vitari's name and ran his analytical gaze over Francis, taking in the creased cassock once more.

"What is your name, Father?" the officer asked.

"Father Francis Scott."

He waved him forward. "Come with me."

Francis walked alongside the officer, heading toward a large plain blue van. There was no obvious writing on this one, but that seemed to indicate its importance among all the branded police cars parked around it. "It's Vitari, isn't it?" he asked, unable to stay quiet any longer. "Is he inside there, is he alive? What happened?"

"Monseigneur," a long-faced, stern-faced woman said, stepping down from inside the van. "We have an active shooter situation inside the hotel and my officer says you may be able to help in more capacity than prayers?"

"That depends." Francis glanced at all the faces staring at him. "Is Vitari Angelini alive?"

CHAPTER TWENTY-SEVEN

Vitari

Little Toni clenched his left hand at his side, while in his right he pointed a gun at Vitari's face.

Vitari held a gun, too, pointed back at the Battaglia underboss, in full view of a dozen witnesses hunkered down behind foyer furniture. He had no doubt live footage was already on the internet. He'd be fucking famous, but for all the wrong reasons.

It might be difficult to retire to a little vineyard in the hills now. But that dream had never been likely anyway, just a dream to hang what was left of his shredded hopes on.

"My son!" Toni sobbed, once, twice, then swallowed his grief and funneled it all into rage. "Salvatore loved you!"

"I didn't kill Sal, *you did.*" Vitari swallowed too. "You and your sick need to fuck kids. I know what's on the drive. I know what you've been trying to hide all this time."

Toni's dark eyes widened. "No, no. You don't. You can't."

"I was there!" Sweat oiled the grip on the gun. He couldn't ease off, couldn't look away from Toni's trigger finger. The second he pulled that trigger, Vitari had to fire too, he had to, even if they killed each other. "My name, Angelini, is the only reason I survived."

"You don't know anything, boy. You're nothing. You're a bitch whore's mongrel. I told Giancarlo you were a bastard child, told him she fucked the Russian."

Vitari almost laughed. He'd heard the same his whole life while living under Giancarlo's roof; those words didn't hurt him now. "Giancarlo knew what you were, Toni. Maybe not at first, but he saw it. You and Sasha Zhokov. Sasha created Stanmore, and you reveled in it. The snuff pictures, you sick fuck!" Vitari's hand and voice trembled. He was coming apart, and knew it, but couldn't seem to stop. God, he was so fucking scared. He'd never been scared before when staring down the barrel of a gun. Not like this. He didn't want to die. He wanted to live, wanted to make wine, wanted to kiss Francis under a starlit sky and make him laugh his stupid, goofy laugh.

Toni's eyes widened. "I... It's lies."

"I know. I know it all, Toni. Your fucking son died for your mistakes. He wanted to honor you, but in the end, he knew it was wrong. That's on you, not me. He'd have followed you, done anything for you, but even Sal saw you for what you are. I don't give a shit what you say about me, but you killed my friend, *my brother,* you sick fuck!" Vitari's voice cracked. Shit, he had to hold it together.

Something dark and cold slithered behind Toni's eyes and the sniveling, emotional act vanished behind the cool, hard glare of a psychopath who only cared for feeding his desires. "I should have fucked you dead like I did the others."

Vitari gritted his teeth. If he pulled the trigger, so would Toni. *It might just be worth it.* Toni needed to die, right here, and Vitari didn't care there were a dozen phones streaming it live.

"You're a filthy abomination. You and that priest, sucking each other's cocks. You disgust me." Toni spat on the floor.

"Shoot me then, in front of all these people. That's what you've always wanted, isn't it? Me dead and out of your way? You never liked how a tainted boy from the back rooms of Stanmore followed you back to Italy."

"I didn't... But Sal, my Salvatore, my boy, I did it for him, my boy, my son. The Battaglia was ours. All ours. Giancarlo was on his way out, and you were distracted, chasing after Father Scott like a bitch in heat. You should have been easy to kill—the destroyed yacht in Spain... even fuckin' Venezuela. Luca was supposed to make you disappear. But you kept surviving, you and Father Scott. Sal... I see now, I see he cared too much. He was weak, in the end. Too weak to do what's necessary for the family."

All this time, while Vitari had been simultaneously losing his mind and falling in love, Sal had been contending with his father's bloodlust. Ever since the yacht had exploded in Puerto Banus. Maybe before that, maybe since the day they'd met, when Sal had made the fights fair. Vitari could see how Toni would make his son befriend the boss's mongrel boy and play the long con. But Sal had too much of a heart. In the end, he'd died to save Vitari. Not his father.

"You're lucky Sal didn't know the monster you are."

"Giancarlo knew the monster *you* are and still loved you. It was his weakness. *You* were his weakness. The stupid boy from Stanmore. I told him to smother you in your sleep, but he never did."

Fuck. "Was I his weakness though? He gave me the drive, and it's about to be in the hands of the police."

Toni laughed. "The polizia? I own the polizia."

"Not Inspector Diaz, you don't."

His smirk died. "What have you done?"

"Stanmore, the boys in the back room? They have a voice now. It's over, Toni. You're over."

Toni's aim wavered. "I... You can't hurt me, boy. I'm the Battaglia. The family is forever."

"I used to think that." Vitari breathed in, filling his lungs. His aim steadied and the screaming panic in his head subsided. "But without love, family is just a word. What we do makes us who we are. And men like you and me, we live as long as the bullet with our names on it. Stanmore is etched on yours." Vitari tugged the trigger.

The gun kicked.

Toni jerked but fired too.

Vitari didn't hear the shot over his own, didn't feel its burn, just a numb punch to the chest. No bulletproof vest this time. But as Toni stumbled and fell, and Vitari staggered, it was worth it.

"Vitari!" He heard Francis in his head, heard him call out. Weakness washed over him. He dropped to his knees, dropping the gun too. But he didn't need it anymore. It was good that Francis wasn't here. But then by some miracle, Francis appeared in front of him. His warm hands touched Vitari's cold face, his doe eyes were wide, and he was yelling from far away.

It was going to be all right, they were going to have a farm in the hills, filled with grapevines, they were going to make wine and everything was going to be fine.

"It's okay, it's going to be okay. I'm all right, Francis."

He tasted blood and touched his lips. Strange, how blood glistened on his fingers. "It's all right. I'm okay." Why was it so cold? "I love you."

CHAPTER TWENTY-EIGHT

Francis

Vitari was dying in his arms and there was nothing Francis could do. Vitari said it was okay, but it wasn't. His face was grey, his lips red with blood. "Vitari, wait, wait, don't go... Stay awake."

Vitari's lashes fluttered. "It's okay, Padre. I'm okay. I'm not leaving, I said... I-I wouldn't." He shivered, teeth chattering.

"Yes, yes, it's all okay," Francis said, echoing his lies. *Oh God, no.* Too much blood stained Vitari's shirt under Francis's hand. He tried to stem it, to slow the flow, but there was so much of it. "Help!" he cried. "Someone help!" But the people in the foyer stared, too scared to move.

"Vitari?"

Vitari mumbled something, but his eyes were blown, unfocused, glassy. Francis knew what this was. He'd seen it in hospital waiting rooms, seen it in the eyes of grieving husbands and wives, and now it touched him too. And it hurt, it hurt so much he wanted to scream. "Why, Vitari, why did you do this? We were almost there, we were almost home!"

"We are home," Vitari whispered. "I see it. Don't you?"

The tears fell now, and the sobs came. Francis tried to hold on, but the hurt was too much. Because he didn't see their home, not like Vitari did. He didn't see the end because it wasn't his time, but it was Vitari's. And it wasn't fair. It wasn't right. "Yes, yes, I see it. The vines, and the... the farm... on the hill. I'll see you there, my love. I'll meet you there, amore mio. We'll be together there. Safe. Sempre." He twined his fingers with Vitari's. "Forever."

"Padre Blanco!" a vicious male voice growled from behind Francis. "Face me, priest!"

Someone yelled "gun!"

Francis grabbed Vitari's fallen weapon, twisted on his knees, aimed up at the man's face, and didn't hesitate, not for a second. He pulled the trigger. The gun kicked, and the man fell. Only then did he recognize him. Little Toni. Sal's father. The gun skipped from Toni's fingers, skidding across the floor, and the man's twitching body finally stilled.

Doors banged. Police swarmed in. A dozen guns pointed at Francis. "Wait." Vitari's eyes were closed. Was he breathing? "Wait!"

Arms separated them, yanked them apart and hauled Francis away. "Vitari! Wait!"

Armed police muscled him against the reception desk, crossing his arms behind his back, cuffing him. Paramedics crowded Vitari, so he couldn't see.

"Is he alive?"

Someone was telling him he was under arrest, telling him his rights, but he didn't care about any of that. The words were meaningless. All of this was meaningless. He closed his eyes and prayed, begged. He knew God didn't make deals, and Francis's soul was surely worthless by now, but he offered it anyway. He'd send himself to Hell to save Vitari. If there was such a thing as divine justice, then God had to listen. He had to. Vitari deserved to live.

When they dragged Francis from the desk, he fought to see and caught a glimpse of the floor where Vitari had fallen. There was nothing there now, just a pool of blood.

Cuffed and thrown into the back of a police car, he bowed his head and prayed until there was no breath left in him.

What sin brought you here?

You did.

His angel could not die.

Francis forced the tears away and steeled his heart and mind.

His angel *would not* die.

He believed it. So, it was true.

God owed him. For Stanmore. For a lifetime of Montague's abuse. For the dead kids. For Vitari's horrible past. God had to make this right, or damn Him to Hell.

Francis bowed his head and sobbed.

CHAPTER TWENTY-NINE

Francis

Four Months Later.

"Padre, Padre, there's a car coming up the hill." Aldo raced into the bottling barn and skidded on the dirt floor. "Padre!"

Francis looked up from the bottle of wine in his hands. He'd told the young lad not to call him Padre, but ever since Francis had volunteered at the local church, Aldo had latched on to the idea Francis might be something more than a local wine maker.

"A car?" he asked in Italian and checked his watch. It was late, gone six. The vineyard rarely had visitors.

He glanced at the bottle-labeling machine. Hidden behind it, out of sight, a shotgun rested against the wall. It was only a car, no need to go for the gun...

He left the gun where it lay, and emerging from the barn, he shielded his eyes from the setting sun and scanned the hillside. A small car was indeed making its way up the track that threaded between the rows of grapevines. Dust billowed behind it.

"Go to the house," Francis told Aldo as he started down the slope toward where the track met the front yard. A glance behind confirmed Aldo had listened and dashed into the house. The boy never did anything at half speed, always running.

He reached the end of the yard, where a small fence separated the garden from the vines, and placed the wine from the bottling barn onto the picnic table as the car rolled to a stop.

The engine died and Catalina Diaz climbed out, dressed in cream pants and a floral, loose-fitting shirt. She removed her sunglasses, smiled, and reached out a hand. "Padre, you look well."

Francis gave her hand a shake. "Welcome. Yes, who knew being outside was good for your health?" They chuckled and traded a few pleasantries, but he couldn't help wondering why she was here. He hadn't seen her since Monte Carlo, since the chaos that had ensued after the hotel massacre. Of course, *that* wasn't over. Not yet. The many trial dates against those accused of multiple crimes had been set for another six months, and he was, technically, in witness protection with a new name and a new life. Nobody from before was supposed to be here, which made Catalina's visit unusual.

"Is this the wine I have heard about?" Catalina asked, noticing the bottle on the table and making her way over.

"Yes, the first run of bottles actually." A thrum of pride warmed his chest as she picked up the bottle and admired the label. "Would you like some?"

"I shouldn't..." She grinned with mischief. "But I will."

"Aldo," Francis called. "Bring out some glasses?"

Aldo emerged about three seconds later, running with two glasses and a bottle opener. He bounded over divots and tree roots, making Francis wince. Aldo welcomed Catalina by kissing her hand, and blurted how she was beautiful and he was delighted to meet her.

"Teenage Italians," Francis half-apologized, watching Aldo sprint off again. "You get used to him."

"He works here?" she asked, watching Francis open the bottle.

"He helps, some. His family doesn't have much, so I offered to teach him about business, keep him busy and out of trouble. Although, I'm beginning to suspect he's more into football than wine."

They sat at the table. Francis poured the wine and tried not to stare as she took a sip.

She nodded, and her eyes lightened. "Bello," she said.

He grinned. It felt good, felt... honest. He'd made something from the earth, cultivated the land, revitalized the farm's mature grape vines, harvested them, invested in the equipment, and now all that toil was coming to fruition. It wasn't going to make him rich, not in money. But the wounds in his soul had begun to heal.

"This is very impressive, Padre. The wine, the house. Your own business. Bravo."

He laughed, a little embarrassed by the praise. "Yes, well, it hasn't been easy, of course."

"No, I imagine not." Her smile faded, and the air cooled as the sun dipped beneath the western hills. A string of light-sensing fairy lights came on, tangled in a nearby tree.

"You want to know why I'm here?" she asked.

"I was wondering, yes."

Nothing remained of her smile now. She placed her glass on the table. "We got him."

His heart thumped. "Him?" He needed to hear his name.

"Sasha Zhokov."

Francis sucked in air through his teeth and held the breath. Sasha's whereabouts had caused no end of sleepless nights. The Russian's absence was the whole reason for the shotgun in the barn. Everyone else connected with Stanmore—and the more recent business based off it—had been arrested, charged, and held in custody. With the weight of evidence from the USB drive and the Vatican's investigations, the Battaglia had collapsed in the chaos after Giancarlo and Antonio's deaths, and once one capo had been apprehended, they all began to fall, eager to make deals for protection or reduction in prison sentences. But Sasha Zhokov had slipped through the net. Vitari's voice message, recorded that fateful night at the casino and sent to Catalina, had given Interpol evidence enough to issue an arrest, and using the evidence on the drive and Antonio's live-streamed confessions, Sasha's web of shell companies had begun to unravel.

But the man himself had been missing since Monte Carlo.

"Have you arrested him?" Francis asked, trying and failing to hide the strain in his voice.

"He's dead, Padre. His body was found in his home in Moscow."

"Dead... You're sure?"

"The body has been identified."

"How did he die?" Francis asked quietly.

"Self-inflicted gunshot to the head."

"Suicide?"

She nodded and said with a faint snarl, "Coward's way out."

Francis had met the foreboding Russian once, when he'd shot Vitari as a warning, but that meeting had left a lasting impression. "He didn't seem the sort."

"His DeSica empire is in ruins, and the world had become small. It was a matter of time before he would be serving life behind bars, Padre. Zhokov knew it was over. Many men like him buckle under justice. They prefer death to a lifetime behind bars, which is exactly what fate awaited him."

Francis sipped his wine, thoughts tumbling. It was good, wasn't it? Sasha was dead. It was over. It didn't feel like justice, though. Sasha had taken true justice from them, from the boys who had died as a result of Stanmore. All those years, the Russian had gotten rich on the suffering of innocents. Francis could only pray God would deliver His vengeance to Sasha in Hell.

"Of course, it was not without sacrifice," she added. "Many did not survive."

"Peace be with them."

"Vitari—"

Francis spoke over her, afraid his emotions might clamor up and choke him. "You didn't have to come all this way. You could have told me about Sasha over the phone."

"I could have." She smiled, and the delight was back in her eyes. "But I wouldn't have seen what you have made here." She looked behind Francis, at the renovated barn and the renovated farmhouse. "This must have been expensive to purchase, no?"

"Oh, the farm?" He laughed and hoped it didn't sound strained. "Not really, it was very run-down, mostly just three walls and a roof."

"Renovations, staff? Not cheap."

"The staff are free, so—"

"Still, the mature vines, equipment, bottle machines, labels?"

This was beginning to feel like an interrogation. "Uhm... I had some savings."

"Because priests are well-paid?" she asked, eyebrows raised.

"Well, no, actually..." He stopped himself right there before saying too much. She was still smiling, as though she knew something more.

"How was your vacation to Panama, Padre?" she asked.

"Oh..." How did she know about that? She must have been watching him—of course she was watching him. But it was just a quick stop. There was nothing to suggest anything untoward had happened there, nothing... illegal.

"You didn't stay long, just a single night," Catalina said, sipping her wine, waiting for his reply.

"You've been tracking me?" Did he sound as guilty as he felt?

"We make it our business to have high-risk witnesses watched, Padre. Especially one who makes a forty-eight-hour trip to Panama."

"It was just..." He waved his hands, groping for an excuse. "You know, memories. We lived there for a while, Vitari and I, and... I wanted to go back."

"For memories?"

"Yes."

"Not for the duffel bag you brought home with you?"

He clamped his mouth shut. Could she hear his pounding heart? Did he need a lawyer? Was she about to arrest him? He had done worse things than bring a bag full of ill-begotten Mafia money into Italy, like shoot a Mafia don dead in full view of a dozen witnesses at the Hôtel de Paris, and she'd managed to wrangle him out of those charges, since he was instrumental in the upcoming prosecutions. The farm, though... He couldn't lose the farm and the business... And the money he'd gone back to Panama for, hidden under Father Federico's church—he had no excuse for that. The money was dirty. But he figured he'd deserved it, so...

She chuckled. "I'm sure you bought all this with legitimate funds, Padre. Besides, money laundering is not my department."

"Money laundering?!" he spluttered. "Oh, no, that's not —I didn't."

Catalina's eye wandered from Francis's flustering toward a lone man trudging up the hillside. His unbuttoned shirt gaped, his tanned chest gleamed in the fading light, and under his arm, he carried a basket of grapes.

Francis sighed. Vitari was a rugged vision of masculine perfection and a welcome distraction from Catalina's barrage of questions.

As he drew closer, it was clear he'd been in the fields for hours. Dust had settled in his dark hair and muddied up his creased shirt. The scar on his chest was a pale reminder of how close he'd come to death, so close to his heart the sight of it choked Francis every time he ran his fingers over it.

"I figure you wouldn't be drinking our wine if you've come to arrest me?" Vitari eyed Catalina, and dumped the basket on the table, rattling the wine.

"Not this day, Angel." Catalina smirked back.

"Francis, why do you look guilty as sin? What did she have you confessing?" His soft half smile tugged on Francis's heart, pulling his thoughts way from the pain of Monte Carlo.

"Oh, nothing, it's nothing..."

Vitari snorted, wrapped a sticky arm around Francis's

shoulders, and kissed him on the neck, but as he straightened, he whispered, "Shall I get the gun?"

"No, no!" Francis laughed too hard. "Definitely, not. Uh, no." Goodness, Catalina was already suspicious, and now she was surely convinced of their guilt.

Vitari's hand rested on Francis's shoulder, a steadying anchor. "So why are you here, Inspector?" he asked, his tone closer to hostile than friendly. "Since we're not supposed to see you?"

"They found Sasha, he's dead," Francis said, covering Vitari's hand with his own.

Vitari stilled, absorbing the news, then lowered himself into the chair next to Francis. "You're sure?" he asked Catalina.

"We're sure," she confirmed.

"It's over..." he muttered and lifted his pained gaze to Francis.

Sasha Zhokov had never physically abused Vitari, but his influence had, and the horror of it showed on Vitari's face in the relief. It really was over. Francis nodded and squeezed his hand.

"We're going to need more wine," Vitari announced, jolting from the chair.

"I don't think we're supposed to drink all the product—"

"Fuck that, I'm celebrating." He started for the house, then spun. "Catalina, you'll stay? I'll whip up a puttanesca."

"You're welcome to," Francis added, in case Vitari's frosty welcome had dissuaded her. "We wouldn't be here without your help. Please, stay."

"I would love to, but I have a flight to catch." She stood and reapplied her sunglasses. "Crime does not stop because you have hung up your guns, Angel—and your cassock,

Padre Blanco." Her gaze fell to Vitari. "This life is more than you deserve. Cherish it, Angelo della Morte."

Vitari's smile slipped but clung on. "I do, ma'am. You have no idea how much."

They watched her climb back into her car and drive through the vineyard, until there was nothing of their old life in the view, just fields of grapes in red-tinged dusk light.

"What did she ask you?" Vitari asked flatly, still standing and staring after the car, despite it being long gone.

"She knows about the money."

"Insurance, to make sure we testify."

"Maybe, or maybe she's telling us she knows, but she's letting us go?"

Vitari grinned, landed a quick kiss to his cheek, and strode up the yard. "You always think the best of people," he called back. "Let's celebrate!"

Francis lingered a while in the quiet dusk under the fairy lights, staring down across the hillside and their small plantation. Sometimes, he'd wake in a panic, thinking *this* was the dream, and the reality was a grimy hotel, alone, knowing Vitari was gone. Now Sasha was dead, he didn't think he'd be having that dream again.

This was their life now. It was wonderful, and much more than either of them deserved. He planned to cherish every single moment. Starting with dinner...

Inside the house, Francis helped begin dinner preparations while Vitari washed the day's dust off himself, then Vitari took over stirring the dishes. Aldo sensed something had happened and asked what they were celebrating, to which Vitari declared in dramatic fashion, *the death of their enemies,* then flashed the boy his stunning, mischievous grin, seeding yet more ideas into the boy's head about their mysterious past life.

After dinner, they sent the boy home before his mother worried, despite his insistence he stay and help them finish the wine. And so, it was just the two of them, sharing a second bottle of their own wine in front of the crackling fire.

"It wasn't enough," Vitari said. He lounged in the chair, glass of wine resting on the arm, gazing at the fire.

"God will punish him." Francis had to believe Sasha Zhokov was suffering eternal damnation in Hell. Justice would prevail, if not in this life, then in the afterlife.

"I know you believe that, but I believe in retribution I can taste."

Francis plucked the wine from his hand, set it down on a nearby table, and stood between Vitari's spread knees. Vitari lifted his gaze. It took a little while, but slowly, L' Angelo della Morte faded, until he was Vitari the wine-maker, relaxed in his chair, smiling up at Francis. Although, Francis's avenging angel was never far away.

"What are you thinkin', Padre?" Vitari asked, smirking, because he knew exactly what Francis was thinking. He even shuffled down in the chair a little, widening the gap between his thighs, where Francis would soon be resting on his elbows, Vitari's dick deep down his throat.

"I'm just admiring my angel."

"You never needed an angel to save you, I just hitched along for the ride."

Francis knelt, like he did at church, rested his elbows between Vitari's legs, and brought his hands together, as though in prayer. "Forgive me, Lord, for all I am about to do."

Vitari's soft lips parted, his eyes filling with need. He leaned forward and pinched Francis's chin. "Are you going to ruin me, Francis?"

"No, I'm going to save you, amore mio."

Vitari's mouth plundered Francis's, his tongue thrust, and Francis rocked against him, with him, pulling him in and pushing back, drowning under a surge of need and want and a passion that burned brighter than any righteous fire.

CHAPTER THIRTY

Vitari

God, if loving Francis was a sin in the crazy game that had been his life so far, then Vitari was all in. Francis pried at his belt, not yet desperate, but the fire in his eyes suggested his desperation was close. When Francis lost control, he was a force of nature, more an avenging angel than Vitari had ever been. When he lost control, he was goddamned divine.

When they'd first met, Vitari never could have known the thousand different ways Father Francis Scott would save him. Kidnapping a priest was the second best moment of his life. But loving him? That was the first.

He loved this man to the point of agony, loved him in ways he hadn't known were possible. And as Francis clutched his dick, freed it from his pants, and swallowed him down while looking up at him with those big, innocent eyes? Fuck, it was too much. Vitari flung his head back, falling so fast and so hard he was weak for him.

Francis pulled off enough to demand, "Look at me," then sealed his lips around Vitari's cock again, like the bad priest he was.

So Vitari did look at him, couldn't look away. This man on his knees had sacrificed his heart, life, and soul for Vitari. He'd killed for him, fallen for him, surrendered for him, and Vitari knew he'd never be worth it, despite what Francis believed.

Everything that had happened—the torture of his past, the wrongness of his upbringing—he'd endure every sickening second of it all again to have Francis standing beside him.

He wasn't scared, not anymore.

They'd faced death and defied it.

Vitari didn't know if God was real, but love was, and he'd worship at its altar for the rest of its days. Worship Francis.

Francis withdrew, leaving Vitari gasping. He stood, whipped off his shirt, then deftly removed his belt and dropped his pants. Long gone was the shy, terrified priest, imprisoned by religious restraints. He stood in front of the fireplace in all his pale glory, unashamedly naked, his cock erect, his body gleaming.

Vitari had no words, and Francis knew it.

"Tell me what you want," Vitari said, finding his voice. "Or I'm going to show you what I need, and I will not be gentle."

Francis's cock twitched. "Stay right there."

He'd die if he had to stay. It was killing him not to lunge, grab him, and devour his every inch until he cried Vitari's name. Francis sashayed back to the chair, placed a knee either side of Vitari's hips, his chest all up in Vitari's face, then his fingers fumbled Vitari's dick.

"If you're about to ride my dick, we need something to slick us up," Vitari growled.

"Oh, I..." He straightened. "I forgot."

Vitari grabbed his naked back, crushing him close, and heaved them both from the chair. Francis hooked his legs around Vitari's waist and clung on. His chuckles tickled Vitari's neck as he carried him to the kitchen. Vitari popped him on the kitchen countertop, grabbed some olive oil, and almost laughed at Francis's uncertain glance.

"It's extra virgin," Vitari said.

Francis erupted in laughter, and Vitari lost it. He had to have him. Now. Had to *own* him, ruin him, bury himself inside his soul forever. They collided, chest to chest. He kissed him, but it wasn't enough. After upending the oil and smothering his hand, he stroked Francis's hard and eager dick, needing him to moan and pant and beg. Francis wasn't rabid with need yet, but he would be.

Francis slung his arms around Vitari's shoulders, locking them together, eye to eye. Lust sparkled in his eyes, color touched his face and chest. "I want to make you come, but never want this to end," Vitari said.

"And I want your cock in my arse, so—"

"Why the fuck didn't you say?

"I thought I was making it obvious?"

He was so fucking precious. Vitari dragged him off the counter, kicked his own pants off, and lathered his dick. But he wasn't about to give Francis what he wanted without torturing him first, even if he was bent over the counter, ass up, so eager to be fucked. Vitari pressed in, pinching his dick between Francis's ass cheeks, sliding upward, teasing him, and at the same time, he reached around and clasped his oiled dick again and gave him long, hard, leisurely strokes.

Francis trembled. Straightening, he leaned back against Vitari's chest. Vitari slowed, pumping Francis's cock while working his own, pinched between them. It was as close to fucking as they could get without penetration, and from Francis's sawing breaths, he was all in.

"Vitari, I want you in me," he whispered.

"You want me to fuck you, Francis?"

He bit his lip and nodded.

"Say it, I need to hear your sweet lips say it."

"Fuck me," he whined.

Vitari loosed Francis's cock, spread his ass, coating oil under his hands, and guided his dick into Francis's forgiving hole. The oil made his tight entry exquisite, and Vitari hissed through his teeth as he slid deeper, widening Francis more with every inch.

"Oh... God," he choked.

"You'd better pray to me, amore, because you're all mine."

Vitari rocked, and Francis moaned, driving his ass back against every thrust. Vitari shallowed his angle, pushing downward, right where Francis would feel his cock inside him the most, and shallow-fucking him, he wrapped his fingers around Francis's dick again. This time, he wasn't going to stop until Francis spilled his load.

"Ti amerò per sempre," Francis said, in passionate Italian. He might have said more, but his panting became grunts of pure animal need. A sound Vitari knew well from him.

"Come for me," he demanded in his ear. "Come for me." He was close too. So fucking close.

Francis whined, not wanting to come but already falling. And Vitari was done, out of his mind, consumed.

Francis bucked, thrusting into Vitari's hand, and warm

cum wet his fingers. Vitari long-stroked him, wringing the last drop of pleasure, then freed his dick, shoved him down, and fucked his hole. With Francis still coming down, his guttural snarls tipped Vitari over the edge. He came so hard it was a good thing they were propped against the counter.

The comedown felt like moving through warm molasses, his head light, his skin tingling. Like a vivid dream. He kissed Francis's back, his shoulders, his neck, and skimmed his fingertips down his spine, relishing his every tremor.

"There is no place, on Heaven or Earth, I'd rather be than here with you."

Vitari wrapped his arms around him. "Except, maybe, a bed?"

"Our bed is also good," Francis agreed with a chuckle.

Vitari opened his eyes and peered into the bedroom's gloom. The dark outside the window suggested it was still late, or early. A few stars twinkled, and a soft breeze teased the drapes.

He wasn't sure what time they'd finally fallen asleep, tangled together, but it couldn't have been long ago. He glanced at Francis's soft face, lashes fluttering as he dreamed. Damn him for being so perfect. Smiling, Vitari eased from the bed, careful not to wake him, threw on a shirt but left it unbuttoned, and underwear, then wandered from the bedroom, down the short back hall, and into the living room.

He stopped.

Dying embers from the fireplace illuminated a broad

figure seated in the chair, and a boy on his knees at the man's boots, hands bound, mouth taped. Aldo.

Sasha Zhokov leaned forward, bringing his face into the firelight, so there could be no doubt.

Light licked over the silenced gun in his hand.

Aldo's eyes widened. He mumbled behind the tape, suddenly animated now he'd seen Vitari.

Sasha smacked the gun across the back of Aldo's head, silencing him, then gestured with the gun for Vitari to sit in the opposite chair.

"Do I explain what happens if you anger me?" Sasha asked, pointing the gun at the back of Aldo's head.

Vitari perched on the edge of the chair. He didn't have a gun—should have taped one under the coffee table, but Francis had said not to, in case Aldo found it. There were knives in the kitchen, but Aldo would be dead before he could reach them, and Sasha would probably put a round in Vitari's back right after killing the boy. Then go after Francis, asleep in their bed.

"What do you want?"

Sasha's smile flashed in the dark, full of white teeth. "Apology."

"An apology?" He almost laughed. "What the fuck for?"

"You ruin my life, my business, everything."

Vitari braced his elbows on his knees and pressed his hands together. "You want an apology from *me* for ruining *your* life?"

"Da."

"You don't see the irony, do you? You're that fucking selfish."

"Careful, Angel. Or I take everything from *you* now." He nudged the silencer against Aldo's head, prompting Aldo's whimpers.

"Like you took my mother? Like you took me, put me in that fucking hellhole."

Sasha tilted his head. "You were popular, one of the most desirable. Those... Italian eyes."

Vitari shot from the chair. Sasha lowered the gun, pulled the trigger, and Aldo barked behind the tape, falling forward. Then he pointed the gun at Vitari, freezing him a few steps from Aldo, who was writhing on the floor. Blood spread through the kid's shirt at his shoulder. But that was good, a shoulder wound wouldn't kill him. The message was clear. The next round would go through Aldo's skull.

"All right." Vitari raised his hands. "I'm sorry." The words burned, but it didn't matter. They were just words. "Let him go. He's nothing to you, it's me you want."

"And the priest." Sasha's gaze skipped to the short corridor Vitari had emerged from.

Vitari gritted his teeth. He had to keep Sasha talking. A half-empty bottle of wine sat on the coffee table between them. He might be able to make a grab for it, smash it and use the edges to cut Sasha, but it would be slow and messy. If he got this wrong, Sasha would shoot him, but not kill him, not yet. He'd make sure Vitari was down, then shoot Francis while he slept. Sasha would kill Vitari only after he'd broken his heart.

It was what Vitari would have done. Vengeance.

"He's not here."

Sasha's laughed rumbled. "I followed the police, watched you. The priest is here."

Catalina Diaz had led Sasha to their front door. They all should have known it wasn't over. Sasha knew how to fake his own death. Catalina should gave looked harder, Vitari shouldn't have let his guard down...

"I said sorry."

"But you are not sorry." The big Russian got to his feet and loomed over Aldo. "I will make you sorry."

"Wait, don't!"

Aldo snuffled, tears streaming from his wide eyes.

"Sasha, wait, fuck, I'm sorry! All right? I'm sorry. My father—Giancarlo shouldn't have snubbed you, you were wronged. We both know he fucked up. You should have stayed in the family, the Battaglia would have been yours. Yours and Little Toni's—that was your plan."

"He turned on me. Betrayed me." Sasha's lip curled. "He did not deserve Stefania, did not deserve the family. "

"He feared you since that day—spent the rest of his life looking over his shoulder. *You* did that. You dropped Giancarlo to his knees. You were always stronger. Better than him." Shit, Vitari would tell him he was a god if he took his aim off Aldo. "I'm his son." Vitari inched closer, maneuvering between Sasha and Aldo, and tapped his own chest, right over where Toni had shot him. "Me. I'm the one who hurt you. You're here for me. Kill Giancarlo's son and win. Vengeance, right?" Sasha looked up and adjusted his aim, pinning it on Vitari once more. Vitari had him. "Justice tastes a whole lot like vengeance, doesn't it?"

Fuck, what was he doing? Sasha wasn't going to leave without killing them all. The kitchen and its knives were now *behind* Sasha, further from Vitari. But Aldo was safer behind him. No more kids were dying for Stanmore. Ever.

What he needed now was a goddamned Hail Mary, some kind of divine fucking intervention, because in the next few minutes, Sasha would pull that trigger.

"I regret Giancarlo is not here to watch you die," the Russian said with a heavy sigh.

Vitari swallowed, hands raised, unarmed, exposed in just a shirt and underwear. He held the Russian's gaze and peered into the man's black soul. Giancarlo had done the right thing, he'd cut out a tumor that would have poisoned the Battaglia from the inside out. Sasha had no honor, no integrity. He was not Family and never would have been. And the Russian knew it.

"Lower your gun," Francis said from behind the kitchen counter, behind Sasha, shotgun shouldered and aimed at the back of Sasha's head.

Vitari had seen him sneak in and deliberately kept all Sasha's attention on him and Aldo.

"Padre Blanco—" the Russian began.

Francis cocked the shotgun with a satisfying *cha-chunk*. "Lower the gun or I will paint the walls with your blood, Zhokov."

Vitari still held the Russian's gaze, who still had his gun pointed at Vitari's chest, close enough he wouldn't miss.

"You will not shoot, priest," Sasha said.

A smile tugged at the corner of Vitari's mouth. Everyone made the same mistake when it came to Father Francis Scott.

"How confident are you of that?" Francis asked, never more calm than in this moment. "Luca Espinosa was confident too, so was Don Antonio, Little Toni. Where are they now?"

Sasha's eyes narrowed on Vitari. Did he want to live more than he wanted Vitari dead? That was the only choice here, because the second he pulled the trigger, Francis would blow him away.

Sasha lowered the gun.

"Drop it," Francis ordered.

Sasha turned, gun still in his hand. He met Francis's dead-eyed glare down the barrel of the shotgun.

This moment, this pause in time, it stopped Vitari's heart.

"For he is God's servant for your good," Francis quoted. "But if you do wrong, be afraid, for he does not bear the sword in vain. For he is the servant of God, an avenger who carries out God's wrath on the wrongdoer."

Sasha's trigger finger twitched—he jerked the gun up.

Francis tilted the shotgun down and fired. The blast tore into Sasha's torso, eviscerating clothes and skin. Vitari ducked and dropped, covering Aldo. A second blast boomed. Sasha staggered, grabbed the chair, and fell into it, mouth gaping.

He still had the gun loose in his fingers, clutching it like a dying man clutched a crucifix.

Francis made his way over, the smoking shotgun now at his side.

Sasha made a weak attempt to try to lift the 9mm, but Francis snatched it from his fingers and held it behind him, for Vitari.

Vitari took it, and with Sasha unarmed and bleeding from every important internal organ, Vitari turned his attention to Aldo. He tore off the tape around his wrists and mouth and checked his shoulder. "You're all right, it's just a flesh wound. Hold here." He placed the boy's hand over the wound on his shoulder. "You'll be fine. All right? It's over." He met the kid's terrified gaze and watched it turn to anger. Aldo glanced past Vitari at Francis, standing beside the fire, with his messy hair and baggy pajama bottoms, staring at the gurgling, dying Russian.

"He's not just a winemaker, is he?" Aldo sniffed.

Vitari snorted and ruffled the kid's hair. "Shh, that's Padre Blanco, God's wrath on Earth. But it's our secret."

The boy nodded, wide-eyed with awe and fear.

Vitari straightened and joined Francis in looking down at Sasha. "Two shotgun blasts to the gut. A fucking agonizing way to go."

"I thought so too," Francis agreed, matter-of-factly.

Vitari glanced back at the kitchen, where Francis had been standing behind the counter. From his position, he couldn't have seen how Sasha had been about to put a bullet between Vitari's eyes. Francis had shot him because he'd wanted to. Because Sasha deserved it. For justice. And maybe a little vengeance too.

The Russian's mouth moved, his lips scarlet with blood. He gurgled something, but Vitari was done hearing his bullshit and slammed the tape he'd taken from Aldo over Sasha's mouth. He'd said his final words.

Vitari braced over him in the chair, eye to eye. "You were never worthy of my father's love, not worthy of the Battaglia. He wasn't always right, but he did the right thing in removing you. And while you robbed me of knowing my mother, what I do know about her makes me think she told you the truth, that you were a sick fuck who had no place among the family." The Russian's eyes betrayed his rage. "For every kid you butchered and abused in homes like Stanmore, for all the lost boys who never saw justice, you're going to sit there and drown in your insides. I know the Hell that's waiting for you. I was raised there." He let those words sink in, tasting their sweet vengeance on his lips. "Nobody is coming to save you, Sasha. Nobody will care when you're gone. You'll be forgotten."

The light gradually faded from his eyes, and Vitari absorbed every single second of Sasha's final moments like a soothing balm to the soul.

Then, in the glow of the fire, with Sasha cold in the chair, it was finally over.

"I suppose we'd better get the shovel," Francis said as he rested the shotgun against the wall.

"I'll do it, you fix Aldo's arm and take him home."

"What do I tell his mother?"

"We don't need to tell her anything," Aldo piped up with a grin, albeit a grin he winced through. "I was running and fell. Mama doesn't need to know about Padre Blanco."

"Lying to your mother is... very bad." Even Francis struggled to justify that since he'd just shot a man twice with a shotgun and watched him die, savoring his final moments.

Aldo glanced between them. "I can tell her the truth—Padre shot a Russian, if you think that is best—"

"No, Heavens no, no, definitely not telling your mama that." Francis took the boy's hand. "Let's get you cleaned up and we'll get our story straight on the way home." He slung a sly little grin over his shoulder, which Vitari caught in his heart, and then they left for the bathroom, already spinning tales.

Francis would come up with some excuse for the wound, he was a fantastic liar.

Vitari eyed Sasha's body, the blood, the gun, and sucked on his teeth. He leaned over the corpse, gripped his limp, cooling chin and peered into Sasha's dead eyes. If there was a Hell, Sasha was surely in it. May he burn for all eternity. "Ciao, motherfucker."

CHAPTER THIRTY-ONE

Vitari

The rusted chain-link fence still ringed Stanmore House like a metal noose. A few more bunches of dead flowers had been fixed to the fence. The trials were long over. People had come and wept for the horrible scandal that had been Stanmore's dark past. News crews had stood on the same spot as Francis and Vitari now, although they likely hadn't been holding two empty gas cans.

Vitari shivered beside Francis, bundled up in a coat, blowing into his hands. "I fucking hate England. Why is it always so cold in this country?"

"It's winter?" Francis suggested.

"You getting sassy with me, Padre?"

Francis smirked, but it *was* cold. But they wouldn't be there for long. In a few hours, they'd be back on a plane to Italy, back on the farm, back living L' dolce vita. But for that to happen, there was one last thing they needed to do. Together.

"Ready?" Francis asked. Earlier in the day, they'd bought a cheap lighter from a nearby store. Francis set one gas can down, and took the lighter from his pocket now.

"I've been ready for this for fifteen years. Light this shit-hole up."

Francis flicked the lighter and locked the flame on, then glanced up and down the street. At 3 a.m., nobody was around. All the houses were dark. Stanmore's grounds were large enough to shield the nearby houses from the flames. Nobody was going to get hurt. But Francis hesitated. It wasn't just about burning it, this place and its old ghosts loomed over them. Its horrors almost too large to burn.

"What if we get arrested?" he asked, gaze lifting.

"Padre. Give me the lighter."

Francis handed it over, sighing his relief now it was in Vitari's hands.

Vitari eyed the little flame, then Stanmore's boarded up windows. Someone had spray painted *RIP* on the left-most window's rotten board, which seemed fitting. This was a cremation, of sorts.

"You want to say something?" Vitari asked. "Something religious?"

Francis grimaced. "Fuck Stanmore."

"I was thinking more like a prayer, but whatever." Vitari snorted and tossed the lighter over the fence.

Flames sizzled the icy dead grasses, and for a moment it seemed as though Stanmore would refuse to burn, but then the flames caught a splash of petrol and roared, sweeping up the front of the house, over the boarded windows, and whooshing into the overgrown ivy and decaying roof. The speed at which it went up stole Francis's breath.

Vitari pulled him back from the surge of heat and out of sight under an opposite tree, and from there, they watched, hand-in-hand, as Stanmore *burned* as though Hell itself had reached up from the depths and devoured it.

Sirens interrupted their moment, but they'd seen enough, hopping back into their rental car, passing the fire truck on their way out of town.

"I hope they don't put it out," Francis said, tracking the truck in the side mirror.

"They won't."

The more miles they got under them, the more Vitari's soul felt at peace. This had been Francis's idea to come back and burn it, and initially, he hadn't wanted to venture anywhere near the bad memories, but now it was done, he could close a door on it for good. He'd needed it, like Francis had known.

"Do you miss England?" Vitari asked, after Francis had been watching the dark countryside scroll alongside for too long without saying a word.

"No. Italy is my home. *Our* home."

Fuckin' right, it was. "What about the Church? You miss that?"

Francis's soft smile grew. "You're my church."

He was sweet, so this was probably a good time to tell him a secret. "So, don't get mad, Padre..."

Francis's eyebrows lifted.

"What?" Vitari asked, adding an innocent shrug.

"I hate it when you start a sentence like that."

Vitari laughed. "Hey, have you forgotten that time in Colombia, when you said, 'Don't get mad, but I called your psycho-father and told him everything'?"

Francis groaned. "I said I was sorry."

"I know." He snickered. "Anyway, like I said, don't get mad, but—"

"Oh God, what is it?"

"It's like you don't trust me."

"Is it illegal?"

Vitari considered the yacht he'd bought without Francis knowing, She was berthed in Southampton marina, waiting for their arrival. He'd kept it from Francis as a surprise. They weren't going back to Italy on a plane. But that wasn't the problem. The yacht itself may have been purchased with some money he'd hidden away, money that may or may not have been earned from criminal activity. Enough money to set them up for a long life together. "It's not *legal*."

"You know that's the definition of illegal."

"Fine then, it's not *bad*."

Francis leveled him under his judgmental priestly glare that demanded he confess all his sins immediately.

"It's not a sin in the Bible," Vitari added. Although, everything they'd be doing between the sheets would be.

Francis huffed but his grin stayed anyway. "Whatever it is, I trust you."

"You're goin' to love it."

"Will we need a gun?"

Vitari had thought of that and stashed a gun along with handcuffs in the yacht's bedside drawer for... emergencies. He smiled, changed the car's gears down, and pushed the accelerator pedal to the floor. "We always need a gun, Padre."

If you enjoyed the Forgive Me series, please do take a few moments to leave a review. Just a few words are enough, and it helps books like this one reach new readers.

Thank you.

ABOUT THE AUTHOR

Rainbow Award winner A. Nash (Ariana Nash) writes LGBTQ+ fantasy and contemporary novels full of morally challenging characters, action, betrayal, and steamy love between two (or more) men.

Sign up to her newsletter and get a free ebook here: https://www.subscribepage.com/silk-steel

ALSO BY ARIANA NASH

Sign up to Ariana's newsletter so you don't miss all the news.

www.ariananashbooks.com

***

Shadows of London

(Five book urban fantasy series)

A sexy assassin, a billionaire boss with secrets, and magic bubbling up through the streets of London. All in a days work for artifact agent, John "Dom" Domenici.

Start the Shadows of London series with Twisted Pretty Things

9 781738 574001